Marion Reynolds attended Trinity College, Dublin where she read English Language and Literature. She was a teacher and lecturer in English Literature and Media Studies in Ireland and the U.K.

Originally from Dublin, she now lives in West Cork with her husband and has two grownup children. She is a regular contributor to Irish newspapers, writing articles, book reviews and interviews with writers. She has had a number of short stories published.

"A Soldier's Wife", was a joint winner in the prestigious Novel Fair 2013, run by the Irish Writers' Centre. It is based loosely on the experiences of her grandparents. Marion is currently working on a sequel.

www.marionhreynolds.com

A Soldier's Wife

Marion Reynolds

Indigo Dreams Publishing

"History begins and ends with the reciting of a tale. Our future is guaranteed by our ability to possess a narrative identity, to recollect the past in historical or fictive form"

Paul Ricoeur
Memory, History, Forgetting (University of Chicago Press 2004)

First Edition: A Soldier's Wife

First published in Great Britain in 2014 by:
Indigo Dreams Publishing Ltd
24 Forest Houses
Halwill
Beaworthy
EX21 5UU
UK

www.indigodreams.co.uk

ISBN 978-1-909357-36-5

Designed and typeset in Minion Pro by Indigo Dreams.
Cover design by Ronnie Goodyer of Indigo Dreams Publications
Original photographs of James and Mary Devereux courtesy of the author.

Printed and bound in Great Britain by Imprint Academic, Exeter

Papers used by Indigo Dreams are recyclable products made from wood grown in sustainable forests following the guidance of the Forest Stewardship Council

For my husband, Patrick Reynolds, for his unfailing love and belief and for my daughter Fiona, my I.T. expert and loyal supporter.

In memory of my grandparents.

Grateful thanks to my daughter, Fiona Reynolds for her advice and suggestions and especially for setting up my web page. My daughter-in-law, Sue Reynolds gave me the English perception of this story. Sinead Daly was one of the first to read it and gave me invaluable support and feedback.

I might never have finished the novel had not the Irish Writers' Centre chosen my novel as a winner at the Novel Fair 2013, so my thanks to them.

Thanks to Joy Devereux Sykes for family photos and to Martin Sykes who researched my grandfather's military records. Niall Devereux, the custodian of his medals, shared them with me.

Nora Owen, former Minister for Justice, television presenter and grand-niece of Michael Collins and my friend for many years has promised to launch this book. My grateful thanks to her.

A Soldier's Wife

Prologue

Bombay,
India,
4th February 1903

Dear Mama,

Forgive me for not writing to you before this. Since we arrived in India, I could not find the words to tell you about the terrible thing that has happened to me.

God has taken my darling Nancy from me. I go to sleep every night cradling her shawl in my arms. It still smells of her and I press it to my mouth to stifle my sobs. My breasts ache for her and my womb is heavy with grief. I can find no consolation because my heart is bitter with God. James cannot bear to look at me; he feels guilty for bringing us to this alien place.

Nancy became ill about one week after we left the port of Liverpool. I thought that she was teething but a few days later, a little boy called John, who was in a cabin near to us, died of measles. His poor mother was out of her mind with grief and all the women were kept below deck for the burial at sea. I was terrified because I remembered when there was an outbreak of measles in Castlebar and you helped to nurse some of the children. I kept Nancy in our cabin and looked after her as well as I could. James brought us food and water and sang to her whenever he was free while I lay on the bed with Nancy beside me, watching for the tell-tale signs of measles. The ship's doctor did all he could but every day Nancy's fever became worse. She was hot and fretful and cried constantly. She would not take my breast and I had to watch her small body grow weaker and the fever stronger.

At first she cried and would not be comforted and I thought I would go mad but then she grew quieter and more flushed. One morning as I watched the sun rising through the porthole window, she turned her little face up to me and closed her eyes. I would not believe that she was dead and screamed at James to get the doctor. He came immediately but just shook his head when he saw Nancy. I held her close to me, cradled her head and rocked her gently. The Major's wife and Violet and some of the other women tried to take Nancy from me. They said that the burial must be quick because of the heat. I fought them and shielded her, holding her close to me, but eventually they prevailed. Oh Mama, do you know what it feels like when your little one is torn from your arms and you know that you will never see her again? The women gave Nancy to James who kissed her and carried her away. I pleaded with them to wait. Another week and she could have been buried on land.

When the ship's engine slowed and then stopped, I knew what was happening. I felt her small body in its white shroud being delivered to the sea-bed and my womb contracted. I cradled her shawl and pictured her puckered face as she suckled, heard her small grunts of contentment, felt the imprint of her downy head on my palm. A kind of howling rose and fell with the notes of the Last Post. I knew it was me howling when the women tried to quieten me. They were holding my hands, making me drink the laudanum that the doctor left, pressing me down onto the bed. I sank into nothingness and when I awoke, my Nancy was gone.

Mama, I do not know how I can endure this pain without even the comfort of you and Papa or my sisters. Every night I dream of Castlebar and how I met James. I wish I was back there. Pray for me.

Your loving daughter,

Ellen

Chapter 1
June 1901: Castlebar

Ellen stole a glance at the three men standing together in front of the fireplace as she laid the table for tea. Her father was deep in conversation with her cousin Jack and Jack's friend, James. The two young men were wearing the scarlet uniform of the Connaught Rangers. The elegant red uniform with its gold braid, high collar and bandolier made even swarthy Jack look handsome, but it was James on whom she focused. He was the shortest of the three men but his upright stance gave him a commanding air. Reflections from the firelight made his blond hair glint; it had a slight curl which the pomade he used did not manage to straighten. His moustache was also blond, waxed and curled at the ends. His deep voice had the inflections of another place, Dublin, she guessed. In the parlour of the gate lodge, with its dark heavy furniture, brocade curtains and ornately framed pictures, her family moved about in their sombre clothes, making the young men look like two exotic birds in a nest of wrens. She caught the intensity of James's blue eyes as he turned and met her gaze and she blushed, almost dropping the teapot in her confusion.

At twenty, she was the oldest of the four sisters and had a reputation for being very ladylike and dainty, mainly because she held herself aloof from the local lads with their rough hands and awkward ways. She knew her mother despaired of her ever finding a husband who lived up to her ideals. Plump and pretty Maggie, the next sister, at eighteen had already found a suitable beau and was engaged to be married to the son of a local jeweller; a good match, according to their mother. Matt, the young man in question, had first paid attention to Ellen. When she refused to walk out with him, he turned his attention to Maggie. The other two girls, inquisitive Jane and shy Annie, were too young yet to be thinking of marriage but, judging by their popularity at crossroad dances, they would not be a worry to their mother.

Their father, Henry Ainsworth, was the lodge keeper on Lord Lucan's estate in Castlebar and Ellen had spent the last four years as nursemaid-cum-governess to Lord Lucan's three young children. Now the older two were being sent away to school in England and she wondered how much longer she would be needed in the Big House. Her sisters occupied themselves with making lace which was exported by a local company to America but she had never been any good with a bobbin or needle. Anyway, she enjoyed being up at the Big House, surrounded by beautiful things, and she was treated almost as one of the family. She modelled her manners on those of Lady Lucan and was far more fastidious than her sisters. Her hands were tapering and white, like those of a lady, she often thought. She wore her dark hair in the style favoured by her mistress, combed back from her face over a frame, and she knew that the dusty pastel colours that she wore emphasised her dark blue eyes. She sometimes read the romances that Lady Lucan left lying around and they fuelled her dreams of meeting a handsome man who would sweep her away from the grey, ordinary life of Castlebar to some exotic place.

"Henry, lads, the tea is wet. Come and sit down." Her mother called the men, took the teapot from Ellen and put it down on the table.

They left their positions in front of the fire and sat down to their tea of boiled eggs, fresh brown bread and scones with butter and jam as they continued their discussion. Jack was describing some of his experiences in India, where he had been with the Connaught Rangers for the previous seven years, the usual tour of duty. He and James appeared to have had many adventures together, the recounting of which provoked great hilarity which

14

they tried to temper because of the presence of her father.

Henry Ainsworth was not given to hilarity. He was a serious man who liked to read. Tall and heavily built with black hair streaked with grey, he had heavy black brows which were usually knitted in a frown although the dark eyes beneath were kindly. A very strict Catholic, he never allowed alcohol into the house, because, he said, it was the ruination of the Irish. His wife, Mary Ann, was a dark handsome woman, as gregarious as her husband was quiet. Originally from Connemara and an Irish speaker, she had come to Lord Lucan's house as an under-parlourmaid. She got to know Henry when he was working as a farmhand but they had to wait eight years before he was appointed lodge keeper and they could marry.

Four daughters were born to them over the next eight years. Henry smiled at the jokes made about his female household. "Blessed art thou amongst women!" simply evoked the response that it was good to have five women looking after a man. If Henry didn't regret the absence of a son, Mary Ann did. Jack was her nephew and since her older sister's death, he had become the son she had never had. She had missed him when he was in India and was delighted when he arrived home to the barracks in Renmore.

"Come and stay with us any time you want, Jack, and bring your friends with you," she told him. Now she fussed around him and his friend, James. "Are you sure you have had enough to eat? Another scone, James? Another cup of tea, Jack?"

When she was satisfied that they had been well looked after, she and the girls sat down at the table. Ellen moved quickly to get ahead of her sisters and managed to sit next to James. He used his hands to great effect when telling a story and she remembered how soft his hands had felt when they had been introduced. Few men had soft hands like that; most had calloused and blistered palms like her own father.

She was covertly admiring James's filbert fingernails when he turned to her, making her blush once more. "I hear that you are working above in the Big House as a governess."

He was looking at her with admiration. "Oh, I am more of a nursemaid than a governess. The children are fairly young."

"Still, you must be very clever."

She wanted the conversation to continue but did not know what to say.

James saw her confusion and changed the subject. "Jack and I have just been telling your father about our experiences in India."

"Yes, I was listening. You must miss India. How long were you there for?"

"Seven years. We, that is, my battalion, will be going back there in a year or so."

"Tell me about India. I would love to travel to somewhere exotic some day but all I do at the moment is read about far-off places."

"You can't imagine how different the life is in India," James said. "The climate is hot and the colours are so intense they would take your breath away. There are beautiful flowers and exotic birds and animals."

"Oh, it sounds wonderful!" Ellen's eyes were shining.

"Yes it is. We have a very good life out there."

"What is it like? Is there a social life? Is it very different?"

"Yes, completely. We sergeants have our own batman, a kind of servant, and the married sergeants have cooks and nursemaids for their children. The social life mainly revolves around regular dances in the mess. The only problem is that there aren't enough ladies, only the married ones and a few daughters who are old enough to accompany their parents." James finished on a rueful note. He was so animated by his memories that he drew his chair closer to hers, and then retreated when he saw her father looking at him.

"I was just telling Ellen, Mr Ainsworth, what life is like in India. You can't imagine how different it is: the heat, the colour, the crowds of people ..."

"Yes," Jack added. "But you didn't tell them about the smells or the flies or the ..."

"It sounds wonderful, so exotic and romantic," Ellen interrupted.

Mary Ainsworth looked at her daughter's shining eyes and flushed cheeks and wondered if it had been such a good idea to let Jack invite his friend to stay. James was a sergeant but, even so, she thought her eldest daughter could do better. "Come and help me clear the table, Ellen. We can leave the men to their smoking."

Ellen got up reluctantly with her sisters and carried dishes into the kitchen where they washed them and put them away. As soon as she could, she went back into the room where the men were and lit the Tilley lamps and then sat down quietly, content just to listen to the conversation which had now turned to politics. Her father was discussing John Redmond and the Irish Parliamentary Party. He had always been a supporter of Redmond and, earlier, of Parnell before his fall from grace.

"Parnell was right," her father was saying. "We must get Home Rule for Ireland. Gladstone introduced it to make sure of Parnell's backing but it cost him the election. Now with John Redmond leading the Irish Parliamentary Party, we have another chance. We can't have people in Westminster, who never set a foot in Ireland if they can help it, making decisions about our country that affect all our lives."

"Why do we want Home Rule?" James said. "The British have been very good to us. I think we should stay as we are." He didn't

17

seem to notice Henry's annoyance.

"The British have been very good to us? Do you know anything about the Famine and how they treated us then?"

Jack looked anxiously from James to his uncle and moved the conversation to a safer topic. "I hear that there is a strong move to reform the land system and allow tenants to buy out their landlords. That would be a great improvement."

Before the discussion could get too heated Mary Ann bustled in. "It's getting late. Would you like a cup of tea, lads, before you go off to bed?"

Ellen made sure that she was the one who handed the tea cup to James and helped him to milk and sugar. She thought he smiled at her in particular as the two young men said their goodnights and retired.

The girls went up to bed before their parents and gossiped about the evening. They were all very fond of their cousin Jack but it was James and his stories about India which were the main topic of conversation. The other three girls took the opportunity to tease Ellen about James; she was usually so standoffish with young men.

"Oh James, I would love to see India! It sounds so exotic and romantic," Maggie imitated in an affected voice.

Ellen batted her away with a hairbrush.

"Can I help you to milk and sugar, James?" Jane lisped and dodged out of her sister's reach.

"Are you a little bit in love with James?" Annie asked shyly as Ellen started to brush her youngest sister's long hair.

"He is very handsome and I do like him. He speaks so nicely and he has such elegant hands! You never know, I might even marry him." Ellen laughed and hugged Maggie.

The next morning was Sunday and the two young men accompanied the family to Mass. Ellen had put up her dark hair to frame her face in the fashionable style that she had copied from Lady Lucan. She hoped that the lavender colour of her dress brought out the blue in her eyes. Sitting between her mother and Maggie, she managed to keep James in view where he sat, beside her father, a little to the side in the row in front of her. The Mass seemed to last forever but finally they were out in the June sunshine, bidding hello to their neighbours.

Maggie's fiancé joined them. Matt was a jovial, good-natured man of twenty-nine. He had gone to school with Jack. He greeted him warmly and was introduced to James.

"Girls, how about a walk before dinner? Jack, let's show James the demesne," Matt said

The two youngest girls decided to go home with their parents to help prepare dinner, which, like most people in a farming neighbourhood, they ate in the middle of the day.

Ellen thought that the countryside had never looked as beautiful as she and Maggie strolled with the three young men. It had rained earlier in the morning and raindrops still highlighted the varied greens of the hedgerow; here and there vertical streaks of purple foxgloves or the delicate lace of elderflowers rose from the brambles and hawthorns in the ditches. The scent of newly mown meadows was in the air and overhead a lark sang. Some of the pedigree cattle in the fields came to the hedge to look at them curiously, their lower jaws moving sideways as they munched. For a while they all walked demurely together, the girls sometimes pointing out an interesting landmark to James or stopping to pick elderflowers which their mother used to flavour the gooseberries.

Eventually, Matt and Maggie lagged behind, delighted to get some rare privacy to talk to each other. They had a lot to talk about; although they were engaged, Matt's father did not want them to get married until he had built a house for them, and the house was no nearer being started than it was when they had first got engaged three months previously.

Jack stopped to chat and smoke with some young men he knew. To her delight, Ellen found herself walking with James. He was shyer and quieter without Jack but soon she found that they were talking like old friends. He told her that he had been in the army for ten years, since he was twenty, and loved army life but found it a bit lonely at times. Ellen did a quick calculation; he was thirty, ten years older than her.

"Why did you join the Connaught Rangers?" she asked him. "Surely a Dublin man like yourself should have joined the Dublin Fusiliers?"

"It's a long story," James replied. "My brother, who went to America after our parents died ten years ago, sent me the money to join him. I thought that I would enjoy myself for a while before leaving Ireland and, somehow, the money all disappeared." James laughed wryly. "I went to stay with a friend of mine in Athlone while I decided what to do. He was about to join the Connaught Rangers. It seemed like a good idea so I signed up too."

The light-hearted story made Ellen laugh but she knew her parents wouldn't be amused by it. "How did you become friendly with Jack?" she asked.

"When I was sent to India I met him when we were both promoted to sergeant. We have been friends ever since."

"When will you be going back there?" she asked shyly.

"In about a year or so." James turned to face her. "Would you really like to go to India"?

"Oh, I would love to," she answered, knowing that the question was about more than going to India. "I've always dreamed of travelling".

"Will you come out walking with me tomorrow if I get your

20

mother's permission?"

She gladly agreed. As they neared the gate lodge, they were joined by the others who seemed to sense their new understanding.

The next day was dark and showery and Ellen despaired of ever getting out with James for the walk to which her mother had reluctantly agreed. Then, when she had almost given up hope, the sun broke through at three o'clock and she hurried to put on boots and a coat and hat.

"Jane and Annie would love to go with you," her mother said, ever mindful of watching neighbours and their good name.

The young sisters were discreet, however, and walked a good distance behind Ellen and James. This time, there was an urgency about their conversation, as though they had little time to get to know each other. He told her about his family, his parents who were dead and his only brother. She told him about her boredom with Castlebar and her desire to travel.

They were so absorbed in each other that they forgot about the two younger girls and were startled when Jane spoke. "We had better turn back now or else we will be late for tea."

James allowed the others to walk ahead and turned to Ellen. "I have to go back to the barracks tomorrow. I wish I could stay longer."

"When will you be able to come back here?"

"I should be able to get leave in about two weeks. I will come back then to see you, I promise." He held her hand briefly before they turned for home.

The two weeks passed slowly for Ellen although she was kept busy preparing two of her young charges to go to school in England. She helped pack their luggage, made last-minute trips into Castlebar to buy forgotten items and tried to reassure the two young boys who were fearful about the journey and about the new school. Finally, everything was organised and the boys were ready. Their sister was to accompany them on the journey with her parents because they were going to spend a few weeks in London before returning home. Ellen had grown very fond of the three young children and she was as tearful as they were when she waved them off.

By the time James arrived she found herself free of any duties. Jack was unable to get leave and her sisters were busy filling an order for lace from America, so Ellen and James found themselves thrown very much into each other's company. They welcomed the opportunity to get to know each other and spent the afternoons walking, sometimes with the two younger sisters, sometimes alone. Evenings were spent by the fireside with the family or visiting the homes of local friends. This time James was not in uniform but Ellen thought he looked just as handsome in his sombre black suit and winged collar.

Friends of the family who were local farmers were having a dance that Saturday night in their kitchen and Ellen thought it as exciting as going to a ball as she prepared. The sisters shared a bedroom so there was much laughing and gossiping as they curled each other's hair with curling irons and tried on different dresses.

"James is such a gentleman, isn't he?" Annie was obviously quite taken with James.

"I think he is in love with you. His eyes follow you around all the time," observant Maggie said.

"What were you talking about yesterday when you came back from your walk? Did he propose to you?" Jane, as usual, wanted to know everything. Ellen blushed but was spared having to reply by the entrance of their mother.

Mary Ann usually joined them while they made their preparations for a social event because she enjoyed the girlish fun but this time she came in briefly, admired the hair styles and called Ellen out to talk privately with her. "Ellen, I want you to think about you and James. You seem to be getting very close. I like James but the life of a soldier's wife is not an easy one. James is just a sergeant and you would find yourself mixing with all kinds of people. I know going to India sounds attractive but what about when he comes back? What is he going to do then? Would you be happy living in a barracks?" She tried to take her daughter's hand.

Ellen took a step back. "Mama, I don't care about any of that. I think I love James. He has asked me to marry him and go to India. We will be going for seven years. He wants to speak to Papa as soon as possible."

"What? You have only known him a few weeks. You couldn't possibly be in love with him." Mary Ann was shocked.

"Yes, I am," Ellen retorted. "Anyway, I have always wanted to travel and see some more of the world. I can't settle down to life in a small town like Maggie or marry a farmer as Jane is likely to do. James is handsome and charming and he wants to take me to India. This is my chance of happiness. If I don't take it, soon I will be an old maid." Her voice was rising with emotion.

"Ellen, don't be ridiculous," her mother said. "You are only twenty. You have plenty of time to think about marriage."

"That is not what you said when Maggie and Matt became engaged."

"Well, that was different," Mary Ann argued. "We know Matt and his family. Besides, he will inherit a jeweller's shop and will provide very well for his wife. I don't think Papa will be pleased when he hears that you want to marry a soldier."

Ellen looked at her mother defiantly. "I will be twenty-one soon and then I can make up my own mind about whom I marry."

"There is no need to speak to me like that, Ellen," Mary Ann said in an injured tone. "Papa and I just want what is best for you."

"I want to marry James. That is what is best for me. Will you talk to Papa about it, please?" Ellen pleaded.

Mary sighed and hugged her daughter. "You've always been different from your sisters. Well, if it makes you happy, I will talk to Papa this evening and then James can talk to him in the morning."

Ellen couldn't wait to get James to herself to tell him the good news. When they reached their friends' house she introduced James to those who hadn't yet met him, smiling to herself at the admiring glances he was receiving and keeping a proprietary hand on his arm. While the fiddler and melodeon players struck up the first tune she drew James into the parlour which had been laid out with a simple supper for the dancers. "James, you can speak to Papa tomorrow. Mama will speak to him this evening and I am sure that they won't object. Oh, I am so happy"

James took both her hands and drew her to him. He kissed her gently on the lips and said, "First thing in the morning I will ask him."

They emerged out into the big flagged kitchen from which the furniture had been removed and as the musicians struck up a Mazurka, they whirled onto the floor. All eyes were on them as they danced; people sensed romance in the air. They stayed on the floor for the Gay Gordons, a polka and a very energetic Walls of Limerick; when the musicians announced a break for refreshment, they were both pink and breathless. Ellen would have wished the night to go on forever except that she was anxious about the next morning's interview between her father and James.

Their house was only a few minutes' walk away so they all

walked home together. James went off to his room while their parents sat in the parlour and had a cup of tea. No doubt they took the opportunity to discuss their daughter's future.

Ellen confided her fears to Maggie as they undressed for bed. "Do you think Papa will give his consent? I often see him frowning at James. Even tonight when Papa saw him drinking some punch, he looked very disapproving. I will die if he doesn't give his consent."

Maggie patted her arm reassuringly as she helped her off with her dress. "Don't worry. If Mama gives her consent then Papa will too."

The next morning, the two men went for a walk together. When they returned, they were both smiling broadly. Henry put his arm around his daughter. "I am very happy for you both. Now, go and kiss your future husband!"

Ellen ran to James and he kissed her as her parents smiled benignly. There was much embracing, shaking of hands and laughing, especially when the other sisters were told the good news.

"I thought I would be the first to get married," Maggie said as she hugged her sister.

"Well, I am the oldest so it is only fair that I am first."

"Can we be bridesmaids?" chorused the two younger sisters.

"You will all be bridesmaids," Ellen promised.

Chapter 2
September 1901: The Wedding

The wedding was arranged for three months later, on 24th September. Ellen spent the intervening weeks in a whirl of activity. There was so much to do: all her trousseau to prepare, the wedding to plan, furniture to be selected, and the wedding cake to be made. Her sisters were making her wedding gown and their own gowns so the house seemed to fill with the froth of lace and silk. Henry made his escape from the feminine excitement to his responsibilities on the estate, as often as possible. Mary Ann had overcome her reservations about James and wholeheartedly directed the preparations. She selected a number of small items of furniture from the overcrowded lodge rooms for Ellen to take to Renmore and went with her to Galway to buy linens, kitchen items and other necessities.

Ellen made her first visit to the barracks in Renmore with her mother two weeks before the wedding. The tall grey buildings with narrow windows which formed three sides of a square were a contrast to the squat, ivy-covered lodge with its tumbling cottage garden. There were a few clipped shrubs in front of the buildings but no flowers to lessen the severity of the angles. The married quarters they had been allocated seemed very small and claustrophobic in comparison to the sprawling clutter of the gate lodge and she found it hard to imagine actually living there.

She wrinkled her nose at the damp dusty smell in the rooms which combined with the stale odours of cooking. "It's very small, isn't it?"

Her mother could hear the anxiety in her voice; she didn't want to betray her own misgivings. "When you have your own things around you it will look different, a stór."

Ellen smiled at the Irish endearment. She knew it was meant to reassure her. There was a small kitchen with a range, a square, empty parlour and a bedroom with a high iron bedstead. There was a shared lavatory down the corridor which was cold and damp and smelled of Jeyes Fluid. She had a moment of panic when she thought of leaving her home and living in this unattractive place but she consoled herself as she and her mother opened all the windows; it was only temporary because they would be leaving for India within the year. When she thought about marriage, she focused on the glamour and exoticism of India and brushed aside the thoughts of living in the barracks. From the window of the parlour she could see soldiers drilling in the square below and hear the barked orders of their sergeant. That at least seemed exciting. She said so to her mother who was looking doubtfully at the small rooms and wondering if the furniture they had brought with them would fit into it.

She had little time to think any more about the accommodation in the barracks during the following two weeks. Each day was a flurry of preparations: cleaning every inch of the house, having fittings for the gowns, packing the bags and small items of furniture which Ellen was to take with her. The night before the wedding was the first pause in the frenzy of activity and Mary Ann sent the girls off to get a good night's sleep before the big day. There was some excited chatting but the other girls soon fell asleep. Ellen lay and listened to their regular breathing. It would be her last night spent in this familiar room with her sisters; the thought made her stomach tighten with anxiety. Moving quietly, she made her way to the kitchen. The kitchen was lit only by the glow of the range: the big clock on the over mantle ticked, the scent of freshly baked bread hung in the air – a smell that always reminded her of her mother. She sat in front of the range in the dark room and found herself sobbing uncontrollably. In her mind's eye she could see the kitchen as it usually was in the evening: her mother sewing, her

27

father reading the newspaper, her sisters at their lace-making. She remembered the drab and uninviting quarters in the barracks; she didn't want to leave her family and comfortable home.

Suddenly, the door opened and her father was beside her, drawing up a chair and putting his arm around her. "Don't cry, my dear. It is only natural to be a bit sad when you are leaving the people and things that you love. But James is a good man and he loves you. Even though we don't agree on political matters, I like him. Dry your tears now and go and get your beauty sleep."

"I'm not really sad, Papa. I love James and I want to marry him." She nestled into her father's arms. "It is just that I know I will miss you and Mama and my sisters so much and Renmore is so far away and then we will be going to India and I won't see any of you for seven years."

"We will miss you too but we will see you as often as we can. Now, off to bed with you and think of the wonderful life you will have with James." He kissed the top of her head. She had always been his favourite daughter and the one he would miss the most.

Ellen didn't see the tears he wiped away as soon as she left the room. She deliberately put the disturbing thoughts of the barracks out of her head and eventually fell asleep thinking about James and the lovely home they would have, the beautiful children they would raise and the wonderful life they would have together in India.

Their wedding day was a typical September one, bright and warmed by the jewel colours of the autumnal flowers and trees but with a hint in the crispness of the air of colder days to come. The house was full of flurry and excitement as the five women dressed for the ceremony. Ellen walked with her parents and sisters the short distance to the church, greeting neighbours as they went. Orange monbretia decorated the hedgerows along the way. When they came to the National School which all four of the girls had attended and where Ellen had been a monitor, the pupils had been allowed out in the yard to wave to the wedding party.

They passed the orchard where the fruit on the apple trees glistened and glinted with dew in the sunlight like baubles on a Christmas tree. Neighbours and friends filled the church and turned welcoming faces to greet them. On the altar, hydrangeas with their faded mauve flowers complemented the dusty pink of Ellen's wedding dress. Late roses provided her small, scented bouquet. Her sisters carried nosegays of sweet pea. James and Jack wore their scarlet uniforms, a counterpoint to the delicate pastels of the sisters.

Ellen moved as in a dream; she felt she was watching herself getting married. She walked up the aisle with her father holding her hand tightly as he did when she was a little girl and in danger of falling; she saw the shy smile that James gave her as he and Jack turned around to look at her; she heard herself and James repeat the wedding vows after Father O'Dwyer; she walked down the aisle with James, holding his hand tightly and saw the congregation through a haze as though a mist had intruded into the church.

"This is the beginning of my wonderful life with James," she thought as she accepted the congratulations of friends and neighbours.

It was only when they returned to her parents' house for the wedding breakfast that she began to have a sense of reality again. The house looked wonderful. A log fire blazed in the inglenook, its warm woody scent filling the house. Big vases of dahlias and hydrangeas decorated every available surface. Neighbours had assisted her mother to prepare the food and it looked delicious, spread out on the big kitchen table which had been covered by their best linen tablecloth. Lord and Lady Lucan had sent word that they were to get any food they wanted from the estate. There was a cooked goose although it was not even Christmas. Jack had provided a punch which her father grudgingly allowed and he and

James and his four comrades who had been invited took up their stand beside the punch bowl which, amazingly, never seemed to get empty.

Ellen circulated around the room and into the parlour where the older people were sitting, enjoying their admiration, accepting their congratulations and showing off her ring. She knew that she probably wouldn't see any of these people for weeks, maybe even months, once she went to live in Renmore. The thought made her feel both sad and elated; she was moving away to a bigger world.

Mary Ann was in her element entertaining the relatives and neighbours. She and her daughters made sure that everyone had a welcoming glass of punch or cup of tea when they arrived. The house seemed to be full to bursting with people chatting animatedly when there was a sudden hush. Lord and Lady Lucan had called to wish the young couple a happy married life. They spoke to Henry and Mary Ann, shook hands with Ellen and James and left quickly, knowing that their presence was inhibiting many of the people there from enjoying themselves. The level of noise and chat began to rise again and Mary Ann encouraged all the guests to come to the table and help themselves to the wedding feast. There were sounds of appreciation and enjoyment as people filled their plates and found a place to sit and enjoy the meal.

Mary Ann waited until they were all replete with the rich food and then announced a singsong, a "Noble Call" where each singer then called on another to perform. Amid good-natured teasing and applause she said that she would begin it herself. Taking her stance by the fireplace she began to sing "An Culainn" in her native Irish. She had a sweet soprano voice and Ellen could feel the tears coming to her eyes as she listened to the haunting tune. Few of the people present could understand Irish but they didn't need to; the traditional song spoke to their hearts.

There was a brief silence when the song finished and then

applause and shouts of "Maith an cailín!" from her own relatives. Mary Ann did a mock curtsy and called on her husband to sing. He was a devotee of Michael Balfe, so people were delighted when he tucked his chin into his chest and sang "I Dreamt I Dwelt in Marble Halls" in his strong baritone. He called on his daughter Ellen to sing next but she agreed on condition that her sisters sang with her. The four girlish voices blended beautifully when they sang the fashionable "After the Ball".

Ellen hugged her sisters and then turned to smile at James. "I call on my husband to sing" caused a ripple of laughter at her first use of "my husband". James consulted with Jack and his other friends and after a bit of discussion, they gave a very lively rendition of a recent barrack room favourite, "The West Clare Railway" by Mr Percy French. Henry glanced at the now empty punch bowl but smiled at the high spirits of the young men. A few neighbours then performed their traditional party pieces with some encouragement from Mary Ann.

When the lamps were lit and the elderly Gannon brothers produced their fiddle and accordion, it was a signal for the tables to be cleared and the furniture pushed back in preparation for dancing. Jack and Ellen were the first to take to the floor and danced an elegant waltz before others joined them for a very boisterous polka. Ellen could have danced all night and was surprised when Jack announced that their carriage was waiting outside. In a flurry of embraces, kisses, goodbyes and good wishes, Ellen and James put on their coats and hats, got into the carriage as their bags were stowed and waved to those of the company who had come outside to see them off. Mary Ann and Henry looked sad and tearful as they waved goodbye to their daughter and Ellen felt the tears come to her own eyes. James put his arm around her and held her close, gently wiping the teardrops away.

The plan was that they would set out for Renmore in the early evening, in a horse and carriage which James had hired, and arrive there to spend their wedding night. Ellen was glad. She felt shy and embarrassed at the idea of spending her wedding night in her parents' house as her mother had suggested. She didn't mind the long journey to Renmore because she would be alone with James for the first time. The dreamlike feeling returned when she found herself alone at last with James in the moving carriage, cocooned in the warm darkness which was scented by the roses in her bouquet. James still had his arm around her and pulled her to him. Their lips met and she curled into him, feeling the sturdiness of his chest. She knew that some women were afraid of their wedding night but she looked forward to it. She wanted James close inside her where she could feel unfamiliar warmth surging through her. They continued to kiss and he stroked her back, then her breasts through her clothes. Suddenly he moved away and fumbled in his pockets until he found something, a silver flask; she could see it glinting in the moonlight which slanted in through the carriage window.

"What is it, James? What are you drinking?"

"Whiskey," he answered. "Would you like some?"

Ellen had never seen anyone drink whiskey from a flask and had certainly never tasted it. But James was holding out the flask invitingly. "Well, maybe I will just taste it."

The liquid burned her throat and she coughed and spluttered as James laughed. "The first time always makes you cough. Next time, it will taste nicer."

"There won't be a next time. It tastes horrible. Anyway Papa would be very angry if he knew that I tasted whiskey," Ellen gasped between coughs.

James took a long drink from the flask, wiped his mouth on the back of his hand, replaced the cap and put the flask in his pocket. He drew her into his arms and kissed her. "You won't have to worry about Papa now. You are my wife so you only have to worry about me."

She could taste the whiskey on his breath as well as the cigarettes which he had smoked earlier. It was both attractive and repulsive, she couldn't decide which. She thought of the sheltered life she had just left; she pictured her family still dancing in the kitchen and tears came to her eyes. But she wanted to be with James, to be his wife, to share his bed, to have his children. She had chosen the life of a soldier's wife and she would go to India with him.

She could feel James's head falling sideways onto her shoulder. He was asleep. She sat upright and guided his head into a more comfortable position. Scudding clouds were obscuring the moon so that there were only odd flashes of light. The wind had got up and she could feel it rocking the carriage, but she felt safe and warm as she cradled her husband's head and thought about the future. The clip clop of the horse's hooves and the regular creaking of the carriage had a mesmeric quality and she found herself dozing fitfully.

The moon had disappeared completely behind clouds when the sudden halting of the carriage woke her up. "We're here, missus!" The driver opened the door and handed out their luggage and she woke James who then struggled sleepily ahead of her with one of the trunks to open the door. He turned up the gaslight and she could see that someone had placed a large vase of flowers on the table and had also lit the range.

She was admiring the flowers when James returned with the other trunk. "I should have carried you over the threshold, sweetheart. Let me at least carry you into the bedroom."

He swept her easily into his arms and did a few twirls before putting her down gently on the bed. "Hello, Mrs Devereux," he said. "I love you."

"Hello, Sergeant Devereux," she replied. "I love you too."

Chapter 3
1901-1903: Life in the Barracks

Next morning she was startled into wakefulness by a bugle call.

"Reveille." James smiled up at her. "You'll hear it every morning."

He pulled her to him and kissed her. Then he rolled out of bed and began to dress. She could see that he was naked and had time to admire his muscular body before he struggled into his drawers.

He caught her appreciative glance and smiled at her as she stretched luxuriously and rolled into the warm place where his body had been. "Sorry love, I have to go. I'm on duty this morning until eight o'clock this evening. I'll just have a cup of tea."

Mindful of her wifely duties, Ellen protested, "No, let me get you a proper breakfast."

Then she realised that she had no idea what food might be in the small kitchen.

James saw her consternation. "I asked Mrs Vaughan to get in a few necessities like tea and milk and bread and butter. She probably brought the flowers too. You'll like her. She is the wife of another sergeant who is a good friend of mine, Des Vaughan."

While James assembled his uniform, she got up and riddled the fire in the range so that flames curled up around the kettle. She dressed in the first clothes she found in the trunk while the water heated and then poured some of the hot water into a bowl so that James could shave. The kitchen was small; she found the bread, butter, tea and milk easily and prepared a simple breakfast. He ate and drank quickly, buttoned up his jacket, checked his uniform in the mirror, kissed her and was gone.

Without his presence, the room seemed empty and alien. For a few minutes, Ellen felt alone. The silence was oppressive. She had never actually spent much time on her own before. There had always been the company of her sisters and her parents or the children up at the Big House. She wondered what she would do for the day until James came home. Her wedding dress, thrown carelessly over a chair, looked incongruous in the small room. There was still some warm water left; she washed quickly and found some more suitable clothes in one of the trunks.

The kettle boiled while she dressed and she made a cup of tea. Slowly, cradling the warmth of the cup in her hands, she moved to the window and contemplated her new life. Down below she could see the soldiers drilling on the square and hear the barked commands of their sergeant. She watched them for a while, marvelling at the precision of their movements. Just as she was deciding to wash the breakfast dishes, there was a knock on the door.

The woman outside was about Ellen's own age, small and sturdily built with inquisitive brown eyes and curly hair that was tumbling out of the combs that tried to restrain it. "Hello missus. I am Violet Vaughan. My husband, Des, is a friend of your husband's." She stepped in, observing Ellen's clothes and the discarded wedding dress which she had not yet put away, noting the opened but unpacked trunks.

Ellen was delighted to see a friendly face. "Oh yes, you are the friend who was kind enough to get in some groceries and those lovely flowers and you even set the fire. That was very good of you. My name is Ellen Ainsworth, I mean, Devereux."

Violet laughed at her stumbling over her new name. "Takes a while to get used to being called Mrs. I still think Mrs Vaughan is my mother-in-law."

Violet had a broad Mayo accent and the red coarsened skin of someone who had worked outside. Her clothes were old-fashioned and well worn. "Would you like a cup of tea? Our quarters are just down the corridor. I don't want to leave

35

Desmond, my little boy, for too long. He is only nine months old and he is teething at the moment so I am not getting much sleep."

Ellen followed her to rooms that were similar to her own but furnished much more sparsely. Her mother had given her some items of furniture and her sisters had made curtains and cushions which made the small rooms quite cosy. Violet's rooms seemed to have only the bare essentials. There were no curtains on the windows and only one chair beside a battered table. In the corner of the kitchen was a drawer which was doing duty as a cot for the small red-faced baby who was screaming and very distressed.

"He has been screaming like that for the past hour. His gums are on fire. If I had a drop of whiskey, I'd rub it into his gums." In the cold light from the bare window, Violet looked exhausted.

Ellen remembered the silver flask from the previous night. "I think we might have some whiskey. I'll run down and get it."

She found the flask easily enough and there was still a few drops in it. Violet had the baby in her arms when she returned and handed her the whiskey. Cradling the baby's head in one arm, she dipped her forefinger in the whiskey and rubbed it on the swollen gums. After a few minutes, the baby quietened down and eventually fell asleep.

Violet sighed. "Poor lamb. He's exhausted. He hasn't slept for nights. Des got very angry with me last night because I couldn't stop him crying. Thank God, he'll sleep for hours now. I might even get a bit of a nap myself before Des gets home. Sit down there on the chair and I'll make that cup of tea."

Ellen sat down on the only chair in the room while Violet bustled about, putting the kettle on the range and finding two cups and a teapot. She continued to talk. "It'll be nice to have someone my own age to talk to. Some of the other sergeants' wives are much older and not very friendly."

Over cups of tea, while the baby snuffled and slept, they told each other a little about themselves. Violet's father rented a small farm, near Pontoon in Mayo, which he was now hoping to buy, encouraged by the new land laws. She had worked on the farm with her brother and two sisters until she married Des Vaughan. She had met him at a crossroads dance while he was on leave and staying with some cousins nearby.

"He was probably my only chance of getting off the farm. I hated it, out in all weathers and working day and night. I was lucky to meet him." Violet grimaced at the memory. "My sisters envy me; a husband with a steady job and us off to India in a year!"

Ellen told her how she had met James and about her family and the lodge and her job looking after the young children of Lord Lucan. Violet was impressed. "No wonder you look so posh and ladylike!"

Ellen thought of the Big House and all the beautiful things in it. She pictured the cosy lodge with her mother and sisters sitting around the fire listening to her father read interesting items from the newspaper. It seemed a world away from the cramped and bare room that they were sitting in. She thought of her own rooms that she had just left; the trunks were waiting to be unpacked and the breakfast dishes to be washed; the range might be out; she had no idea what they were going to have for their tea when James returned. She asked Violet a few questions about where to buy basic foodstuffs and said goodbye, promising to call the following morning. Violet was already lying down on the bed hoping to get some sleep before Desmond woke, when she closed the door and returned to her own quarters.

The rooms looked welcoming after the frugal comfort of Violet's, even if they were untidy. She set about unpacking the trunks, making the bed, washing the dishes and relighting the range. By the time James came home she had set the table and arranged a tea of eggs and scones which they had brought from the lodge. The look on James's face when he opened the door and saw the table laid, the range blazing and her welcoming smile made her feel very warm and excited. Then she thought of the new life that was ahead of them and she was confident that she had made the right choice; she was a soldier's wife now.

Ellen soon settled in to the routine of the barracks. When James left in the morning she cleaned the small rooms and put away the breakfast dishes. Sometimes she had some washing to do which she then hung out on the communal washing line. She was a bit shy about hanging her underwear in such a public place but others didn't seem to have such qualms. She smiled to herself at the size of some of the drawers on display and wondered at the raggedness of some of the skirts and dresses.

Violet, carrying Desmond, usually accompanied her to the local shops where they bought many of their provisions. Some things could be bought in the sergeants' mess but Ellen enjoyed the walk to the shops and the banter with the shopkeepers. Violet always seemed to be short of money and bought the cheapest cuts of meat. Sometimes Ellen had to lend her a few pennies to make up the price of her shopping. She wondered at that because Des earned the same amount as James, yet they never seemed to have enough money. Clutching her baby close to her and looking away, Violet confided to her that Des liked to gamble. Any kind of gambling attracted him: cards, horses, wagers on boxing matches; they all seemed to hold the same attraction. Gambling and drinking were all part of the social life which the men enjoyed in the sergeants' mess. James enjoyed a few evenings a week in the mess with Jack and Des and some of his other friends and sometimes came home loud and garrulous and smelling of porter, but Ellen knew that she could always rely on getting the same amount every week for housekeeping. Another one of the wives that she got to know, Nan Murphy, appeared a few times with a black eye, the result she said of her baby kicking her as she was changing his nappy. Everyone knew that Dan Murphy had a temper after a few drinks and often picked fights with one or another of his comrades. It seemed that he also took out his anger on his wife.

"He'd want to watch himself," Violet said. "If he gets into trouble and is demoted, he won't be allowed to bring Nan with him to India. Enlisted men can't bring their wives. Des says he is on his last warning."

"But what would Nan do if she couldn't go with him?"

Violet shook her head. "I don't know, go home to her family in Dublin, I expect. I don't suppose she would like that anymore than I would."

Ellen began to realise that her upbringing in the lodge in Castlebar had been very sheltered; she knew very little about life. She missed the company of her mother and sisters and having someone to talk to about her new experiences. When her mother came on a visit before Christmas, Ellen was delighted to see her and hear all the news about home. She showed her mother all around Renmore and they stopped in a little tea shop where they settled down in a corner and enjoyed some tea and fruitcake.

"Nice, but not as good as mine," Mary Ann pronounced as she pressed her fingers into the last crumbs of the sticky cake. She smiled at Ellen, who was looking happy and well. She had been observing her daughter all day and could see that she was content. Over several cups of tea, Ellen told her mother about her friendship with Violet and the concern she had for her friend because of Des's gambling. She also mentioned Nan and the story about her baby kicking her and giving her a black eye.

"That sort of thing happens more often than you might

imagine," her mother said. "I sometimes visit families on the demesne with Lady Lucan and we hear some awful stories. Drink is a terrible curse and leads to violence and gambling and all sorts of abuse."

"Is that why Papa doesn't drink?" Ellen knew the answer but wanted to hear the story again.

"Yes, when he was born just after the Famine, people had nothing, yet they often spent what little they had on drink to escape their misery. His own father drank and lost the little land they had when old Lord Lucan started land clearance. Luckily, the present Lord Lucan is a very different man from his father. As you know, he gave your father a job and a house to live in and has always been very good to us."

Ellen looked shyly at her mother. "Mama, there is something else that I would like to ask you."

She began to describe some of the symptoms which she had been noticing over the previous two weeks; her mother confirmed what she suspected with tears of joy in her eyes. She was going to have a baby!

Mary Ann hugged her and laughed and cried at the same time. "My first grandchild! Oh, my darling girl. What wonderful news; I am absolutely delighted!"

Her mother's joy was contagious but Ellen realised that she felt both frightened and elated at the idea of giving birth. Her mother seemed to know that instinctively when Ellen asked her, "Will you be here with me when the time comes?"

Mary Ann held both her daughter's hands. "Of course I will. I'll come a week before the baby is due. That should be about the end of July. Don't look so worried. Having a baby is perfectly natural and you will have the best of care here in the barracks. Did you say anything yet to James?"

"No, I wanted to be sure before I told him. He will be so

excited."

Her mother was able to stay and have tea with them before being picked up by one of Lord Lucan's carriages. James fussed about his mother-in-law, admiring her hat and flirting gently with her. The happiness between the young couple was palpable and the mother was glad to see that her instincts about James had been right. He was a good husband and would be a good father. As she said goodbye to the young couple she could feel the suppressed excitement in her daughter.

"God bless you and take care of yourself, a stór. And you take care of her too, James."

Putting his arm around Ellen as they waved out the window to her mother as she got into the carriage on the square, James realised that there had been an extra depth of meaning in his mother-in-law's words. He looked questioningly at his wife who was flushed with excitement. "James, we are going to have a baby!"

"Are you sure? When did you find out?"

"I wasn't sure until I talked to Mama."

Ellen could see the tears in his eyes as he drew her gently to him and kissed her. "Oh my love! You have made me very happy. I can hardly believe it! When is the baby due?"

"In July. I can hardly believe it myself! Would you prefer a boy or a girl?"

"I don't mind which, my love. As long as you and the baby are well, that is all that matters to me," he said as he sat down and gently guided her onto his lap.

James was very solicitous of his wife and Ellen's pregnancy was an easy one apart from the odd bout of morning sickness. Her mother sent her some bigger skirts and she made a wrap-around pinafore from some material which Lady Lucan sent her. Her sisters were making a layette including a hand-embroidered

41

christening outfit, so Ellen contented herself with knitting small bootees and matinee jackets. She was hoping for a girl, mainly because she had no experience of boys, but she knew that James would like a son.

When her waters broke, it was two weeks early and she was shopping with Violet in Moon's Department Store in Galway. Luckily, they didn't have baby Desmond with them because Violet's sister, who was visiting, was looking after him. In spite of having had a baby herself, the other woman flapped about, urging Ellen to sit down and looking helplessly at the shop assistants in Moon's.

"Violet, call a carriage to bring me to the hospital and then go back to the barracks yourself. You have to tell James and he will let my mother know." Ellen wrapped a towel around her which one of the shop girls had given her and, with as much dignity as she could muster, walked out to where there were waiting carriages.

The pains began to get stronger on the way to the hospital so that she had to clutch Violet's hand and wait for the contraction to pass before she could speak. "Get back and tell James as quickly as you can. I don't think my mother will get here on time now." She waited until another wave of pain passed before she could get out of the carriage.

"Are you sure you will be all right?" Violet obviously couldn't wait to get away and she helped her friend down and quickly got back up into the carriage herself. "The nurses will help you. I'll tell James to come as quickly as possible. God bless you."

Ellen had never felt as lonely as she did when the carriage pulled away and she allowed the nurse to guide her inside. The smell of the hospital was making her feel sick. She knew that James wouldn't be able to see her until it was all over and her mother was far away in Castlebar. An even stronger wave of pain made her cry out and double over.

The nurse put an arm around her. "Come on, my dear, don't look so frightened. Women are having babies here all the time and you are no different. Have you any bag with you? No, don't worry, we will soon get you into a nightgown and ready for the midwife. It looks as though it won't be very long."

Ellen found herself being changed into a rough, well washed cotton nightgown. Her own things were taken away, even her wedding ring. The ward that she was brought to was full of women in various stages of labour, some screaming for their mothers, others lying stoically waiting for the next pain.

Ellen became hysterical. "I don't want to stay here. I want my mother. I want to go home."

"You'll be going home soon, love, with a lovely baby of your own," the nurse said patiently. "Come on now and lie down and let me have a look at you."

Ellen allowed herself to be led to a bed. She lay down just as an overwhelming pain washed over her and she thought she was about to split open. She could only see black in front of her and then there was nothing. She was vaguely aware of people moving around her, of being pulled and then a tearing sensation and a baby crying.

When she woke up, James was leaning over her with tears in his eyes. "Ellen, my love! The baby is beautiful and so are you. I got here as quickly as I could but the baby had already been born. It was all over very quickly, it seems.

Ellen fought to focus on James. "The baby. Where is it? What is it?"

"A girl!" James held her hand. "They just took her away for a few minutes to clean her up. She's perfect. She has a great pair of lungs and I think she looks like me."

A nurse appeared at the side of the bed with a bundle

wrapped in a blanket. "Here you are, Mrs Devereux, your lovely baby girl!"

She helped Ellen to sit up against the pillows and put the baby to her breast. She immediately started to suckle, making a contented snuffling sound. Her tiny hands clutched her mother's fingers, her head was covered in a golden down and her eyes were navy blue. Ellen though she had never seen anything so beautiful.

The nurse was smiling at the baby. "She's a beauty! What are you going to call her?"

James and Ellen looked at each other. They had thought of many names but hadn't made a final decision. Ellen made up her mind. "I'd like to name her after my mother, Mary Ann. But we will call her Nancy."

James looked at his daughter. "Nancy! Yes, she looks like a Nancy. Your mother will be delighted."

Oblivious to all the attention she was getting, baby Nancy gave a big yawn and fell into a contented sleep.

Ellen must have fallen asleep herself because when next she woke, her mother was smiling at her and down at the small bundle she held in her arms. "She is beautiful and so big! The nurse let me hold her because you were asleep. I got here as soon as I could. Luckily, the carriage was coming in to Galway for some provisions. How are you feeling, a stór?"

Ellen smiled at the familiar Irish term of affection and took the baby from her mother. "I feel wonderful, Mama. We are going to call her Mary Ann after you, but Nancy as a pet name so there is no confusion. Won't Papa be pleased?"

"He will be delighted." She tried out the name. "Nancy Devereux! What a lovely name!"

Mary Ann was able to stay for a couple of days and she persuaded James to let Ellen go back to Castlebar with her for a week's recuperation. Ellen didn't want to leave her husband but the thought of being looked after by her mother and sisters was more attractive than going back to the grim barracks.

James agreed and Ellen found herself tucked up snugly in the carriage with baby Nancy cocooned in a large blanket on her lap. Her mother was seated opposite with three large bags beside her, two of them Ellen's. James kissed his wife and baby goodbye and motioned to the driver to drive on. Henry and his daughters were overjoyed when the carriage arrived and Ellen and the baby emerged. Maggie insisted on carrying the baby once her father and the other girls had got a good look at her. During the following week, Ellen only held the baby when it was time for her to feed. Otherwise, one of the girls appropriated her and very often it was Maggie.

It was the custom to have a baby baptised as soon as possible so Mary Ann thought it would be a good idea to have the christening there in Castlebar with all the family if James could get leave to travel. Usually women were confined for two or three weeks after the birth and did not go to the christening. Ellen felt so well that she insisted on going even though it was only two weeks after the birth. Maggie and Jack, who was travelling with James, were to be the godparents.

The local parish church was full when they arrived. Ellen hadn't been there since her wedding and was delighted to see that the altar vases were filled with hydrangeas just as they had been almost a year previously. A happy buzz echoed around the church until Father O'Dwyer arrived. There were six babies from the parish to be christened. When it came to her turn, Nancy slept peacefully in Maggie's arms, swaddled in her christening shawl, until the cold water was poured on her head at which she gave a loud yell.

The whole family and some of the friends who had attended the ceremony went back to the lodge where Mary Ann and her daughters served a dinner of ham and cabbage followed by apple tart and thick cream. Jack produced a bottle to "wet the baby's head" and all the men with the exception of Henry drank a toast to the baby's health. Lord and Lady Lucan called in to the lodge to see the new baby and brought a present of a silver christening mug.

James never left his wife's side and managed to hold his daughter for much of the afternoon. He was glad when the time came for them to be tucked into the carriage with Nancy in his arms and a drowsy Ellen by his side and he could have his family to himself. He watched his wife and daughter sleep for almost the whole journey, only waking up when the carriage slowed and then stopped before entering the barracks square. Nancy immediately started crying; it was an hour past her feeding time. Violet had once again lit the fire and put some flowers on the table. Ellen sat in the armchair in front of the fire and fed Nancy.

James watched the firelight play on the warm brown hair of his wife and glance off the blonde down which covered his daughter's head. He bent and put an arm protectively around them. "You are both so beautiful. I love you very much."

Chapter 4
1902-1903: Nancy

Nancy was a delightful baby and the days now flew by for Ellen. She enjoyed bathing her baby in the mornings and dressing her in one of the little layettes that her sisters had made. When she sang to her, Nancy gazed at her mother solemnly. She looked around her and seemed to want to absorb as much as possible on their daily walks. When James came home and lifted her up, Nancy gurgled with joy and played with the shiny buttons on his uniform. Ellen thought that she had never been so happy and was content to stay in the confined quarters of the barracks. Some days the winter weather made it impossible to go out for more than a few minutes but she was happy to sit in front of the range, playing with Nancy or reading while the baby slept.

Maggie wrote to her that she and Matt were planning their wedding for the following May; the house that his father had been building for them would be ready by then. Ellen had a fleeting feeling of envy as she read her sister's description of the small house. She had always dreamed of having a house of her own and here she was, living in cramped married quarters. Now Maggie, her younger sister, would have a house of her own. Even though she had never wanted to stay in Castlebar, she was a bit envious; she was also happy for Maggie. She was looking forward to going home for the wedding and was waiting to tell James the news when he came home.

However, he had news of his own when he came home that evening looking very excited. "Ellen, at last! We will be leaving for India in two months!"

He waltzed Ellen around the room and then picked up Nancy so that she was being waltzed between them, shrieking with delight.

"But, James! Then we will miss Maggie's wedding! I had a letter from her today and they are getting married in May. Could we postpone going for a couple of months? She will be so disappointed if we are not there."

James looked concerned. "I'm sorry love, but I have no choice about the departure date. The battalion will all travel together. Will you be very disappointed to miss the wedding?"

"Yes, of course. I would love to be at Maggie's wedding and she will be disappointed if I am not. But this is what we have been waiting for. I'll miss my parents and my sisters and my friends here but I am looking forward to living in India."

"We will have to start packing as soon as the trunks arrive. You will get a list of the kind of things you should bring for yourself and Nancy. And you won't be leaving all your friends behind. Des and Violet will be coming too."

"What about Jack? Will he be travelling with us?" Ellen's mind was racing ahead, imagining the journey.

"I am afraid not. His division is going to northern India a month later than us."

The next few weeks were hectic and James was very busy. They managed to fit in a trip to Galway to buy lighter clothes and some necessities for the journey. They also had to have photos taken for their passports and while there, they had Nancy's first photograph taken. It was an elegant study of the three of them: Nancy in a lace dress made by her aunts, James in his scarlet uniform, Ellen in what had been her wedding gown with her hair swept up to frame her face. She arranged for a copy to be sent to her parents and got an ornate frame for their own copy.

Ellen and the baby also went to Castlebar during the weeks before they left. James accompanied them on the outward journey to say goodbye to Ellen's family. He had to return to the barracks a day later. Nancy was teething and not sleeping very well so, when James left, Ellen was happy to let her sisters take over so that she could rest and have some time with her mother.

On her last afternoon, Ellen sat in the kitchen with her mother while Nancy was taken for a walk by her aunts. "I can't believe that I won't see you or Papa or my sisters for seven years! It seems like a lifetime. I am looking forward to going to India but I am afraid that I will be very lonely." She brushed away some tears and reached for her mother's hand.

Mary Ann put down the teacup she was holding and drew her daughter to her. "Nonsense, a stór. Won't you have James and Nancy and the new friends you have made for company? Before long, Nancy will have brothers or sisters and then you won't have any time to be lonely."

"That's just it. You and Papa won't be there. Nancy won't even know her grandparents." Ellen was sobbing.

Mary Ann stroked her daughter's hair and choked back her own tears. "We will be thinking of you and praying for you every day. You and I will write to each other as often as possible and you can keep me up to date on Nancy's progress. The girls will be back soon now, so dry your eyes and come and have tea with your sisters. We only have a few days together so let us enjoy them."

When the time came to leave, Ellen focused on trying to calm Nancy, who was red-faced and crying, so that she would not cry herself. They left in a flurry of hugs, tears, kisses and last-minute messages. She managed to control her grief so that it wasn't until the carriage turned into the barracks square that she allowed the sobs to escape, frightening Nancy into a moment of silence. James came to meet them and carried a wailing Nancy into their quarters followed by the driver and some of the bags.

He put his free arm around Ellen and kissed away some of her tears. "I know, sweetheart. It must have been hard saying

49

goodbye to your family. But you will love the life in India, I promise. Now I better get the rest of the bags. They must have given you half the house!"

Packing clothes for herself and the baby, saying goodbye to Jack and some of their other friends and selecting a few personal items to take took up the last few days, and suddenly they were ready for departure. Violet and she read the instructions and advice they had been given and helped each other with the last items of packing. Thankfully, Nancy was now the proud owner of a brand new tooth and had reverted to her former sunny disposition.

The ship which was to take them to India was leaving from Dover so they were to make the journey from Ireland by ship and train. Their husbands saw them safely on board the train from Galway with the other wives and children. The train journey passed uneventfully; the younger children slept, the older ones played up and down the corridor and the mothers chatted and viewed the scenery which was new to many of them. Neither Ellen nor Violet had ever been on a ship before; they were very excited when they arrived in Dublin and boarded the vessel which would take them across the Irish Sea. They were to share a cabin for the crossing and would not see their husbands until they boarded the vessel in Dover which would take them to India. The cabin was small but they managed to fit themselves and their babies and their baggage which had arrived before them into it with the help of some enlisted men. When they had fed and changed their babies and settled them down to sleep, Ellen and Violet lay down in their bunks themselves, tired but too excited to sleep.

"I have thought of nothing but India for the past few weeks and now I can't imagine what it will be like. Will it be very, very hot?" Violet asked her friend. "Will we be able to wear our

50

ordinary clothes? I hope so because I haven't got many light things, you don't really need them on a farm in Mayo!"

"It will be very, very hot, James said. Don't worry about clothes. I have some extra clothes you could have. My sisters made me some new ones and I won't need them all."

Violet smiled. "You are very good but I don't know if they would fit me. Anyway, Des says that you can get clothes made in India for nothing. The wives get dresses made for the dances in the sergeants' mess. Are you looking forward to the dances? I am. I never got to go to dances much before and now we will even have someone to mind the babies."

Violet was bubbling with girlish excitement. Ellen smiled at her friend's innocence. She was thinking of the dance in the kitchen in Castlebar, the night before James asked her father for her hand. "Yes, I love dancing and so does James. Now, we better try to get some sleep because we have another busy day tomorrow. Goodnight, Violet."

Neither of them could sleep. The cabin was airless and claustrophobic. The sea seemed to get rougher in the middle of the night and Ellen could feel her stomach churning from the tossing of the ship. She got up but found she couldn't keep her balance.

Violet was sitting up with her hand over her mouth and her eyes large and frightened. "I'm going to be sick!"

Just in time, Ellen found a sick bag and held it for her friend as she vomited violently into it.

Next morning Violet was still feeling very ill so Ellen had to wash and dress the two babies. Desmond was now toddling so he was quite a handful and squirmed and cried as she dressed him The sky was grey over Liverpool when they docked, almost as grey as the faces of the women who were disembarking. There was a special train to take them to Dover and they were grateful for its smooth regular rhythm and the sash windows which could be opened in each carriage. By the time they were walking up the gangplank to the ship which was to be their home for three weeks, Violet was cheerful again.

The cabins which they had been allocated were next to each other and were small but a lot bigger than the one they had been in on the crossing of the Irish Sea. Their husbands had some free time before the ship embarked so they were able to help with stowing the trunks and unpacking some of the things they would need for the long journey. James was delighted to be with his daughter again and played with her and sang to her while Ellen made the cabin as homely and comfortable as possible. Most of the women and children were up on the deck as the ship pulled away from the dock. People on the shore waved and as she returned their waves, watching the shoreline become hazy, Ellen had the feeling that she was waving goodbye to her old life.

The two friends were glad that they had cabins next door to each other. During the first week at sea, they wrapped up warmly every morning and took the babies up on deck for some fresh air, laughing and helping each other as they struggled up and down the gangways or looked for a sheltered place on the windy deck. They met other mothers who were doing the same thing and they made some new friends. After the first few days, neither of them suffered from seasickness and the babies seemed to thrive on the sea air and slept deeply. Some afternoons as the babies slept, Ellen showed Violet how to put her hair up in a fashionable style and how to use lemon juice to remove the freckles from her weatherworn skin.

Every night James held Ellen in his arms and told her stories about India, about the exotic birds and beautiful trees and flowers, the dramatic landscape. She loved listening to the strange names of the flowers, bougainvillea, lotus, jasmine; there were only two that she had heard of before, orchid and marigold, but she imagined the vibrant colours of all of them. He described birds with vivid plumage whose names he did not know, trees like the Flame tree and animals such as tigers that she had seen only in picture books. India began to sound more and more like a fairy tale that she and James and Nancy were about to become part of. James had a lot more time to spend now with his wife and child and he took full advantage of it. Sometimes Des called for him to come to the sergeants' mess for a drink and a game of cards but James usually declined, good-naturedly joking that Nancy wouldn't allow him out of her sight.

They had been one week at sea when the first rumours of an outbreak of measles among the children were heard. At first, Ellen did not worry too much. She was still breastfeeding Nancy and believed that that gave the baby some immunity. Neither she nor her sisters had had measles although she remembered her mother visiting families on the demesne in Castlebar where children had contracted the disease and died. Violet had had more experience and was frightened; her two youngest sisters had died of measles when there had been an outbreak in their village. Ellen thought of her mother and the precautions she took when returning from visiting sick people on the demesne; she would wash her hands thoroughly with carbolic soap, change her clothes and wash them and scour any bowls or utensils which she had brought to the stricken house. Ellen and Violet resolved to do the same.

A few days later, they heard that a little boy called John, whose mother Lily they had become friendly with on their walks on deck, had died. Almost as soon as they heard, an order came for all the women and children to stay below deck. Violet joined Ellen in her cabin and the two women cradled their children protectively as they tried to ignore the images which were coming into their minds. Whispers from other mothers had informed them about burials at sea, the necessity for them and the ceremony which accompanied them. The sudden silence made them realise that the engines had stopped. Then they heard the haunting notes of the Last Post and they could no longer block out the reality of what was happening. They heard the heartrending screams of Lily before the engines started their drone again and drowned her out. Ellen and Violet looked at each other in terror. Ellen made no move as Violet picked Desmond up and silently returned to her own cabin. Each woman was now concerned only for the safety of her own child.

Ellen wouldn't leave the cabin and became obsessed with cleanliness. She made James wash thoroughly before he picked up Nancy. She scoured every surface in the cabin and washed her own hands until they were raw. Nancy was teething again and became very fretful. She wouldn't sleep and the only rest that Ellen got was when James was free and looked after Nancy, rocking her and singing to her until she fell into a fitful doze.

After two days she began to run a temperature and became lethargic; she didn't respond to James no matter how he sang or talked to her. Ellen was giving the baby a cool bath to try to bring down her temperature when she saw the tell-tale signs of measles; a red rash had appeared behind Nancy's ears. In spite of the heat in the cabin she felt her blood freeze. Wordlessly, she showed the rash to James.

"I'll get the doctor. He'll know what to do." His normally ruddy skin was grey; he looked terrified as he kissed Nancy's head and hurried out the door.

The doctor was reassuring and comforting when he came. "She is a strong little girl. Don't let her get dehydrated and try to reduce her temperature. The worst will be over in a day or two. Bathe her eyes if they get crusty and keep the cabin dim; the light may be hurting her eyes. Call me if she doesn't improve and try to get some rest yourselves."

James thanked the doctor and closed the door after him. "I'll get some compassionate leave so that you can get some rest, sweetheart. I'll go and see the major now. Try not to worry. We will look after Nancy together."

While James was gone, Ellen tried to feed Nancy. She wouldn't take her breast and screamed and twisted her head from side to side. She had more success with some boiled water which she fed to the baby off a spoon but it was a very slow way of getting liquids into her. James returned and took over the task of feeding the water to Nancy. She was obviously exhausted and began to nod off in his arms.

James looked at Ellen's strained face. "You try to get some rest now, sweetheart. She will sleep for a while and may feel a bit better when she wakes up."

Ellen lay down and covered herself with a shawl. She must have gone to sleep immediately and slept for a couple of hours because when she was woken up by Nancy's screams, the cabin was dark. James was still holding the baby who was twisting her head from side to side and pulling at her ear. Ellen cradled the small head and looked into her right ear. It was red, inflamed and angry looking. In her medicine bag, she had a small amount of olive oil which her mother had always used for earaches. She warmed some on a spoon over a candle and managed to pour some into the affected ear while James held the squirming bundle. It seemed to soothe the baby because she stopped crying and lay, looking listless and exhausted in her father's arms.

Ellen took her daughter gently from James and settled into the chair by the porthole. "You have a rest now, love. I will try to feed Nancy again later. She might sleep for a while now."

James lay down and soon fell into an exhausted sleep. The

only light in the cabin was coming from the moon which was shining through the porthole, highlighting Nancy's flushed face. Ellen focused on her daughter, watching for the smallest change in her condition. They remained like that for a few hours, until she could see the sun just nudging up over the horizon. She leaned over to close the curtain over the porthole, mindful of the doctor's advice about light, when Nancy made a small sound. She opened her eyes and looked up at her mother. Then she closed them and sighed.

"James, James. She is not breathing! Oh my God, quickly, do something!"

James leaped to his feet and in one movement had taken Nancy and was putting his cheek to her mouth, checking for her breath. Then he felt her small body. "Her heart is not beating. Take her quickly. I'm going for the doctor."

Ellen was left holding the still warm body of her daughter, murmuring to her and stroking her downy head.

"Let me take her, Mrs Devereux." The doctor was beside her, taking her baby. He examined her gently and shook his head at James. "I'm sorry. There is nothing I can do."

Ellen screamed and took her baby back. She cradled her, wrapping her shawl around her, holding her close. Suddenly, the cabin seemed to be full of people, the Major's wife, Violet, other women that she had got to know on the voyage. They were trying to take Nancy from her. She resisted with a strength that she did not know she possessed. Then James was beside her, gently taking the small form, talking to her soothingly. He moved away and was gone out of the cabin. She tried to follow but was held back by someone.

Time seemed to stand still. She could hear the murmurs of the women who had stayed with her. It was daylight in the cabin now. Something was different. The ship's engine had stopped.

Suddenly, she knew what was happening. She screamed and tried to get at the door. Hands held her back. A terrible screaming rose from her and mingled with the notes of the Last Post. She was screaming, screaming and then strong hands pushed her down on to the bed and poured something sweet into her mouth. She recognised the smell – laudanum. Then there was nothing.

As she struggled to wake up, she had trouble remembering where she was. Her head felt heavy and her eyes sore; her tongue felt thick and her shoulders ached. Light coming through the porthole reminded her, they were on a ship, bound for India. She could hear Nancy stirring; she would be wanting her morning feed. She put out her hand; James was gone already, probably to an early duty. With some difficulty, she pulled herself into a sitting position. There was a movement in the dim corner of the cabin.

"Mrs Major! What are you doing here? You gave me a fright!"

"It is all right, my dear," the older woman soothed. "I didn't want to leave you alone."

"Alone? Where's James?" Ellen was trying to clear the fog from her head.

The older woman looked distressed. "He couldn't be here with you."

"I am sorry. I have to feed Nancy. I can hear her stirring." Ellen swung her legs over the side, stood up unsteadily and walked the two paces to the cot. "Where is she? Did you take her? Has James got her?" She could feel the fear rising in her and something else, a nameless dread.

Mrs Major was beside her with her arms around her. "Do you not remember? Nancy died last night. The doctor gave you laudanum and you have been asleep ever since."

Ellen stumbled back to the bed. Jumbled memories came into her mind: Nancy red-faced and crying, James pale and distraught, Nancy lethargic and unresponsive, the doctor examining the small body, the emptiness as Nancy was taken from her, someone screaming, the terrible wail of the Last Post.

She pushed her jumbled thoughts away. "No, it's not true. I want my baby. I want Nancy. Where is she? I want James."

Mrs Major was holding her hand, trying to calm her. "James was very upset last night. He had too much to drink. For his own good he has been confined to a place where he is safe. I told him I would stay with you."

The terrible events of the previous night were coming back clearly now. She wanted James to hold her, to make it go away, to say that everything would be all right.

"Oh, my Nancy! I should have looked after you better. Where is James? I want James." Ellen was crying and trying to open the cabin door.

"Come now, my dear. I will help you to wash and dress. James will be back with you this evening."

Ellen didn't resist as the other woman filled a bowl with water and selected a clean nightdress for her. Obediently, she washed and put on the nightdress. Clear images of the previous day were now chasing through her mind. She could hardly breathe with the ache in her heart. The bottle of laudanum was on the bedside table. "I want to sleep again. May I take some more of that?"

"If it helps you, my dear." Mrs Major poured the medicine and sat beside her as she drifted off to sleep again.

Hours later she woke to hear James creeping into the darkened cabin. This time she didn't have the luxury of forgetting. "James, I want my Nancy! Where were you? I needed you."

"I know, love. I am so sorry. After the ... After the ... I couldn't come back to you without Nancy. I went to the mess and ..."

She reached her arms out to him but he didn't see. He had covered his eyes and was sobbing, immersed in his own grief. She lay down on the bed, her back to him and wept.

Chapter 5
1903-1904: India

The next few days seemed like a nightmare from which she could not wake. At the insistence of Mrs Major, she dressed and accompanied her for walks on the deck. The atmosphere felt malevolent; the sky was dark and lowering; the air was oppressive. She stared out to sea to avoid the kind, curious stares of the other women but then imagined that she saw drifting white shapes in the water and had to close her eyes. She rebuffed any attempts at sympathy, fearing to hear the platitudes that she herself had often offered bereaved mothers. At night she slept heavily, in a laudanum-induced stupor, not even aware of James lying wakeful beside her. Every night she dreamed of Nancy and in the morning felt afresh the terrible grief as though the death of Nancy had just happened.

When word came that they were due to dock in Bombay, she assembled on deck with the other women. Most of them had a baby in their arms or a child by the hand. She threw bitter glances at them. She felt jealous and angry that God had taken her child but not theirs. The heat was oppressive, sucking the breath from her lungs before she could exhale. Trickles of perspiration ran down between her breasts and from under her hat. Most of the other women had changed into lighter clothing; she had abandoned her coat but otherwise was still dressed as she had been when they left Dover.

The ship slowly docked and she could hear the shouts of the dark-skinned men who were waiting on the quayside. The sun was harsh and lit the kaleidoscope of colour that moved about, colours with brightness and clarity such as she had never seen before, saffron, yellow, scarlet, indigo and turquoise, colours that hurt her eyes. The clamour of noise battered her ears and she realised as they inched into their berth that the rotting, sickly smells in the air were overpowering. Her big brimmed hat was little protection from the sun which was high overhead and burning through her clothes. She felt faint and would have collapsed but for the strong arms of Mrs Major and another woman who linked her and helped her down the gangplank.

Soon they were in a train, bound for Pune, and she had a sense of lush tropical countryside as she sat looking out the window, between sleeping and waking. Slim figures made bright slashes in the landscape as they tended herds of long-horned cattle in the fields or worked, knee deep in water in the paddy fields. Then they were at the station where there seemed to be utter chaos; masses of people shouted and moved about in the intense heat; the all-pervasive smell hung like a heavy cloud over everything. They were ushered into open horse carriages by some of the enlisted men and started the short journey to the barracks. Once again, the motion of the carriage made her sleep.

Mrs Major woke her gently. "Come along, my dear. We are home. Let me show you to your quarters."

She was dimly aware of long low buildings with gardens around them. Mrs Major knocked on the door of one of them. It was opened by a young dark-skinned girl, dressed in a dark red sari. Her black hair hung in a long plait down her back and her feet were bare.

Mrs Major introduced her. "This is Prithi. She will look after you now. She understands a little English."

The girl smiled shyly at Ellen. "Namaste, memsahib." She brought her hands together in front of her heart as she said this.

Ellen managed a weak smile.

"Now, Prithi, memsahib is very tired. She would like a bath and then some light food. Sahib Devereux will be here in about an hour." Mrs Major put her arm around Ellen. "My dear, you must rest now. Prithi will prepare a bath. Then you must change and join your husband for supper. I will come back tomorrow to see how you are settling in. God bless you."

Prithi motioned Ellen into an inner room as the older woman left, where there was a commode and a large bath and various basins and ewers. Ellen began to undress and found that her clothes were soaked with perspiration. She was reluctant to undress completely with the young woman in the room but Prithi was filling the bath with jugs of hot water and sprinkling in aromatic herbs and seemed unaware of any awkwardness. The bath looked so inviting that Ellen forgot her shyness and quickly stepped out of her underclothes and lowered herself into the water. Prithi moved behind her and started to sponge Ellen's body, then poured water over her hair. She produced some sweet smelling unguent and combed it through. Ellen sank back into the water as Prithi rinsed her hair. Her muscles relaxed for the first time in a week. She could have stayed there indefinitely but for the lingering presence of the young girl. Eventually, she enveloped herself in the big towel that Prithi handed to her and unpacked some light clothes from the trunk which was already open.

She was dressed and combing the water out of her long hair when James appeared in the doorway. "You look much better, sweetheart. I am sorry I couldn't be here sooner but I had to see my men settled first. Mrs Major tells me that Prithi is excellent and will look after you very well."

The familiarity of James after the strangeness of the day brought tears to her eyes. She threw herself into his arms, her wet hair drenching the front of his uniform as she did so. "I want to go home, James. I don't think I could live here."

He stroked her wet hair gently. "It's all right, love. You will get used to it. Now, let me show you around our new home and then we will have something to eat."

He kept his arm around her shoulders as he showed her around their quarters. There was a long living room with an ornate sideboard and chairs and a dining table which was already set for a meal. A fan in the ceiling whirred and created a cool breeze. A small kitchen was off to the side, obviously the domain of the man who was clattering dishes about until they entered, whereupon he saluted them theatrically and went back to his noisy pursuit. The bedroom was large, again with a fan whirring above the bed. A net hung down over the bed – a mosquito net, she supposed. She had already been in the bathroom which was now tidy when they looked in.

In spite of herself she was intrigued. "Who is that man?" she asked James.

"He is the cook – Vinod is his name. He is Prithi's uncle. He was the cook for friends of mine, the Gallaghers, when I was here before. We are lucky to have got him and Prithi. Now let us see what Vinod has made for our supper."

Supper turned out to be an omelette which she was just about able to eat. It felt very strange to be sitting down opposite James without Nancy gurgling in the background. She knew that he felt it too. They made several attempts at conversation which petered out very quickly. Eventually, James stood up. "Let's go to bed, love. You look exhausted. Things will seem better in the morning."

He helped her to climb into the high bed and showed her how to arrange the mosquito net. He kissed her and held her close to him but she didn't respond. Nothing could take the pain away.

Next morning was like a reprise of the morning after their wedding, when reveille sounded and James leapt out of bed. This time she didn't attempt to get his breakfast but turned over and went back to sleep.

Blinding sunlight woke her some time later as Prithi opened the curtains, then turned and smiled at her. "Hot water for memsahib?

You are vanting breakfast?"

The thought of breakfast made her retch. "No, thank you. Just some tea, please."

She felt nauseous again when she tried to sit up. It was a familiar feeling. This wasn't seasickness. She had been breastfeeding Nancy so she hadn't had a regular time of the month. Could she be with child again?

Prithi entered with a tray. "Chai, memsahib."

The smell of the tea answered her question. She hadn't been able to bear the smell of tea for the first three months when she was carrying Nancy. "Thank you, Prithi. I will just have some water."

Thoughts chased through her mind. How could she be carrying another baby so soon after losing Nancy? Would she be able to love this child? Had she done any damage to the baby by not eating and taking so much laudanum? She felt none of the excitement or love that she had felt when she first realised that she was carrying Nancy. She didn't believe she would ever love this child. But she still had a duty to it. There would be no more laudanum and she would eat properly; that much at least she could do for this poor child.

She got out of bed carefully, keeping the nausea under control. Prithi was by her side with jugs of water. She had already laid out some of the light cotton clothes from the trunk. She helped Ellen to dress and brushed her hair and then watched as she put up her hair over the frame.

"Memsahib is going out?"

"Do you know where the Major has his quarters? I want to see his wife."

"Yes, memsahib. Major always being in same place. I bring you."

Prithi walked ahead of Ellen, looking back encouragingly from time to time. Once outside, the heat was overpowering. They

63

walked in the shade of the bungalows as far as possible until they came to one that had a purple plant that she recognised as bougainvillea growing outside. Prithi knocked on the door and stepped back.

Mrs Major didn't look at all surprised to see her. "Good morning, my dear. Come inside and have some tea. I am delighted to see you out and about."

Prithi disappeared as she followed the other woman into the livingroom. She couldn't wait to confide in her friend. "Mrs Major, I think I am with child. I wasn't feeling very well before we started the journey but I thought it was just the upset of leaving. I might be in my third month."

Mrs Major sat down on a large sofa and drew the younger woman down beside her. "Oh, my dear, that is wonderful news. Have you told your husband yet?"

"No, I just realised myself. Besides, I don't think I can love this child. It is too soon. It will always remind me of Nancy. I could never love another baby like I loved Nancy." The tears were streaming down Ellen's face.

"Of course you could. One baby doesn't replace another. They are all different and have different places in your heart. This new baby will be a blessing. Once it is born you will love it just as much as you loved Nancy."

Ellen was still sobbing and mopping her face with her sleeve.

Mrs Major took her hand. "Did I ever tell you about my babies?"

Ellen was startled and stopped sobbing. "I thought you had no children."

"Oh, I did. I had four lovely babies but they all died a few weeks after birth. I couldn't carry any of them to full term. They were all born prematurely and died within a few weeks. I remember them all as individual little people, two boys, Edward and William, and two girls, Alice and Emma. They all have a place in my heart and I think of them and pray for them every day."

"How could you bear it? To lose four children? You didn't even have as long with them as I had with Nancy."

For a moment the older woman looked sad. "I wouldn't have missed the few weeks I had with each of them for the world."

Ellen was shocked out of her own misery. She had always thought of Mrs Major as a childless woman who devoted her life to good deeds.

"Now, we must get you to see the doctor," Mrs Major said briskly. "He is on duty at our little hospital this morning so we will go there now."

The little hospital turned out to be quite big, a white haven of peace with friendly nurses and a jovial doctor who was from Galway, like her mother. He and the nurse gave her a thorough medical check-up and pronounced that she was indeed into her third month and perfectly healthy. Ellen was both relieved and sad. In one way she had hoped that something would go wrong so that she wouldn't have to carry this baby. In another, she was glad that the experience of the previous few weeks hadn't done any harm to the baby.

Mrs Major was waiting for her and walked her back to her own quarters. She stopped at the door and took Ellen's hand. "You will never stop loving Nancy, my dear. But now you have another child to love. Take care of this baby."

The next day she had a visitor. Violet looked nervous and anxious as Prithi showed her in." Hello, Ellen. I wanted to see how you were. I hope you don't mind me coming. I couldn't come to you while there was a danger of measles. Only women with no children were allowed to look after you."

Ellen was delighted to see her friend and embraced her. "I understand, Violet. I would have done the same. Don't be upset.

65

How is little Desmond?"

"Big and bold and driving me mad. Oh, I am sorry." She looked guilty at mentioning her son.

"I am going to have another baby, Violet. I am in my third month," Ellen blurted out.

Violet embraced her. "So am I! Oh, we will have our babies at the same time. I am so happy for you. You must be delighted."

Ellen didn't want to tell her friend about her mixed feelings. She thought she might be shocked.

Once she was into her fourth month the sickness passed and she began to eat voraciously. There was always a big bowl of fruit in the living room, fruit that she had never seen before. She tried them out, one by one. Her favourite was the pomegranate with its jewel-like seeds inside an outer leathery skin. Vinod turned out to be a good if temperamental cook. She loved his chicken which was slightly spicy and served with rice. The variety of vegetables was amazing and Vinod told her their names as she watched him prepare them in the kitchen.

The heat outside was intense so she didn't venture outside very much. When James left in the early morning, she sometimes took a stroll with Violet around the gardens while it was still reasonably cool. Desmond was tactfully left with his ayah. Violet chattered about the new baby she was expecting and how she hoped it was a girl before looking guiltily at Ellen who simply patted her friend's arm.

She was beginning to feel a little better. Her nights were still filled with dreams of Nancy and there were times when her grief was so overwhelming that she screamed at James and blamed him for bringing them to India and causing Nancy's death. Letters from home detailing the festivities of Maggie's wedding caused a fresh paroxysm of grief and loneliness, when she pictured her family in Castlebar, happy and celebrating, probably still unaware of the terrible thing that had befallen her and James. Eventually, a stoic acceptance of the loss of Nancy began to take over her mind, helped by her frequent talks with Mrs Major. Her loss was still like an open wound but she was learning to live with it.

James was very busy with his duties and was often gone for days as he and his men visited hill stations or areas where there had been some trouble. Prithi was very attentive and seemed to know Ellen's needs before she knew them herself. Her English was fairly limited but Ellen made some efforts to get to know her. She was intrigued by the fact that Prithi spent all her time in their quarters and never seemed to wish to visit her home. She tried asking questions about her family, her parents, whether she had brothers and sisters but Prithi just smiled shyly and seemed not to understand. Vinod wasn't much more forthcoming. He would talk to her about the strange fruit and vegetables: tell her their names, even teach her how to cook her favourite dishes, but was reluctant to talk about his family. Ellen wondered about this and asked Mrs Major about it.

"Most of the servants come from villages which are quite far away. They don't get to see their families very often, perhaps only once in two years, if that. I know Vinod has a wife and children but he has been here with the regiment for a long time and I don't suppose he has seen them for years."

Ellen was shocked at this revelation. "That is awful! How can they bear to be away from their families for so long?"

Mrs Major looked resigned. "You must see it in the context of India, my dear. The poverty here is so terrible that people like Vinod and Prithi count themselves lucky that they have enough to eat, a comfortable life and some money to send to their families."

"What about Prithi? Do you know anything about her life?"

"No, except that she is the niece of Vinod. That is how she got the job. A girl like her hasn't too many choices in life. She needs a dowry to get married and perhaps she is saving for that now. If she gets married and her dowry is not large enough, she could be killed by her in-laws. It happens more often than you would imagine. She is probably better off staying here and working."

Ellen knew the kindness of Mrs Major and could not believe the matter of fact way that she was discussing the cruelty of the servants' lives. "Do you mean that the government knows that things like that are going on and does nothing about it?"

Mrs Major shook her head. "That is their culture and we cannot change it, I am afraid."

The monsoon season coincided with the last months of Ellen and Violet's pregnancies. They could no longer go for their morning walks and both were confined to their quarters by the incessant, torrential rainfall. Ellen was grateful that it was at least cooler and lay on her bed under the fan writing to her mother and sisters or reading some of the novels with which Mrs Major kept her supplied.

Violet was the first to have her baby, a little girl who she named Julia. Ellen had just arranged to go to visit her friend in the hospital when she was rushed in there as a patient herself. This experience of childbirth was very different for her. She knew the doctor and nurses from her visits for check- ups and the birth was faster and much easier. She was awake for the whole experience and held her new baby as soon as he emerged into the world. In spite of her fears she was overcome with love as soon as she saw the tiny face and felt the little fingers grip hers. She had a son and the first thing she registered was that he looked very different from Nancy; he was a very long baby with a head of thick, black hair; his eyebrows were knitted in a frown which made him look very serious. He reminded her of her father. She said as much to James when he came to visit.

He held his son briefly and then handed him back to Ellen. "Yes, he does look like your father. Maybe we should call him Henry."

Ellen was delighted. "Do you think so? Or would you like him called James after you?"

"Let's call him Henry James."

"Papa will be so pleased. But we will call him Harry as a pet name. I always liked the name Harry."

Ellen and Harry were soon home and Mrs Major visited every day. She was delighted when Ellen asked her to be godmother to the new baby; Des Vaughan was to be godfather. Harry and Julia were christened on the same day and they had a joint celebration in the sergeants' mess. Ellen tried to enjoy it but could not help but compare it with Nancy's christening, with her parents and sisters and Jack present. James saw the faraway look in her eyes and felt sad.

Harry was a demanding baby; he was only happy when he was in Ellen's arms. Most nights he woke and would only go back to sleep if she held him and sang to him. James became accustomed to Ellen spending most of the night pacing up and down with Harry in her arms and then sleeping in the morning when the baby finally fell asleep. Prithi did her best to do her duties as an ayah but Harry screamed whenever Ellen tried to hand him over. He suffered from colic and Ellen made many visits to the doctor in an attempt to discover what was causing the colic. Then, when he was six months old, the colic disappeared and he suddenly became a placid, happy baby. Up to this, with sleepless nights and feeling exhausted all the time, Ellen had little time or energy to think about Nancy. James avoided talking about her as did most people except Mrs Major. She still saw Nancy in her dreams and was grateful for these small glimpses of her beloved baby. Now she realised that Harry was coming up to the age that Nancy was when she died.

Prithi was able to look after Harry now that he no longer suffered from colic so Ellen enjoyed much more freedom. James had been anxious for her to come to one of the regular dances in the mess. Violet already had been to one and was full of enthusiasm and gossip about it. They arranged to go together with their husbands to the Christmas dance, a special date in the social calendar of the regiment. They both engaged the services of a local Indian dressmaker who came to their quarters with swathes of materials to choose from, measured them and then had the dresses ready in a week. Ellen chose a beautiful pale blue silk which emphasised the blue of her eyes and Violet a pale green which made the most of her red hair and brown eyes.

The evening of the dance Prithi helped Ellen to dress and she was just putting the finishing touches to her hair when James came into the bedroom. "My darling, you look wonderful. I will be a proud man tonight!"

Ellen was warmed by the love and admiration in his eyes. "You look very handsome yourself, Sergeant Devereux!"

James was in his dress uniform and did indeed look handsome. In fact, as she looked at their reflections in the mirror, Ellen thought that they looked like their old selves, the people they were before the tragedy, but she knew that Nancy's death had changed them and affected their relationship. She wondered whether they would ever regain some of the happiness that they had enjoyed in the small rooms in Renmore.

Ellen's heart lifted when they entered the mess and heard the dance music. She had a momentary pang of guilt at feeling happy again but hadn't time to think about this as James swung her onto the dance floor and they danced the Gay Gordons. They were on the floor for almost every dance and only stopped to catch their breaths and drink some punch.

The major approached as they were sipping from their glasses. "I wonder, Sergeant Devereux, if you would allow me the honour of dancing with your wife. I have been watching you both and I think you are the best dancers in the regiment."

James looked proudly at Ellen, took her glass and watched as she and the major danced the Mazurka.

That evening as they walked back to their quarters, Ellen stopped to kiss James in the moonlight. She could see the tears in his eyes as he said, "We will be happy again as we used to be, I promise you, my love."

Chapter 6
1904- 1907: Harry

Ellen began to enjoy their life in India. The two servants looked after the cooking and housework so she devoted herself to Harry. He walked and talked much earlier than most children He was curious and anxious to learn about everything and Ellen found that her years of teaching the children of Lord Lucan had given her valuable experience. She got some children's books from the regiment stores and read to Harry every evening before he went to sleep. Soon he was trying to pick out words himself and she began to teach him to read. He loved counting and she taught him simple mathematics using coins. She taught him colours when they went on walks from the beautiful flowers and plants which seemed to grow everywhere. He also picked up some Marathi which was the local language used by Prithi and Vinod. He loved to watch Vinod preparing food or Prithi as she swept the floor or polished the furniture. They doted on him and chatted away to him as they worked, chats that Ellen could not understand because they were in Marathi. James did not approve of Harry spending so much time with the servants but spent little time with the child himself. Reflecting on how devoted he had been to Nancy, Ellen found herself wondering if he was afraid to become too attached to Harry for fear of losing him too.

Letters from home came regularly, telling her all the latest news. Jane was now walking out with a young man called Tom. He was a civil servant who had been sent to Castlebar from Dublin as part of the new Land Reform commission. Her mother thought that he was a very suitable beau for Jane. Maggie and Matt had settled into their new home. Annie had taken over the role of governess with the small daughter of Lord and Lady Lucan. Her mother was suffering from arthritis but otherwise was well. Her father had become involved with the foundation of a branch of the Gaelic Athletic Association in the town. Sometimes he added a postscript to her mother's letter but he wasn't really fond of letter-writing. He had received little formal education but was self-educated; he was well read but self-conscious about his writing. Jack also wrote but not regularly. When his letters did come they were lively and amusing and made Ellen and James laugh. They were both surprised that Jack had not yet married but he seemed happy.

By the time Harry was two, Ellen found herself with child again. She welcomed the news when it was confirmed by the doctor. James also seemed delighted with the idea of another child. She hoped for another boy, company for Harry she told herself, but knew that she could not bear the thought of replacing Nancy with another daughter. She and James were now regular patrons of the dances in the mess which were held every week. Her figure, even when with child, was so neat that she continued to attend well into her sixth month. They were a popular couple and their dancing was much admired.

Her friendship with Violet continued. Violet was by now as she said herself "as big as a house" having delivered twin girls the previous month. The twins were a handful and even with the help of the ayahs, Violet found it difficult to manage. Ellen went to visit her as often as she could and helped with the babies.

She also continued her friendship with Mrs Major, a woman who had come to mean almost as much to her as her own mother. Mrs Major was indeed a kind of unofficial mother to the wives in the regiment, especially those who were very young or on their first tour in India or who had difficulties in their marriage.

Nan Murphy, who she had first got to know in the barracks in Renmore, was one of the wives that Mrs Major tried to help. Ellen had not seen much of her since they arrived in India; Nan seldom

73

came out. There was also the fact that James did not like her husband, Dan. When she did appear, she often had fading bruises on her face; once she had a broken arm. She still had just one child although it was known that she had had a number of miscarriages. Mrs Major encouraged her to report Dan's violence to his commanding officer but Nan was reluctant to do so.

"I don't want him to be demoted. If that happens, I will be sent home. The life I have here is better than the life I had at home. I know you find that hard to believe but it is true. Anyway, Dan loves me. It is only the drink that makes him violent."

Mrs Major discovered that Nan's family lived in a tenement in Dublin and she had been happy to escape the squalor and degradation of that life. She had scraped a meagre existence in Dublin, finding the lowest kind of cleaning jobs whenever she could and going hungry when she could not. Her father had been a docker; he was badly injured in an accident when Nan was a baby and had not been able to find work since. Her mother worked in a factory but the wages she earned just about kept them alive. Her brother left home as soon as he could and they had not heard from him since. Nan was able to send home money to her mother from time to time; Dan was generous even if he was violent when he had drink taken.

There did not seem to be any solution to Nan's difficulty, Mrs Major confided to Ellen. The problem was that there was so little to do that many of the men drank more than was good for them. Even some of the wives succumbed to drink and were known to spend the afternoon in bed, sobering up before their husbands came home.

When the new baby was born they called him Joseph after James's father. Joseph was small and resembled his mother very much. He had the same earnest blue eyes and silky dark hair. Harry was delighted with his little brother and called him Jo-Jo. He talked to the baby as though Joseph could understand him and had to be prevented from hugging him in a very boisterous way. James too seemed taken with the new baby and spent more time with him than he had done with Harry. It warmed Ellen's heart to see the three of them together and she wished that Nancy was there too. She still had Nancy's clothes and even though girls and boys wore much the same clothes as infants, she had never been able to dress either of the boys in the small garments. She imagined that they still smelled of Nancy and occasionally took them out and buried her face in them.

While she was in the hospital having Joseph she made a new friend, Ada, an English girl who had met and married a sergeant from the Connaught Rangers while he was on duty in Aldershot, England. She too was delivered of a son, her second. She was older than Ellen, tall with black hair and was very glamorous. Their backgrounds were quite similar in many ways. Ada's father had been a footman in a Lord's house in Kent and her mother had been a parlourmaid. She had lived independently in London, working in a factory. She had a passion for painting in water colours and told Ellen all about it when they were in beds next to each other after the birth of their babies. Although she had never taken any interest in the crafts at which her sisters were adept, Ellen liked the sound of painting in water colours. Ada promised to give her some lessons when they were both home after their confinements.

A few weeks later, Mrs Major arrived at the door early in the morning just as James was leaving. She looked distressed and Ellen asked Prithi to make some tea for her friend. "I don't imagine that you have heard the news yet, my dear. It is bad news I am afraid. Nan is in the hospital with a fractured skull. Dan is under guard and will be court-martialled. Apparently, he went home quite drunk last night. Neighbours heard a lot of noise and called the military police. By the time they arrived Nan was unconscious and her little boy was hysterical. I have been to the hospital already this morning but no one is allowed see her yet."

Ellen could not believe it. "Oh my God, is she going to be all right?"

"It is too early to tell. They will know more in a few days."

"We should have done something before this. We knew that this was likely to happen. Why didn't we do something?" Ellen asked.

Mrs Major looked sad. "Nan wouldn't allow us to do anything, my dear. We did try."

Mrs Major left shortly after and Ellen was left alone with her own thoughts. She wondered what they could have done to protect her friend. Now it was too late.

Nan took months to recover and was never the same again. She had lost the sight in one eye and was a shadow of her former self. Dan was court-martialled, demoted and sentenced to six years in military prison. As soon as she was well enough to travel, Nan and her son were sent back to Ireland. Ellen and Mrs Major accompanied them on the carriage journey to Pune. From there, she and her son would take the train to Bombay from where they would journey, first to England and then on to Ireland. She looked a forlorn figure as she stood on the platform before boarding the train, clutching her small son's hand, her few bags at her feet.

When they asked Nan where she would go, she was vague about her plans. "I'll probably go to my mother's first. Then I will have to try to get a job. I want to have a place for Dan to come home to when he is released."

She promised to write to them but somehow they knew that she wouldn't.

Ellen kissed her friend goodbye and turned to Mrs Major in tears as the train pulled out. "I find it hard to believe that Nan is still worried about her violent husband. She is being punished as much as her husband, even though she did nothing wrong. It is very unjust. Why could she not have stayed here with the regiment?"

"The army would not allow a woman on her own to stay here. It would be very bad for discipline and morale," Mrs Major said.

Dan's incarceration and Nan's departure cast a shadow over the whole regiment, especially the wives. Ada tactfully tried to distract Ellen by introducing her to water colour painting. One afternoon, while the children were having a nap, she arrived with her paints, brushes and easel. She had also brought a selection of her paintings, carried awkwardly by her cook. Ellen was struck by the luminous colours and delicate brush strokes in the pictures, which were mainly of flowers. Soon their painting sessions were a regular feature, with Ada coming twice a week, usually in the cool of the morning, when James and Laurence, Ada's husband, had reported for duty and the children were on walks with the ayahs. Sometimes they painted outside in the gardens, other times they set up in the cool living room. Ada was different from the other friends that Ellen had made. For one thing, she was English and had lived in the big city of London for a few years. Like Ellen, she loved to read but her reading was wider than the novels which Ellen loved. She was interested in politics and was amazed at how little Ellen knew about the subject. She professed to be a socialist and a suffragette and said that she had met the Pankhursts in London at a meeting. Ellen didn't know who the Pankhursts were and was embarrassed to reveal her ignorance.

"They are the leaders of the suffragette movement in England," said Ada.

"What is the suffragette movement?" Ellen asked. She had a vague idea but wanted to know more.

"They are a group of mostly women who are fighting for women to be able to vote. In countries like New Zealand and

Australia, women already have the right to vote, the same as men."

Ellen knew enough about voting from her father to feel able to discuss this. "But men have more experience of the world; they know more about politics and things than we do. We trust them to make decisions for the family so we should trust them to make decisions about the country for us."

"We have to make sure that we are as well informed as they are. Anyway, who usually makes the most important decisions about the family?" asked Ada.

Ellen thought about her mother and the way her father always deferred to her when it came to decisions about the family. "Maybe you are right. I never thought about it before."

The two women continued to have painting sessions every week but now as they painted, Ada told Ellen about her political convictions. In a letter to her sister, Maggie, she mentioned the fact that Ada was a suffragette, expecting her sister to know as little about it as she did. To her surprise, Maggie had been to a meeting of suffragettes in Galway with Annie and knew quite a lot about the subject.

Mrs Major's knowledge of the suffragettes was gleaned from the newspapers that her husband received in the post from England. "Nothing good will come of this, my dear. Men and women have different roles to play in the world. That is God's plan."

"Ada says that some of the women have been imprisoned for demonstrating. When they went on hunger strike, they were force fed." Ellen expected her friend to share her horror.

"They were imprisoned because they broke the law. They were force fed, as you call it, because they couldn't be allowed to die. Now, that is quite enough about that subject. Tell me about my godson's latest exploits." It was clear that Mrs Major didn't like Ada or the ideas that she was disseminating.

Ellen began to feel that living with the regiment in India was like living in a bubble where they were protected from any dangerous ideas circulating in the outside world. Even living in India wasn't real; they might just as well have been living somewhere in Britain: the food they ate was mostly British, the clothes they wore were British, their social life was British, the people they mixed with were British except for the odd Maharajah who paid a courtesy visit and, of course, the servants. It was a continual source of annoyance to Ellen that no matter what she did she could not get close to either of their servants. She compared the situation to the one at home where the people in the Big House knew all about their servants and took an interest in their lives. She knew that not all of the landowners in Ireland were as good to their tenants and servants as Lord and Lady Lucan; she had heard many stories about the evil deeds of the previous Lord Lucan and other members of the landed gentry. At home, she and her family were in a similar position to Prithi's; they were not gentry or landowners, they too were servants. She knew that some of the people in the regiment treated their servants badly, even hitting them or threatening them. There were rumours that a girl as young as Prithi had left her position as an ayah because she was being interfered with by a certain officer. Nothing was ever done about it; the family got a new ayah and everything went back to normal. The only person she could talk to about these things was Ada. Even James seemed to find this situation normal and told Ellen that the regiment would look after it if there was a problem.

She began to feel more and more confined and wanted to see more of the country. She and Ada made forays into the surrounding countryside, supposedly for painting trips but really to see what the real India looked like. They always had an escort of course, soldiers who made sure that they did not stray into dangerous territory. Even so, they saw the ramshackle villages that were nearby, saw the hungry children and the filthy beggars, and realised that the majority of the local people were living on the very edge of existence.

Sometimes they saw villagers going to work or returning from work. Many of them were women and it was obvious that they had been working in stone quarries or on road-building. They saw women walking to the nearest well, which was often miles away, or returning with large vessels of water balanced on their heads. The people in the villages were not friendly like the servants but stared at them and were resentful of their intrusion. It reminded Ellen of the way people looked when Lord Lucan and his family drove through Castlebar in their fine carriage. At school she had been aware of other children who were obviously hungry and who came to school without shoes and wearing ill-fitting, threadbare clothes. She and her sisters had grown up in the shadow and protection of the Big House but many of their neighbours were as poor as the Indian people in the villages. Ada told her that there were people in parts of London and other cities like Liverpool who were just as poor.

When they went home and saw their own healthy children, they felt guilty and could not get the pictures they had seen during the day out of their minds. The beauty of the country was in sharp contrast to the poverty and they saw many things which inspired them to paint: beautiful sunrises, trees with fantastical shapes, herders with their small flocks, women in flaming saris, birds with plumage that looked as though it had already been painted, and of course jewel-coloured flowers. They made sure to bring home plenty of paintings to show as the fruits of their excursions; they did not discuss the disturbing sights they had seen with anyone except each other.

Chapter 7
1911: Returning Home

Kathleen was born when Joseph was three. Ellen was relieved that when she held her new daughter in her arms for the first time, she felt the same overwhelming sense of love that she had felt for her other three children. Kathleen was uncannily like Nancy in looks, with the same golden down on her head and the same navy blue eyes. Her personality, however, was different. Where Nancy had been placid, Kathleen was demanding. She slept very little and was only happy when Ellen or James held her in their arms. James and the two boys were delighted with her and couldn't wait to get her home. Ada and her husband Laurence were the godparents. They had two boys themselves, Albert who was six and George, the new baby. Ada had converted to Catholicism when she married but didn't seem terribly interested in the intricacies of the religion. However, she was delighted to be godmother to Kathleen.

The first letter Ellen got from Maggie after Kathleen was born shocked her with its sadness. She knew that Maggie and her husband wanted children very much. Now they had been married for six years and there was still no sign of a baby. The words she wrote to express her sorrow were heart-rending. "Every month I hope and every month my hopes are shattered."

Ellen knew she was lucky to have three healthy children. Even in countries where women were well cared for the death rate for babies was high. During the first few years of a baby's life there were all kinds of hazards such as the measles that had killed Nancy. Which was worse, she wondered, never to have a child or to watch your child die? Ellen felt her sister's pain and was conscious that when she wrote to Maggie her letters were full of news about the children. Maggie was the sister to whom she was the closest but she wondered if the fact that she had three children was driving a wedge between them. Maggie's own letters were about their parents, the goings-on in Castlebar and her experiences in the jeweller's shop where she was now assisting Matt. The underlying sadness in those letters made it clear that there was a void in her life which her parents or Matt could never fill.

The other news from home concerned her second sister, Jane, who had been going out with Tom O'Regan who worked for the Land Registry, the part of the Civil Service which was helping Catholics to buy the land they had previously rented. He was being transferred back to Dublin and they were planning to get married within the year. Her mother's letters were full of Jane's plans. Tom had bought a house in Dublin in the suburb of Glasnevin, a place, according to her mother, full of the best kind of people. Ellen loved her mother dearly but knew that she was a snob at heart. She was resigned to the fact that this was another family wedding that she would miss although she had never been as close to Jane as she was to Maggie and Annie.

Jane herself wrote very seldom. She was too busy with trips to Dublin with her mother to buy her trousseau and the furniture for her new house. In one of her few letters she explained how difficult it all was.

"I am absolutely exhausted with all the trips to Dublin. We are ordering all our furniture from Clery's and I am having my gown made by a well-known dressmaker, Madame Yvette. Lady Lucan recommended her to me. Mama and I travel up on the train every second week. Tom has already been transferred and is very busy in his new job. Still there is so much to do. What a pity you and James will miss the wedding! It will be quite a big affair because Tom is so well known. The reception will be in the Imperial Hotel in Castlebar and we are spending our honeymoon in Westport. The Connaught Telegraph is sending a photographer so we will be able to send that on to you."

Annie, the youngest sister, wrote regularly. She had replaced Ellen as governess to Isobel, the youngest child of Lord and Lady Lucan. With only one child to look after it was easy work but a bit lonely at times with only the little girl for company and her mother and Jane so pre-occupied with the wedding.

She kept Ellen abreast of all the new developments on the demesne. "You will never guess, Ellen! Lord Lucan got rid of his carriages and bought a new car, a model T Ford. He has employed a chauffeur to drive the car, a man from Dublin called Albert Dunne. He is very handsome and the girls in Castlebar are fascinated by him. He lives in a flat above the coach house which is now called the garage. He lives alone and doesn't really mix much with the locals. I have spoken to him a few times and find him quite charming."

Ellen smiled at her sister's innocence. No doubt her mother would keep a close eye on the charming Albert and her youngest daughter! Letters also came less regularly from Jack. He was enjoying his time in Northern India but missed the company of James. He had made some new friends and went hunting with them. He sent a present of a tiger's tooth to Harry, from a tiger that he had shot on one of his expeditions. Ellen put the tooth away with distaste and thought of the beautiful animal that she had shown Harry in picture books. Her son would have been distraught at the idea of his beloved Jack killing a tiger.

After her confinement with Kathleen, Ellen found that she was very tired and busy, with little time for the painting excursions with Ada that she had enjoyed so much. She could have employed another ayah for Kathleen but decided that she only needed Prithi. Harry was now five and attending the school in the barracks where he was the star pupil. Thanks to her tuition he could already read and knew his numbers when he started there. He was also a beautiful singer and took the starring role in the school's Christmas concert. Joseph was a quiet and shy three year old and Prithi could easily manage the new baby and him. James had been promoted to Sergeant-Major and enjoyed his new role. Kathleen adored him and was very happy when she got his attention but screamed and wanted her own way when he wasn't there. Violet had had her fifth child, a boy she called William, and had a second ayah, so she and Ellen were able to spend time together with the two babies.

Soon there was talk of returning home and they realised that there was less than a year left of their time in India. Both of them started to buy small presents of silk scarves and brass ornaments to take home to relatives. They each had a wardrobe full of silk dresses that had been made especially for them.

"Do you think we will ever wear these dresses at home?" Violet asked one evening when they were taking a rest between dances in the mess.

"I don't know; fashions will have changed a lot there. Maybe we could have them altered. I can't see myself wearing this on a chilly evening in Castlebar! Anyway, people at home would be scandalised at the low-cut tops and flimsy material!" Ellen was remembering the Victorian primness of fashions in her home town.

"Are you looking forward to going home, Ellen?" Violet obviously had mixed feelings about the prospect.

"Of course I am. I want to see my parents and my sisters very much. I want them to see and get to know my children. But I am nervous about what will happen to us when we return and where we will live. Once James and Des leave the army our lives will be very different."

"Are you talking about us?" James and Des had returned from the bar in time to hear the last few sentences.

James put his arm around Ellen. "Don't worry about what will happen to us when we leave the army. We have been promised jobs once we are demobbed. We will also get help to find a suitable house. Once we get back to the barracks in Renmore we will start looking for jobs and accommodation. In the meantime, will you do me the honour of dancing with me, my love?"

Ellen relaxed into his arms and let the music transport her as it usually did.

In the months that followed, she found her concerns coming more and more to the forefront of her mind. She discussed the situation with Violet and Ada. Violet's only concern was where they would live. She wanted to live in Mayo, near to her family, but knew that the chances of Des getting a job in Mayo were slim. Ada and Laurence planned to return to England and didn't mind where in that country they eventually settled. Ellen hoped that James might be given employment in Galway where she would be near to her family. There would be no ayahs for the children and she knew that they all faced a very different kind of life. She loved India, the heat and the colour and the easy lifestyle, yet she had also found India stultifying because of the restrictions on the movements of the wives. She resolved to enjoy the months left in India but found herself looking forward to seeing her family again and introducing them to her children.

The months flew by and she began to prepare Harry for the changes their return to Ireland would bring; Joseph was too young to understand. She showed Harry pictures of his grandparents and aunts and talked to him about Castlebar and Galway. As soon as Prithi realised that their departure was drawing near, she was inconsolable and went about their quarters crying silently. Even Vinod was upset and spent a lot of time talking to Harry and Joseph in the kitchen and making them special sweetmeats.

They had accumulated quite a lot of possessions in the seven years and Ellen packed as many of them as possible, all the time wondering if she would find a use for them in their new home wherever it might be. While she was packing she found the box with Nancy's small clothes in it. Holding them close to her face she imagined that she could still smell Nancy from them. She wondered how she would feel on the voyage home; whether it would bring back the terrible trauma of her loss. She had her other three children to look after now so she would have to cope with her feelings privately rather than upset them.

When the day of departure came, Joseph and Kathleen were hysterical with excitement; Harry was calm and helpful to his mother. Prithi was beyond being of help, crying and hugging the two younger children alternately. Most of their luggage had gone ahead; they only had the things necessary for the long sea voyage. Vinod had been crashing dishes loudly in the kitchen but suddenly appeared and clasped Harry to him, muttering what sounded like prayers over him. The other two children clung to Vinod and set up a loud wailing. James had to detach the children and carry all three of them to the waiting carriages. Prithi and Vinod were left sobbing as the carriages moved away. James waved his family off; he would re-join them at Bombay before they went on board their ship. It was a short trip to the train that would take them to the port.

Ellen sat back and drew a deep breath; the previous few days had been exhausting. The two younger children had been upset with the disturbance to their routine. The two servants had been inconsolable and Harry had asked questions incessantly about their new life. James had been busy with the organisation of the men who were travelling back to Ireland and could spare little time to help. Ellen just hoped that she had remembered everything; the changes of clothes that would be necessary as they approached the colder climate, the small medicine chest, the books and toys to keep the children occupied.

The train was waiting for them at Pune and, as arranged, Ellen,

Ada and Violet and all their children piled into one carriage. The three older boys, Harry, Albert and Desmond, were soon involved in an intricate card game, Violet's twin girls played with their dolls, Joseph fell into an exhausted sleep and the three babies were held on their respective mothers' laps. Ellen had little memory of the journey they had made when they arrived in India and looked out the window with interest at the changing landscape. All the things she loved about India were there to be seen: the blue sky, the luscious green growth, the vibrant colours of the flowers, the jewel colours of the clothes of people in the fields, the stark outlines of oxen drawing ploughs, the silhouettes of women gracefully bearing burdens on their heads, the barefoot children playing. She also remembered the stories of the ill treatment and murder of women by their own people, the exploitation of women and children; she remembered seeing the inadequate shelter, the terrible poverty and malnourishment, the cripples and the beggars, the inexplicable way that Indians accepted this as their fate.

Ada's voice woke her from her reverie. "I'm not sorry to be leaving India. I feel as though I have been living in a hot house in Kew Gardens for the past seven years. I can't wait to get back to real life."

"Life will not be as easy at home. I will certainly miss the ayahs! I'm not looking forward to the cold and rain either. I have got to like the heat." Violet was smiling wryly at her five children and wondering how she was ever going to manage them on her own.

"It will be nice to be back with my family. They have never seen my children and I have missed two weddings of my sisters." Ellen was thinking of the cosy lodge with the fire lighting and tea and scones on the table. The children would love the freedom of the garden and the demesne. Her parents would be proud to show off their grandchildren. The aunts would be delighted to spoil their nephews and niece.

The squabbling of the boys, now getting tired of their game, was interrupted by the hoot of the train as they drew into the station. Soldiers were on duty to help the women and children on board the ship. Making sure they had all their bags and shepherding the children kept Ellen occupied until they were shown into their cabin. First the airless smell struck her, then the layout of the cabin. Although bigger, it had the same layout as the cabin they had occupied on the outward journey. She was overcome by nausea and had to sit down. The scenes surrounding Nancy's death came back to her with all the vividness of a nightmare.

She thought she was going to faint when a small hand stroked her face. "Are you all right, Mama? Would you like a drink of water?" Harry was already pouring water from the bedside flask and handing it to his mother.

She took a long drink then picked up Kathleen from the floor and held her on her lap, put an arm around Harry and Joseph nuzzled up to his mother. "I will be all right, my darlings. Thank you, Harry; you are such a thoughtful boy."

By the time James arrived at the cabin, they were all ready for bed and everything was arranged in the small space.

The journey home was uneventful. They began to feel the cold when they were a week's sailing out from Dover. Ellen got out the heaviest clothes they had but still the children shivered; they had never been exposed to cold before. They spent less time on deck and more in the cabin. She was thankful that she had packed books and games for the children to keep them occupied. James played with them whenever he was free while she rested. Most nights she slept uneasily and dreamed of Nancy. When they were on deck she looked into the deep ocean and wondered where her baby was but the needs of her other children prevented her from becoming melancholy.

One morning, word came that land could be seen; she dressed

the children warmly and took them up on deck. They stood in the watery sunshine and saw the ghostly white silhouette of the cliffs of Dover looming through the mist. "That is England, my loves, the white cliffs of Dover. We are not very far from Ireland now. Soon we will be home."

Harry looked up at her, shivering in the early morning mist. "Mama, will we see Prithi and Vinod again? Will we go back to India?"

"No, Harry. Ireland is our home now. Remember all the stories I told you about Ireland, your book about the brave warriors of the Fianna and the story of Diarmuid and Gráinne? Soon we will be there and you will see how wonderful it is. It is very green and beautiful in a way that is quite different to India. The weather is cool so that you do not need to sleep in the middle of the day. There is no danger of snakes or poisonous insects so you can play outside alone if you wish to. The rain is light and misty, not like the monsoons."

Kathleen began to squirm in her arms. "Papa, Papa, want Papa."

Joseph's face looked pale and anxious. Ellen smiled at him. "Don't worry, children. Papa will be with us when we arrive in Ireland. We will all go together to the barracks in Renmore. That is where we will be living for the moment."

By midday they had disembarked and were safely on the train to Liverpool. As before, Violet, Ada and herself travelled in the same carriage with their children. By the time they boarded the ship, exhaustion and the strangeness of everything made the children sleep so that their mothers found themselves confined to their own cabins looking after their children. The children woke early the next morning, cold and hungry. Ellen left Harry to look after them and went to get some warm milk and bread from the galley.

Harry looked thoughtful as he drank his milk. "Have we no Prithi now? Who will look after us? Who will cook for us like

Vinod did?"

"I will, my pet. In Ireland we will not have servants. I will look after you and cook for us. You can help me. Won't that be fun?"

Harry was unimpressed. "I like Vinod's cooking. Can you make sweetmeats?"

"No, but I can make cakes and scones. My Mama taught me. Now, let us get dressed. We will be docking in Dublin soon."

The final leg of their journey, from Dublin to Galway, was easy. The children looked out the window of the carriage with interest. They had never seen sheep before or cows with such small horns and were amazed at the numbers in the fields. Going through the Curragh, they saw the racehorses on their morning gallops. The stone walls, the green fields, the tall crops of wheat and barley, the small cottages, the donkeys, the odd motor car on the roads all fascinated them and they chattered and talked for most of the journey. James appeared at Galway to help them and their luggage in to the carriages which would take them to Renmore.

The forbidding grey buildings of the barracks looked like home to Ellen after the long journey. They were shown to their quarters, bigger and in a different wing of the building from those they had occupied seven years previously. The children, and Ellen herself, were now drooping with tiredness and she immediately undressed them. Basic provisions had been left in the kitchen so she gave them a light meal and then put them to bed. All three were to share a bedroom. They were asleep when James arrived, free at last from his duties. They undressed and lay together on the feather mattress, nestled under the eiderdown, their arms around each other.

"I am glad to be home" Ellen murmured sleepily. "I can't wait to see my parents and sisters again."

James kissed her. "I am glad to be home too but I will miss the army. It has been my life for so long; I can't imagine being a civilian again."

Chapter 8
1911-1912: Reunions and Partings

The trunks arrived the next day just after James had left. The quarters could not possibly accommodate all the contents so Ellen decided to unpack some necessities and also some items which would make the rooms look more like home. Warm clothes were the first priority. Automatically, she looked around for Prithi to help her, then realised that, in the future, she would be doing all the household tasks herself. She found some heavier clothes and then selected a silk bed cover and a beautiful woven tablecloth of jewel colours and a few small brass vases. They brightened up the drab rooms considerably. Then Harry helped her to wrap some of the presents they had brought for her parents and sisters. The trunks were too heavy for her to move so she left them where they were until James came home.

The children were excited and keen to see their new surroundings. The day was bright and sunny so she dressed them warmly and took them out for a walk. Once outside the environs of the barracks, the countryside revealed its springtime beauty. The sweet smell of turf fires mingled with the scent of freshly cut meadows in the cool blue air. The banks on each side of the roadside were awash with the delicate yellow of primroses and here and there a slash of the darker yellow of forsythia. Whitethorn gleamed through the fresh green of the hedges over which cattle gazed at them, chewing contentedly. Harry and Joseph were enchanted with the new sights and revelled in the freedom of being allowed to run and chase through the fields like frolicking lambs, picking flowers or gazing at cows. Their lives have been as constricted as mine, thought Ellen, as she remembered all the precautions they had to take when they took the children out in India.

Her parents could not wait to meet Ellen and the children and sent Lord Lucan's new automobile to bring them to stay for a few days. Lord and Lady Lucan were in London visiting their sons and had taken their young daughter with them. They left instructions that the automobile was to be sent for Ellen and her children whenever she wanted to visit. Harry and Joseph were very impressed with the Ford car when it arrived and jumped up and down in the back seat. It was driven by the new chauffeur, Albert Dunne, and he turned out to be as handsome as Annie had said if a little taciturn. He was probably not too pleased to have his free time interrupted by the child and grandchildren of a fellow servant.

When they arrived at the lodge, Henry, Mary Ann, Maggie and Annie were waiting outside. Ellen was shocked at the changes that seven years had wrought in her parents; they looked like much older versions of themselves. Her father's once black hair was completely grey and had receded from his forehead. He was thinner and slightly stooped. Her mother retained the same lively expression but her hair too was grey, whereas before it had been just sprinkled with grey. She walked with some difficulty; her arthritis was obviously worse. Maggie looked much as she had always looked except that now she was plumper and wore her hair up in a more matronly style. Annie however had blossomed from a shy young girl into a beautiful young woman with strawberry blonde hair and laughing blue eyes. She chatted to Albert as he handed out their luggage and helped the children to alight. He suddenly became charming and wished them all a good holiday as he drove the car away to the garage.

Her parents were delighted with the children and smothered them with kisses and hugs. "Harry, what a handsome boy you are! Come and give me a kiss." Mary Ann kissed and hugged Harry and then stood back. "My, you are the image of your grandfather!"

Joseph was looking up shyly at his grandfather who scooped

him up and hugged him. "You look like your mama when she was your age."

Maggie immediately appropriated Kathleen, kissing her and admiring her blonde curls. Kathleen was pleased with the attention and clasped her aunt around the neck. Joseph was holding hands with both his grandparents and Harry was chatting to Annie like an adult.

The door was open and the lodge looked as welcoming and homely as ever. Even though it was May, a log fire burned in the grate and the smell of baking hung in the air.

"Oh I love the smell of the log fire; and I can smell the scones!" Ellen linked her mother's other arm and they all went inside.

Ellen began to feel as though she had never left. The table was laid for tea and soon they were all sitting down, chatting, laughing and exchanging information. Mary Ann sat beside Ellen, holding her hand and wiping away the odd tear. Harry had engaged his grandfather in conversation and was soon being taken out to see around the garden. Joseph struggled down from his chair to follow them and soon the four women were left sitting around the fire almost as though the previous seven years had never happened. Ellen felt the warmth and affection cocooning her like a familiar quilt. Later, the children were put to bed with much hugging and kissing, just as Matt arrived to accompany his wife home. He too was plumper than Ellen remembered and just as good-humoured as he always had been. Annie went to read to Harry and Joseph who could still be heard talking excitedly and gave her sister the opportunity to be alone with her parents. They were keen to know what plans Ellen and James had because, of course, they hoped to keep their grandchildren nearby.

"His tour of duty is finished so he will be looking for a job," Ellen told them.

"A job in Galway would be ideal," her mother said. "Then we

could see you and the children frequently."

Ellen didn't want to raise the hopes of her parents. "The regiment will help James get a job. He asked for something suitable in Galway or Dublin but of course, most of the jobs are in Dublin."

Ellen for her part was anxious about her parents and how they were managing in the lodge. Her father admitted that he found the work quite onerous at times and found himself short of breath quite often, but his work was easier now that Lord Lucan spent more time in London.

Mary Ann said as she was pulling herself to her feet to go to bed, "I find it difficult now to stand for long periods and I get very stiff. Annie is a great help to us around the house. But I am afraid that the arthritis has put paid to my gardening!"

Later as the two sisters prepared for bed, Ellen took the opportunity to talk to Annie about her own life. "Is there any young man in the background, waiting to whisk you away?" she asked light-heartedly.

"There are not very many eligible men left around here now," Annie said ruefully. "Many of them have gone to Galway, Dublin or Belfast or further away for work. Anyway, I have other ambitions. I want to train as a nurse."

Ellen was surprised at her sister's revelation. She had never heard anything about this before. "That sounds like an exciting idea. Have you done anything about finding a training place?"

"Yes, about a year ago I applied and was accepted for a place in the Mater Hospital in Dublin. I was delighted and was going to write to tell you but then Mama's arthritis got worse and I had to refuse the place. She is not so bad now but the winter is very difficult for her. I would have to go to Galway or Dublin for training. I couldn't do that at the moment because Mama and Papa are so dependent on me. I will just have to postpone my plans."

"Oh I am sorry, Annie. I can see how difficult it must be for you."

Annie looked patient. "I am resigned to it now but please do not say anything to them about it."

The family had so much to talk about that the few days in Castlebar passed quickly. Soon they found themselves back in the automobile heading for the barracks at Renmore.

Albert was more talkative this time and told Ellen a bit about himself. He was originally from Dublin but had worked in London as a chauffeur. "That is where Lord Lucan met me when he hired me and my car for a few weeks. When he was buying his new car he asked for my advice and then engaged me as his chauffeur. I was getting a bit tired of London at that time so I took the job."

Harry interrupted the conversation, wanting to know all about the car and how it functioned, so Ellen amused the other two by playing games with them.

James had news when they arrived home. The children were excited to see him so it wasn't until they were in bed that he got the opportunity to talk to Ellen. "I've been offered a job in Dublin. It's in the Post Office as a sorter. The pay is not bad and they want me to start in a month's time."

"In Dublin? Could you not get anything in Galway? My parents were hoping that we would be nearby at least for a while. Where would we live in Dublin? We don't know anybody there." Ellen couldn't hide her disappointment.

"I have a few old comrades in Dublin. I think Des is hoping to get something in Dublin and there are a few others who might be going there. I got a form to fill in for the Artisan Dwelling Company, you know, the people who are building the houses for ex-army and civil servants. If we got one of their houses we would be all right."

Ellen didn't want to dampen James's enthusiasm. "Well, if you think it is the best thing I suppose you should accept the job. I wish we didn't have to leave so soon though."

"It is just as well to get settled in the summer," James said. "Harry will be starting school in September so it will give us a chance to get to know the place. You will like Dublin, I know. I love it even though I haven't lived there for about sixteen years."

During the next few weeks, Ellen and the children spent as much time as possible with her parents and sisters. She had always thought of her parents as they had been when she left Castlebar and now it pained her to see their slower progress around the house and their stooped walk. She could see how much pleasure they derived from watching the three children tumbling and playing around the house. They loved talking to the children and were amazed at the precociousness of Harry when he insisted on reading to them. She consoled them that Dublin was not so far away and made them promise to visit as soon as the family was settled. For her part, she was determined to visit her home as often as possible, particularly when the children had school holidays. The parting after their last visit before leaving for Dublin was difficult. The children did not really understand but both parents were very tearful when they kissed their grandchildren goodbye, more than they had been when she left for India all those years before.

"Promise that you will visit us often, a stór." Her mother wiped away her tears.

Henry was holding Joseph by the hand and said gruffly, "We were getting used to having the children around. They make us feel young again."

Harry reached up to kiss his grandfather. "Don't worry, Grandpapa, we will come to visit you soon again."

Her parents looked forlorn as they stood in the gateway, waving goodbye. They were getting old and felt partings more keenly. Within a few days she and James and the children would be on their way to Dublin, their last upheaval for a long time, she hoped.

Chapter 9
1911: A Home in Dublin

Ellen had been through Dublin when she travelled to India but only as part of a British army contingent. She had never seen anything of the city and she looked curiously around her as the train stopped at the platform. Kingsbridge Station looked huge. Crowds of people walked purposefully towards trains, carrying bags and children; others like themselves were alighting from trains, lifting down bags, looking for porters or searching their pockets for tickets or tips. The steam engine of the Galway train from which they had just alighted was still puffing gently, emitting thick smoke which smelt of bad eggs.

James was looking around for a porter. He wouldn't be able to manage all the bags on his own and Ellen had the three children to look after, Kathleen in her arms, Joseph clinging on to her skirts and Harry holding Joseph's other hand. She had been used to crowds of people in India but there they had been kept at a distance, while here the family was jostled and pushed as soon as they stepped onto the platform.

"Good man!" James had managed to catch the eye of a porter. "Here, give me a hand with some of these bags. We are being met outside."

James led the way through the imposing granite station house to the street outside where all manner of horse drawn vehicles were waiting. A man wearing a bowler hat and smoking a pipe was waving to them. James tipped the porter and put down the bags to greet his friend. They shook hands energetically as James said, "Me oul' comrade, how are ye?"

"Pullin' the divil be the tail, Jimmy. Are these all your care?" The other man was smiling at the children as they admired the horse.

97

Ellen was startled by James's sudden lapse into Dublinese but smiled at Mick as they were introduced. She knew that he and James had served together in India on his first tour there.

"This is my oul' horse and cart. Come on now, chislers. Let me lift you up. Here missus, you can use one of them bags as a step up," Mick said as he helped her up.

Ellen found herself sitting with the children at the back of a cart which was none too clean and smelled as if it had been used to carry pigs. The bags were piled up all around them and James hopped up beside Mick, who shook the reins and clucked the horse into movement and immediately started a commentary on the places that they passed.

"We haven't far to go, just here along Parkgate Street, then right along Infirmary Road, up the hill and into Aberdeen Street. Do ye see that pub over there, Ryan's? That's a grand place for a good bottle of porter. The Ryans is great friends of mine. That shop, there, missus, half way up the hill is a grand place to get the victuals. Now down there, if we went straight on we would come to the gates of the Phoenix Park, the biggest park in Europe, or so they tell me. It's a grand place for the chislers to run around and there's a duck pond an' all." Mick was waving expansively as he described the area.

Ellen half listened to him, looking at the houses as they turned into Infirmary Road. They were two storeys high, with granite steps leading up to them and a small garden to the front. All the windows seemed to have lace curtains shielding the occupants from the gaze of passers-by with plant pots strategically placed in the space between the drapes. Their own house would be smaller, she knew. It hadn't been easy finding a decent place to rent in Dublin. Most people around the city lived in one or two rooms of a rundown tenement building where they shared one lavatory. Ellen had never seen a tenement but had read about them in the newspaper when two houses had collapsed in Dublin, killing ten of the occupants.

Because James had been in the British Army he was able to secure a house which was owned by the Dublin Artisan Dwelling Company. Many of the people who rented the houses were employed by Guinness, a major shareholder in the company. Other tenants were ex-British Army, like themselves, or skilled workers and professionals like teachers and civil servants. Thanks to the army, their furniture had been delivered the day before and Mick, who lived in Black Street, just behind the street where they were to live, had been entrusted with the key and had supervised the unloading and arrangement of the items.

Ellen's heart sank as they turned up the hill into Aberdeen Street. Her first impression was of greyness unrelieved by any greenery. Her eyes had been accustomed to the lush greens and the gentle pastels of the demesne at Castlebar and then the exotic patchwork of vivid reds, oranges, saffron and yellow which was India in her imagination. Now the colours seemed to have leeched away, leaving only greys, charcoals and blacks. Though it was August, the sky was dark and low and was met by smoke swirling down from chimneys. The houses were terraced and very closely packed together with no front gardens. They were two-storey and looked solidly built of redbrick with granite window sills and front steps, but they were very small with front doors uniformly painted dark green with one window to the side of the door and another above that.

A number of the houses had their front doors wide open revealing a woman with arms folded over her chest peering out at the new arrivals. In a few moments the children, some of them with bare feet, who had been playing Toss Ha'penny in the gutters, crowded in around the cart eyeing them curiously and offering to help with the bags. Other children, dangling in

99

makeshift swings on the gas lampposts, stopped their swinging to watch.

Ellen felt self-conscious as Mick gave James the key and handed down first her and then the children from the cart. James opened the door and ushered them in, and they stood together in the tiny hall. To their right was a very small room whose window looked out onto the street. It was empty of furniture. Straight ahead, the kitchen was quite a good size with a large black range to the right and a window which looked out to the small yard at the back. Their table and four chairs had been left in the middle of the room. Their two armchairs were positioned each side of the range. To the left of the window was an alcove where they could see the bottom of the stairs and to the right of that, the back door. To the left of the alcove was a cupboard, the larder she supposed. Mick began to bring the bags in to the kitchen and then closed the door on the audience outside.

"Well, what do you think?" James looked nervously at Ellen. "It'll look different when we have our own bits and pieces around, won't it?"

"It's very small, but it is a start. Come on, let's have a look upstairs." Ellen was determined to make the best of it. She lifted the baby while James held the hands of the other two as they all climbed the steep stairs. At the top was the largest bedroom, with a window which looked out onto the street, big enough for two double beds although there was only one in it at the moment, flanked by the cradle which her father had made originally for Nancy. The back bedroom was much smaller, big enough for the other double bed with a window looking out onto the small yard and a dark curtained alcove which reached back under the eaves.

Ellen looked into its spidery interior. "It's like the Black Hole of Calcutta."

The children looked nervously at her. She forced herself to

sound cheerful. "Children, do you want to see the yard?" She carried Kathleen carefully down and James carried Joseph, leaving Harry to climb down himself, holding on to the banister.

Ellen lifted the latch on the back door. The yard was surrounded on three sides by a whitewashed wall which was about five foot high and made it impossible for anyone to see into their neighbour's backyard. At the far end on the left was a lavatory with a flushing toilet. On the right, near to the back door, was a big stone sink with a brass tap. Opposite that was a storage area, covered in from the weather, empty now but presumably for fuel.

It was a better house than most people in Dublin had, Ellen knew, but she couldn't help but be disheartened. The quarters in the barracks in Renmore hadn't been much better but at least she had had her family nearby. Dublin felt as alien to her as India had when she first went there, but in India she had grown to love the sun and the heat and she had the protection of the British Army and the luxury of servants. Here she would have to look after the children herself and do all the cooking, cleaning and washing. She didn't know a soul in Dublin and wouldn't know how to find her way around it.

"Mama, I'm hungry." Harry broke into her thoughts. Joseph was sucking his thumb and Kathleen was crying.

"All right, children. I have some milk and buttered soda bread in one of the bags. Sit down there at the table and I will get it for you."

She found the bread and gave a piece to the two boys and then passed the milk bottle from one to the other. Kathleen stopped crying as soon as she picked her up.

Mick and James were looking at her anxiously. "Ellen, you don't mind if me and Mick slip down to Ryan's for a quick one? On account of him looking after the furniture and meeting us ..."

"You two go on. I have to make up the beds and settle the children down for the night. What are we going to do for coal and kindling for the range? I'd like to be able to boil the kettle for a cup of tea tonight." Ellen couldn't keep the disapproval out of her voice.

"If May's on the hill is open we might be able to get a bag there which will keep you going until the coalman calls. We'll bring it back on the cart, missus," Mick said as he was already half way out the door.

James gave each of the children a kiss and followed him. Once the men had gone Ellen turned up the gaslights and settled down to feed Kathleen while keeping the boys amused with a story about a train. Then she found the bedclothes for the little cradle in one of the bags and carried the now sleeping baby upstairs and placed her gently down, cocooned amongst the blankets. She found a facecloth and the nightgowns for the two boys in the same bag.

Once she had changed them, she went out to the yard to wet a cloth under the tap so that she could wipe their faces and hands. The night was mild and she could see the glow of the city lights in the sky. The air smelled of coal fires. A toilet flushed in the adjoining yard and someone coughed. A dog barked close by and an answering bark echoed further away. Down the street a baby cried. In the distance she could hear the shunting of trains coming from Kingsbridge.

She turned to find Harry watching her from the doorway with Joseph behind him. The anxious looks on their faces made her put her arms around them and kiss them. "Don't worry, my babies. We will soon make a home here and you will make friends and we will all be very happy."

They stood in front of her while she wiped the grime of the day from their faces and hands.

102

"Will you tell us another story, Mama, about the train?"

"I will but only when you are both in bed. Harry, you help Joseph up the stairs while I bring the bedclothes."

The two boys clambered up ahead of her and waited while she made up the bed in the small bedroom. Once they were tucked in, she began the story but found that they were asleep before she had uttered four sentences.

"Poor lambs, you must be exhausted," she said as she tucked them in.

Wearily she made her way downstairs again and opened the second bag which had their own bedclothes in it. She would have loved a cup of tea but she had no kindling for the range. She didn't want to drink the last of the milk in case the children woke up thirsty in the night so contented herself with a glass of water. There was no sign of James and it was beginning to get chilly; she quickly made up the bed, changed into her nightdress, checked on the two boys, tucked the blankets securely around Kathleen and sank back onto her own bed. She must have fallen asleep immediately because she woke up what seemed like hours later to hear noises downstairs. She lit a match and went to peer down the stairs. James was at the bottom of the stairs, holding on to the banisters, his body listing to one side.

"Hello, sweetheart. Me and Mick had a few jars and we met a few butties that we knew. I'm all right; I just don't know me way around this house." He began to climb the stairs, pulling himself up one step at a time.

"Don't wake the children. They are exhausted after the journey and everything." She helped him up the last few steps. The sweet, cloying smell of porter filled her nostrils.

James was smiling a silly, foolish smile. "Do you know I love you?" he said as she helped him onto the bed and removed his boots. He was asleep and snoring before she settled beside him.

Chapter 10
1911: Living in Dublin

The sun streaming in through the un-curtained window woke her early the next morning. Beside her, James was spread-eagled under the blankets, still fully clothed apart from his boots. Kathleen began to stir and make anxious little noises but the two boys in the next room seemed to be still asleep. Ellen got up, put her overcoat over her nightdress and picked up Kathleen. She went down the stairs as quietly as she could, treading lightly when a step creaked. In the kitchen she found that Mick and James had left a bag of coal and some kindling beside the range. Still with Kathleen in her arms she found some matches in one of the bags and some paper which had been used to wrap crockery. Kathleen cried when she put her on the floor but she couldn't manage to light the range and get some water from the tap in the backyard while still carrying her. The range blazed up quickly enough and she put the kettle on to boil.

While she was waiting she sat down in one of the armchairs with Kathleen and fed her. She could hear the street coming to life outside: doors banged shut, voices passed by the window, a train whistle shrilled, a factory horn sounded in the distance. The sounds of the city were new to her.

The kettle had boiled by the time Kathleen was satisfied. She pushed the two armchairs together to make a safe nest for Kathleen and made herself a cup of tea. The tea revived her so that she began to search some of the bags for foodstuffs and kitchen ware. A bag of oatmeal and a jar of her mother's strawberry jam were the first things that came to hand. In another bag she found a cooking pot and some cups so tightly wrapped in newspaper that the ink had come off on the pottery. She measured out some oatmeal and water and put it on to cook for James and the children. Above her head she could hear the children stirring; James slept on.

The two boys were just waking up, their eyes anxiously searching the strange room, when she went upstairs. She pulled them to her and talked brightly about their new house and their new life. Once they were dressed, she took them downstairs to have breakfast. The familiar routine seemed to calm them down and they chatted to her about the train journey of the previous day. She had everything done by the time James came down, bleary-eyed and shamefaced: the range was blazing, they were all washed and dressed, and the kitchen was tidy apart from the boxes not yet unpacked.

"I should have been down to help you. Why didn't you wake me up? Sorry about last night. Mick and me met a few auld army butties and I didn't feel the time passing. Anyway, we got ye the coal!" He was trying to placate her.

Ellen didn't reply immediately. She was afraid that if she said anything it would simply start a row, something that was happening more and more frequently, usually instigated by his drinking. Since they had returned to Ireland, she knew that they had both been feeling insecure, concerned about their future and worried about getting a house. James hated leaving the army and his unhappiness had expressed itself in regular drinking sessions.

After a while she said, "We need to buy some things for the house: curtains, something to put the clothes in, somewhere to keep the delph and some food. Have you any money left?"

"Of course I have money left! Did you think I would spend every penny? Look, here's your housekeeping. Anyway, I'll be starting in the Post Office next Monday and I'll get me wages the following Friday. Mick says there's a grand little shop up the top of the street and turn right. Do you want to go up there this morning and I'll mind the children?" He was trying to make up for his neglect of the night before.

"Yes, I better get some food. We have very little left. There's a

105

bit of oatmeal in the pot there for you. Is there anything you need?" Ellen didn't look at him.

"Get me a few ounces of tobacco – Mick McQuaid's. Oh, and some sweets for the chislers; they were very good when we were travelling."

"Will you stop calling them that?" She immediately regretted being so sharp with him.

Being alone with the children the previous night, in a strange house in a strange city, had left her feeling lonely and abandoned; it was an irrational feeling she knew. James was a good husband and a caring father even if he did succumb sometimes to drinking sessions.

James continued to look at her anxiously as she put on her hat and coat, put the money in her purse and picked up a basket. She closed the door more loudly than she intended and walked up the street, turning right as Mick had directed.

The shop was identifiable by a Johnson, Mooney and O'Brien sign hanging outside. It was really a small cottage which had been converted to a shop. The door was held open by a woman who looked as though she was just leaving. She looked curiously at Ellen and followed her back into the shop. Their footsteps echoed on the worn wooden floor. A counter stretched right along the right wall with an array of dried goods in large containers on display on shelves behind. A tall, imposing looking woman stood at one end of the counter dressed in the old-fashioned style that her mother favoured, high-necked blouse with a cameo brooch at the neck, tucked into a long black skirt. Her grey hair was held up in a high loose bun and she wore eyeglasses low down on her nose.

She peered at Ellen. "Hello, my dear. What can I do for you today?"

"I want a pound of butter, a quarter of tea, a pound of sugar and a pint of milk, two ounces of Mick McQuaid and a box of matches, please. Have you fresh bread?"

The woman put a brown paper bag on a weighing scales and started to fill it with sugar. She cut a slab of butter from a large piece which stood in water and shaped it with two butter boards and then wrapped it in grease proof paper, talking all the time. "The bread will be in soon. We don't keep milk; it goes off too quickly. Christy Murphy comes around every morning and delivers milk. He'll be here soon and I'll tell him to call to you if you like. Are you living around here? What's your address?"

"5, Aberdeen Street. Thanks, we just moved in." Ellen was grateful for the friendly help.

A group of three women had been standing at the far end of the counter; one of them was being served by the young assistant. She moved over to stand beside Ellen. "We heard youse were coming. British Army, ain't youse?"

Ellen was startled by the animosity in the tone. "Yes, my husband was in the British Army. He will be working in the Post Office from next week."

"Ah, they always look after their own. My Bill is a cooper with Guinness. He got the job for himself." The woman was staring at Ellen.

The imposing looking lady interrupted. "My name is Miss Ormond. I own the shop. That is Rose, my assistant over there."

A fresh-faced young girl smiled at her from the far end of the counter where she was slicing rashers.

Miss Ormond proffered her hand to Ellen. "The fresh bread will be here any minute. Is there anything else that you want?"

Ellen focused on the friendly face in front of her and tried to ignore the eyes burning into her back as she gave her order. "A half pound of back rashers, a half pound of sausages and a dozen eggs. Oh, and a package of salt." The jar of barley sugars caught her eye. "Give me two of those barley sugars as well."

107

Miss Ormond started cutting the rashers, weighed them and then the sausages and wrapped them all in white paper. While she put the eggs in cardboard boxes, Ellen put the rest of the groceries in her basket.

With the eggs safely stowed, Miss Ormond made a great show of totting up the sums which she had written on a sheet of white butcher's paper and then tore off the piece of paper and presented it to Ellen. "You can pay me now or you can start a book."

"A book?" Ellen didn't understand.

"Yes, most of the women have a book," Miss Ormond explained. "We write in their book what they buy, keep a copy ourselves in the big book and at the end of the week they pay me."

Ellen smiled at her. "Thank you but I don't need a book. I will pay you now."

She heard the deliberately loud whispering as she waited for her change. "It's well for some!"

"Thinks she's better nor the rest of us!"

At that moment the door was nudged open by a large bread board full of turnovers, loaves and ducks, followed by a short man in a brown shop coat. He manoeuvred awkwardly because of a pronounced limp.

"You're a bit late, Peter," Miss Ormond scolded. "These customers are all waiting for bread."

Peter started to unload his bread, bantering with the women in a good-humoured way as they selected what they wanted and paid. Ellen took a turnover which was still warm and smelled enticing; she hadn't eaten any breakfast. She paid and hurried out of the shop, tearing off a piece of the skin which formed on the bread and letting it melt on her tongue as she walked home. Some of the front doors were open as she passed, women were sweeping out the hall or simply standing, arms crossed, heads stuck out like geese, watching for any movement or items of interest on the street. No.

108

6, the house next door, was open; a stately looking woman with upswept grey hair and a pinafore around her wide body was polishing the brass door knocker.

She turned when she saw Ellen. "Hello, I am Bridie Kelly. You must be Mrs Devereux. We heard you were coming."

"Pleased to meet you, Mrs Kelly. We just moved in last night. I was up in the shop getting a few things." Ellen was relieved to see a friendly face.

"I heard that you are not long back from India. It must be quite a change for you, the weather and everything." Mrs Kelly continued to polish as she spoke.

"Yes, it is, but we are happy to be back in Ireland. My husband is starting a new job in the Post Office next week," Ellen told her.

"I am a widow, myself. My husband used to work in Guinness's. He was a cooper but was killed on the job in an accident." She looked sad. "We have five childer. The company looks after us though. If there is anything you need to know, just ask me."

Ellen thought. "Well, there is something. My son Harry is seven and should be starting school in September. Where is the nearest boys' school?"

"Brunswick Street Christian Brothers. That is where my two lads go. You need to go and see Brother O'Keeffe. He is the head teacher. You would probably catch him in any morning." She collected her polishing cloth and turned to go in.

"Thanks, Mrs Kelly. I better get in with these messages. Good day, now."

The children were waiting to see what she had brought them. "They are for after tea, now," she warned as she gave them the barley sugars. While she unloaded her basket she told James what Mrs Kelly had said.

"Brunswick Street?" James said. "I know where that is. We can go there this week if you like before I start in the job."

"Maybe we could see about the things we need for the house. I wouldn't know where to go." Ellen wanted to make up for her brusqueness that morning.

"Don't worry, love. We can take the tram into the city and I will show you where to shop. It will be an outing for the chis- children as well." James was delighted to be back in favour and started planning their trip to the city. "Wait till you see the trams, Harry. The city is very big, much bigger than Castlebar, and full of lovely shops."

"Will we be going in a car like the one that Albert drives?" Joseph was remembering his trips from Galway to Castlebar.

"No, Jo-Jo. Didn't you hear Papa saying that we would be going in a tram? They are much bigger than a car." Harry was excited at the thought of a trip.

That evening they had their tea in front of the range and James told them stories about Dublin. He told them about the zoo which was nearby, the big shops with all kinds of things for sale, the street markets, the buskers who played music on the streets in the hope of getting some money from passers-by, Carlisle Street which was said to be the widest street in Europe and the theatres where there was all manner of entertainment. Ellen found herself almost as entranced as the children by her husband's stories. When the children were in bed, they sat each side of the range, drinking tea and talking about what their life in Dublin would be like. In bed that night, the apprehension she had felt about living in Dublin disappeared and she curled into her husband as he kissed her and made love to her.

Next morning as they ate their breakfast, the boys remembered the stories of the night before. "Papa, Mama, are we going on the tram? Are we going to the zoo?"

James was delighted with their enthusiasm. "We need to get some things for the house so the first outing will be down to the quays. I know some good second-hand shops there where we will get a few bits of furniture. Then we will go to the city centre so that you can get to know Dublin."

After breakfast, the family walked to the Park Gate where the tram left for the North Quays and Carlisle Bridge. Ellen had never been on a tram before and was as excited as the children when they paid their one penny each and climbed on board. They managed to sit together at the front of the tram from where they had a good view.

The boys were fascinated by the city; they had never been in a city in India except for going to the port and had seen little of Galway which was considerably smaller than Dublin. The roads were busy with horses and carts, people on bicycles, others pushing handcarts and an occasional motor car. When they got to the North Quays it was even busier with the footpaths thronged with people and barges gliding down the River Liffey.

They alighted from the tram at Carlisle Bridge and made their way along Ormond Quay where there were a number of shops selling furniture and household goods. They went into one of them where James seemed to know the shop assistant. While they were talking, Ellen wandered around the shop with the children. There was a good display of furniture at what seemed reasonable prices.

"James, there is a wardrobe here that I like but would we get it up the stairs of the house?" Ellen was excited.

James joined her with one of the assistants, who immediately said, "Don't worry, missus, we have a crane and we put big items of furniture through the window."

"That's right, Ellen. Mick was saying the same thing."

Ellen had picked out a few other pieces. "There's also a small dresser and a few stools for the children. And maybe a dressing table. Is that too much?" she asked him.

"No, Ellen, love. I have most of my demob money so we can

111

well afford them items." He turned to the assistant. "When can you deliver them?"

"This Friday, I think. Will that suit youse?" He looked from James to Ellen.

Ellen looked happily at her new purchases. "That would suit very well. Thank you."

James paid and the family walked back along the quays to Carlisle Street. At the bridge they turned up D'Olier Street where they stopped to admire Trinity College.

"I know a great sweetshop up here," he said. "Who would like a lollipop?"

They walked up the length of Grafton Street to a shop called Nobletts. The children were amazed at the display of lollipops of all shapes and sizes and other sweets that looked very inviting. The two boys were allowed to pick their own lollipop and Ellen got a bag of jujubes.

James pointed across the street as they came out of the sweet shop. "That is St. Stephen's Green over there. It is a lovely park though not as big as the Phoenix Park. Will we have a walk through it?"

Ellen slipped her hand through her husband's arm as they crossed the street, both of them with a son by the hand and James carrying Kathleen. There were children by the duck pond, feeding bread to the ducks that were setting up quite a noise. Joseph was enchanted with the ducks. A mother, who was handing bread to her children, gave some to Joseph and Harry so that they could participate in the noisy proceedings. Kathleen was waving her hands in the air and making gurgling noises. Ellen looked at her handsome husband and three lovely children and tried to capture that moment of pure happiness in her memory forever.

Chapter 11
1912: New Beginnings

James had only a few more free days before he started in the Post Office so they decided to visit the school to arrange for Harry to begin there in September. Once more they set off for the city but this time they walked to North Brunswick Street, as Harry was to do every day. The distance seemed very far for a small boy to walk, thought Ellen, as they went down Infirmary road, into Arbour Hill and on into Brunswick Street. The tall building looked grey and forbidding as they waited at the front door. The chanting of pupils could be heard as a young brother opened the door and asked them their business. He disappeared inside and after about ten minutes they could see a tall figure dressed in a soutane gliding towards them.

James moved forward. "Brother O'Keeffe? We have a boy who would like to start school here, Brother. His name is Harry Devereux." Harry moved forward to stand beside his father.

The brother had a long narrow face and gimlet eyes through which he stared at them suspiciously. "Hmm, I see. And where are you living? Where was he at school before this?"

"Oh, we have just returned from India. We are living off the Infirmary Road, in Aberdeen Street. He ..."

The brother interrupted. "India? So you are a member of the British Army?" The disdain in his voice was unmistakeable.

"I was in the British Army. I will be working in the Post Office for the future." James's pride was equally unmistakeable.

"Has he made his First Communion?"

"Not yet, Brother. He is only seven."

"All right. We will start him off in the First Class, the Communion class. We may have to demote him to High Babies if he is not up to it academically." He peered down at Harry.

113

"He is very good at the reading and writing and the sums too. My wife …"

The brother cut him short. "Indeed. Well, he will also have to study Irish, our own language."

"When can he start, Brother?"

"Bring him here on the first of September at nine o'clock." He turned and glided away, his feet hardly seeming to move under the long soutane.

On the way home, Ellen told the two boys to walk ahead of them. She turned to James with tears in her eyes. "That brother seemed so unfriendly; he wasn't very pleased with the fact that you were in the British army. I hope Harry will be all right in this school."

Ellen was thinking of her own happy school experience in the convent school in Castlebar run by the Mercy nuns.

"Don't worry, love. He is obviously a bit of a nationalist. Harry is a bright boy and I am sure he will be all right." James tried to allay Ellen's fears.

"It is such a long way for him to walk. He is not used to the city. I am afraid he will get lost."

"I will walk him to school before I go to work myself for the first few days. After that, maybe he could walk with Mrs Kelly's boys, I'll ask her."

Ellen spent the next few days worrying about how Harry would fare in his new school. She was distracted on the Friday by the delivery of their furniture. A big lorry drew up outside the house, attracting the attention of all the children of the neighbourhood. One of the two delivery men went upstairs and had the window frame out in two minutes. In the meantime, the other man was attaching the wardrobe to a winch which was on a crane on top of the lorry. To the cheers of the children, the wardrobe was winched up and in the window to be followed by the dressing table and the window frame replaced. The remaining items came in through the front door. The house suddenly seemed more furnished and homely and Ellen and the children spent the rest of the day unpacking the trunks and arranging their clothes. James spent his last day of freedom out with Mick, playing cards in the Hollow in the park and having a few pints in Ryan's.

On Saturday, they took the children to the Phoenix Park. The People's Gardens, as the nearest part of it was called, was a short walk away. Ellen loved it as soon as she saw it. The grass was beautifully kept and the flowerbeds were full of late flowers, among them her favourites, dahlias. There was a hill leading down to the duck pond and the boys gleefully rolled down it over and over again. She had remembered to bring some bread so she distracted them from their rolling with promises of some bread to feed the ducks.

When it was time to go home, they were reluctant.

"Can we come here again, Mama?"

Joseph was enjoying the newfound freedom.

"Of course we can, my pet. We will come every week if you like."

James accompanied Harry to school for the first week and after that he walked with the two older boys from next door, Paddy and John Kelly. His teacher was a kindly old man, Brother Tuohy, who seemed very fond of Harry. Yet some days he seemed very quiet when he came home but would not tell Ellen what was troubling him. In desperation she asked Paddy, the older of the two Kelly boys. "Ah, he gets a bit of aggravation because of his da, being a British soldier and all that. Me and John look after him though."

Harry's first report at Christmas was excellent. He was first in the class in English, second in Maths and even in Irish he had done very well. By the following summer he was confident enough to walk to or from school on his own sometimes, especially now that he was a member of the Palestrina choir. Brother Tuohy had encouraged him to go for an audition when he heard him singing in class. Ellen went to the Pro Cathedral with him for the audition which was conducted by Mr O'Brien, the founder of the choir. He was accepted immediately and discovered that membership of the choir brought a small annual payment. Ellen resolved to put that by for Harry's education. Whenever she could, she attended Mass on Sunday in the Pro Cathedral. Her heart was bursting with pride the first Sunday that Harry was the chief boy soprano and the whole family heard him sing the Panis Angelicus.

She wrote to her parents and Annie frequently and encouraged them to come to Dublin on a visit. Her sister Jane was also living in Dublin and her parents had not visited her either. They promised to come at the end of the summer when Lord and Lady Lucan would have returned to London. The first of September was the date they decided to travel.

James was now working five and a half days and sometimes more because of overtime. He was reasonably well paid; Ellen only realised that when she went to the local shop and saw what other people could afford to buy. Many of her neighbours had large families of eight or ten and they seemed to live on a diet of bread and tea, supplemented by a pot of coddle or pig's feet on a Saturday.

Ellen herself had become a good cook, remembering her mother's recipes and adapting Vinod's. She enjoyed the cooking but the cleaning was a different matter. Sometimes she looked at her hands, which had once been soft and white and were now raw and chafed, and thought how her life had changed. Even at home in the lodge, she had never done much cleaning. She used her duties up at the Big House to avoid the domestic chores which her sisters were expected to do.

Now there was the range to be cleaned and black leaded every

116

morning, the beds to be made, the tidying and dusting to be done, the clothes and bedclothes and towels to washed every Monday in the sink outside and then dried and ironed on the Tuesday, the floors to be washed and polished every week. Sometimes, due to the weather, the clothes were hanging around the kitchen for days, wet and steaming, or else she had to wait another week or two before she could wash them. She had given up the elaborate hairdo that she had worn in India and now wore her hair in a simple coil at the back of her neck. She covered her clothes with a pinafore and put her silk gowns from India at the back of the wardrobe.

James managed to retain his smart, military appearance even when wearing civilian clothes. He pressed the crease into his trousers by putting them under the mattress, brushed his clothes and his Homburg hat every morning and burnished his shoes and hers and the children's every Saturday. He walked to work because he liked walking but also to save the daily tram fare and his military step could be heard leaving and arriving home at exactly the same time every day. He didn't say much about his work but was obviously bored although he didn't complain.

Violet and Des had arrived in Dublin six months after them and were now living in Prussia Street. They had only been able to get a three-roomed cottage but were happy with it. Des was also working in the Post Office so James saw him frequently. Desmond was due to begin in Harry's school in September.

During that summer, Violet and Ellen often met up in the Phoenix Park and the children played together while they watched them and chatted. Harry and Joseph played out on the street with the other children and through them Ellen got to know her neighbours. Sometimes the older children arranged concerts and all the mothers came out into the street with a stool to sit on and became their audience. Harry was a great hit when he sang the popular tunes of the day and Ellen was proud of her handsome boy.

117

Chapter 12
1913: Unrest in Dublin

Ellen was looking forward to her parents' visit to Dublin and began to make plans. She decided to give her parents the bedroom that she and James slept in when they visited and to buy a mattress which she could put in the small parlour for their own use. One morning, she asked Mrs Kelly to watch the boys who were playing on the street while she made a quick trip into the city. She carried Kathleen and made her way by tram to the shop on the quay where they had bought their furniture. She found a mattress which was reasonably clean-looking and negotiated with the assistant who remembered her previous visit. Satisfied that she had got a bargain, she arranged for the delivery and made her way back to the tram stop. Kathleen was getting heavier and heavier and was also crying because she was hungry.

There was a small crowd at the stop talking urgently together. A woman turned and saw Ellen. "Have you heard, missus? There's a strike on the trams."

"A strike? Why? Will there be no trams stopping here?"

A man who seemed to have the attention of the crowd spoke importantly. "The owner of the Tramways Company forbade his workers to join the Union, so they downed tools and left their vehicles. You won't see a tram for many a day, missus."

Ellen didn't know what she was going to do. It was a long walk home with Kathleen in her arms and she didn't even know the way. She rested Kathleen on the quay wall while she thought about it. Mrs Kelly would take care of the boys until she arrived home. She knew that Kingsbridge was on the river so if she kept walking along the North Quays she would come to the station. She knew her way home from there.

Hoisting Kathleen back up into her arms, she started the long walk. The quays were thronged with people all walking like herself while exchanging news of the strike. Along the way she could see into public houses with inviting stools but lone women didn't go into public houses and certainly not women with a baby.

Her back was aching and her feet burning by the time she got to Kingsbridge. Gratefully she entered the station and sat down on a bench. Kathleen was crying because she was uncomfortable; her nappy was soaking wet and she was hungry. Ellen needed to use the toilet and managed with some difficulty with Kathleen in her arms. There was a bench in the toilet so she managed to feed Kathleen. She drank some water and tidied herself and set off for home with an exhausted Kathleen asleep in her arms.

The boys were anxious and hungry when she arrived. Mrs Kelly had indeed taken them in but they had refused her offers of bread and dripping. She slipped off her shoes, changed Kathleen and then sat down to feed her. Harry poured two cups of milk and made a jam sandwich for himself and Joseph. When James came home he was surprised to see her looking so tired and worried.

"James, there was a tram strike today. I had to walk all the way home from the quays with Kathleen in my arms. I heard people saying that there was going to be a general strike. Mama and Papa were supposed to be travelling in a few days. They wouldn't be able to walk even if the train gets them as far as Dublin."

"I know, love. I heard all about it at work. There is talk about a big meeting in Sackville Street in a couple of days to be addressed by Jim Larkin, the union leader. Are you all right?" James was looking at her with concern.

"Yes, just a bit tired. What will we do about Mama and Papa? They may not know what is going on in Dublin. How will we let them know?" Ellen was almost in tears.

"The papers will be full of the strike so they will know. I'll call into Tom's office on my way home tomorrow and he can telephone

Lord Lucan's house. We can arrange another date for them to travel," James reassured her.

The strike, or "The Lockout" as the newspapers were now calling it, escalated. Big factories like Jacob's biscuit factory locked out its workers because they joined the union. Riots broke out around the city, one man died and the police were accused of brutality in their dealings with the strikers. James had to be careful which route he took to walk to work because if anyone was suspected of being a "blackleg" or strikebreaker, they would be set upon. Ellen kept the children close to her and was glad that the school term had not yet started. Then one evening James came home with the Evening Herald and showed it to Ellen. Large black headlines proclaimed "Two Houses in Church Street Collapse; Seven Dead, Many Injured."

"I'm not surprised a house collapsed," James said. "Some of those tenements have as many as ten people living in one room. The houses are in a terrible condition. The landlords don't care about the tenants and the tenants have no other choice. It's a disgrace."

A list of the dead and injured followed the article. Ellen was reading through it when she was stopped short by a familiar name. "Dan Murphy! James, is that the Dan Murphy we knew in India, you know the one who was court-martialled for beating his wife?"

"Well, it could be. He would have been released from prison over a year ago. Still, it's a common name." James looked over her shoulder.

Ellen was running her finger down the list of dead and injured. "It is him! Look, among the injured, Nan Murphy and her son Frank! Oh, I will have to go to see her. It says the injured are in Dr Steevens' Hospital. I am sure Violet will want to come with me. Oh, poor Nan, I often wondered what became of her."

The following evening Ellen and Violet left their husbands

looking after the children and made their way to Dr Steevens' Hospital. On the way they came across angry-looking groups of people with placards. Keeping their heads down they hurried along to the hospital and were directed to the women's ward where they found Nan. At first they didn't recognise her. All they could see above the bedclothes was a thin grey-haired woman with a nose that looked as though it had been broken. When she turned to them, one eye was unfocused and the other was sunken and dull.

"Nan, do you not know us? It's Ellen and Violet, remember us, we were friends in India?" Ellen whispered.

There was a long pause while Nan tried to focus on the two women. "India? That was a long time ago. Poor Dan is dead, you know. A wall fell on him. God love him, he never meant to do anyone any harm. Frank is here in the hospital too. Me mother was killed as well."

They had brought some sweets for Nan but somehow sweets seemed an unsuitable offering in the circumstances.

"Is there anything we can do for you, Nan? Is there anything you need?" Ellen and Violet looked at each other helplessly.

"I don't know where me and Frank are going to go when we get out of here. Could youse help me to get another room?" The woman was looking at them pleadingly.

Ellen had no idea how to go about getting a room for Nan. She looked at Violet who shook her head. "We will see what we can do, Nan. How long do you think you will be in hospital?"

"About two weeks. They will keep Frank until I am well enough to leave. If we have no place to go, we will be put into the Union." Tears rolled down her cheeks as she said this.

The bell went to signal the end of visiting time and the two women were glad to leave the fetid smelling ward with its rows of closely crammed beds. They walked home, discussing how they might help Nan.

Violet was shaking her head. "Des won't have anything to do with getting her another room, I am sure of that. He won't want to get involved. We could bring her in some clothes for herself and Frank and maybe some food the next time we visit."

Ellen was very quiet when she returned from the hospital. James and the children were sitting in front of the range and he was reading to them. She sat and listened until the story ended and it was time for the children to go to bed. She washed their faces and hands, put on their nightclothes and tucked them in, all the time thanking God for her small cosy house, her healthy children and her good husband.

When they were alone she told James about Nan. "How will she get another place, James? If she can't, she and Frank will end up in the workhouse."

James shook his head. "She might manage to find another room in a tenement but she would have to have a week's rent in advance. Some landlords wouldn't be too keen to rent to a woman."

"Can we help her, James? I feel so sorry for her. Maybe, maybe we could look for a room and pay the first week's rent. We still have a little money left in our savings. We have been so lucky ourselves." She could see from his faraway look that James was thinking of Nancy as she said that.

"We can have a look for a room for her, anyway. We might need that money ourselves some day, but if you want to help her, we will."

Ellen hugged her husband. "I knew you would say that. Thank you, my love."

Violet and Ellen went to visit Nan a few times during the following two weeks. They brought her clothes for herself and Frank who was about the same size as Violet's son Desmond. They were shocked at the old, filthy clothes that Nan discarded. Ellen told her that James was making enquiries about getting a room for her and she broke down in tears.

"The blessin's of God on ye. If I can only get a room for Frank and meself, I'll find some way of making a few shillin's to pay the rent."

A few days before Nan was due to be discharged, James planned to go to Church Street where he had been told there was a chance of getting a room. He didn't want Ellen to go with him but she insisted, saying that she wanted to see how suitable it was. Church Street was where Nan had lived previously and where the two houses had collapsed. The ruins of the houses were the first thing they saw when they reached the street. There was something almost indecent about the way the interiors of the rooms were open to full view with the front walls missing: torn stained wallpaper hung down in mocking garlands over ruined fireplaces and bits of rotten furniture, stairways leaned drunkenly over collapsed floors, once sturdy Georgian doors hung adrift from their hinges. Mindless of the danger, ragged children played among the debris or scrabbled for any salvage that might be of use. Ellen tried to imagine what it must have been like for Nan to live in such a place and felt sick.

James was holding her arm tightly as they walked further down the street to where the houses were intact. He stopped at number 12. "This is it. The landlord said he would meet us here, on the third floor where there is a room available."

The fanlight above the door was broken; the door was wide open revealing a dark hall and a stairway with uneven steps leading to the first floor. Once inside, the smell of urine was overwhelming; there were traces of faeces in the stairwell. Ellen touched the banister which was greasy and then managed to climb the three flights of precarious steps without touching it by holding on to James. Their progress upward was watched from open doors, ragged women with babies, children with ill-fitting clothes and bare feet, consumptive-looking men. Each room seemed to be home to a family.

On the third floor a well-dressed man stood in the doorway of one of the back rooms. "You must be Mr Devereux. I'm John Fitzpatrick, the landlord. Step inside. This is the room you were asking after. I must have a week's rent in advance as I told you. Any failure to pay the rent on time will result in eviction."

James was taking money from his pocket as he entered the room. "The room is for a friend of ours, herself and her son. She will be taking up residence as soon as possible, next Saturday if that suits. Here is one week's rent in advance and the first week's rent. Is there any furniture with the room?"

The man was pocketing the money. "Just what you see the last tenant left. We don't offer furnished accommodation."

Ellen looked around the small room which was in the attic of the house. A filthy mattress was on the floor with a few rags thrown over it. A blackened pot sat in the fireplace which was overflowing with rubbish. A filthy chamber pot was in the corner.

She turned to the landlord. "Is there a lavatory? Where do people get water? How do they cook?"

The man smiled condescendingly at her. "There is a water tap and a closet in the back yard. People cook on the fire, that is, when they can be bothered to cook. Most of them live on tea and bread. You are obviously not from the city, ma'am, or you would know these things. Here is the key and good day to you both now."

Ellen waited for the sounds of his footsteps to vanish before she began to cry. "How can people live like this, James? It is inhuman. That man seems to be well off but he is taking rents from unfortunate people who have nowhere else to go."

James put his arms around her. "That's the way it is in the city, love. They say that Dublin has some of the worst living conditions in the British Empire. I am sorry you had to see this."

"Is there nothing better we can get for Nan?"

"Even if we could, she wouldn't be able to pay the rent on anything better." He wiped the tears from her face.

"At least we could make it a bit more comfortable and clean. I have that mattress I bought and some spare bedclothes and a few other bits and pieces." Thinking of the small things she could do for Nan made her feel better.

The following Saturday, Ellen and Violet brought Nan and Frank from the hospital to the room. Nan was still so weak that it took the two women all their strength to support her on each side as they walked the short distance to Church Street. Frank walked beside them and James went ahead with Mick who helped him with the mattress. They threw out the old one and the foul rags, cleaned the fireplace, emptied the chamber pot and swept out and washed the floor. They fetched water from the communal tap and opened the window to let in some fresh air.

When the three women arrived the room was looking considerably better. Ellen and Violet made up the bed into which Nan collapsed. Her gratitude for the little they had done was embarrassing. Her son, Frank, was obviously still in a state of shock and sat, expressionless, beside his mother. They left, noticing that the old mattress which James had thrown out had already been claimed by two young boys who were dragging it up the stairs.

What had seemed like a short strike meandered on through the autumn and into the winter of 1913 before it petered out in January 1914. In October groups of starving children of the strikers were sent to England to be fostered by English workers. The Archbishop of Dublin condemned the plan on the grounds that it threatened the Catholic faith of the children. Angry mobs gathered at the docks to try to prevent the departures of the children and in some cases, succeeded. Harry often shared his lunch with hungry classmates and Ellen felt embarrassed when she went to the local shop for groceries and heard customers being refused more credit because their husbands were on strike. Neighbours sometimes sent a child to beg for stale bread for their dog. In some cases there was no dog but it was important to go along with the pretence to preserve the neighbour's pride.

One of the women who had been antagonistic towards her on her first visit to Miss Ormond's shop, she now knew as Mrs Brady. Her husband, Tom Brady, was a cooper in Guinness. That company had been one of the few which did not forbid its workers to join the ITGWU but entered into negotiations with the union. However, at the very beginning of the Lockout, Brady and a handful of men had gone on strike and had been dismissed by the company. One day in the week before Christmas, Ellen visited the shop for her groceries.

Mary Brady was leaning over the counter pleading with Miss Ormond. "Please, just once more. I have nothing to give the kids. Just some bread, please, for the love of God."

"Mrs Brady, I have given you credit for the last few months. I can't give you any more. You owe me enough already." The shopkeeper was adamant.

There was a bread board full of loaves on the counter. Ellen picked one up and thrust it into the hands of Mary Brady. The woman looked shamefaced but grasped the bread and was out the door.

"Put it on my bill, Miss Ormond, please," Ellen said.

The shopkeeper felt the need to explain her lack of compassion for the woman. "I have been giving her credit for the last few months. She thought that Tom would be reinstated. But in spite of Jim Larkin intervening, Guinness wouldn't take him or the other few back. She has pawned everything they have to pay the bills but they are going to be evicted this week. God help them, I don't know what they are going to do."

Ellen and Violet had kept up their visits to Nan and brought her whatever they could spare from their own kitchens. To their surprise, Nan had got a job in the fruit market in the city. It was back breaking work, hauling boxes of vegetables and fruit, but she got some of the fruit that was going bad as well as her small wages and it kept Nan and her son alive.

Travelling through the city in the cold evenings on their way to Nan they saw the terrible effects of the Lockout on the people of Dublin. Pale faced children scavenged for anything they could find; even dung from the horses pulling the carts was saved and brought to well-off areas where it was sold as compost for well-tended gardens. Women waited at the end of the day in street market areas like Moore Street to gather up cabbage leaves, green potatoes, rotten fruit or any discarded food which they could take home to their families. There were queues outside shops with the five ball sign, shops Ellen learned were pawn shops. There were beggars everywhere, especially on Sackville Street and Grafton Street where the well-off did their shopping. In spite of the poverty in the city, the hansom cabs still disgorged well-dressed people at the Imperial Hotel and other fashionable places. It reminded Ellen of what she had seen of Bombay and the small shanty towns around Pune. By the beginning of January 1914, the strikers had used up whatever resources, physical and mental, that they had and began to return to work and an uncertain normality. For some, like the Bradys, it was too late.

Chapter 13
1914: Partings

Ellen's parents never made the promised visit to Dublin. When the Lockout was over, Mary Ann wrote to Ellen saying that she didn't think that Henry would be able for the journey; he was experiencing problems with his breathing and was finding it difficult to work. Lord Lucan had sent a young boy from a family on the demesne to be his assistant. Mary Ann sounded worried about her husband so Ellen resolved to visit Castlebar with the children as soon as Harry got his summer holidays from school.

James took a couple of days off work when Harry and Joseph started their holidays. They made a visit to the zoo on the first day. The children were enchanted with the animals. Harry loved the lions and would have spent hours in the lions' house but for the very overpowering smell. Joseph liked the monkeys and was only a bit scared of them. Kathleen was happy to have a day being carried around by her father. They picnicked where they could see the sea lions and only went home when they were all exhausted.

On the second day they made a trip on the tram into the city to get some clothes for the children. The streets were quiet now that the strike was over. Broken windows in shops showed evidence of some rioting but generally it looked as though life had gone back to normal.

The third day James was working a late shift so he was able to accompany his family on the tram to Kingsbridge station and see them off to Galway. The children were excited by the bustle in the station and the huffing of the train as it was stoked up ready for the journey. James arranged the bags on the overhead racks and kissed the children. He alighted and Ellen leaned out the window to kiss him. "Take care of the children and yourself, love," he said.

"Of course I will, James." She wanted to say how she loved him but was shy in front of the other people in the carriage. The boys were jumping up and down with excitement, raising dust from the upholstered benches in the carriage as the train pulled away from the station and James became a small figure, waving until he disappeared.

At Galway they took the train for Westport where Matt, Maggie's husband was waiting for them with the chauffeur, Albert. Harry was excited about riding in the car and asked Albert endless questions as they made the short drive to Castlebar.

When Ellen asked Matt about her parents he was reticent. "You will find them changed," was all he would say.

There was no one waiting at the front door of the lodge so Ellen had time to look at the flower garden as she walked up the pathway. Neglect was evident everywhere she looked: weeds grew up through the Canterbury bells and the honesty, the roses had not been deadheaded and were full of greenfly, the delphiniums leaned over and rested their long necks on the mallow, the pathway was slippery with moss. The front door opened slowly and in the dim light of the hall, Ellen could see her mother, whose face lit up when she saw her daughter and grandchildren. Painfully, she moved to embrace them, steadying herself on a walking stick as the children almost knocked her over.

"Harry, my, you are so big! Joseph, my little man! And Kathleen, my beautiful angel! Ellen, you look well. I am so delighted to see you all!"

Ellen lifted Kathleen and put her other arm around her mother. She felt the birdlike bones and realised that her mother had shrunk. "Mama, it is so good to be here. Where is Papa?"

"He is having a nap so that he will be in good form for the children. He gets tired now, you know. But seeing them will cheer him up." Mary Ann moved slowly into the kitchen. There was no smell of baking but a vase of sweet pea exhaled their sweet scent.

She put the kettle on the range and started to collect teapot and cups.

Ellen went to her. "Let me do that, Mama. I still know where everything is. Sit at the table children and talk to Grandmamma and I will get you some milk."

"There are scones and jam in the cupboard. I am afraid they are not mine, Maggie made them. I haven't the energy now to bake or make jam like I used to."

Ellen found all she needed in the familiar kitchen. It felt strange to see Mary Ann sitting down with the children, being waited on. In the old days, she never sat down and enjoyed ordering everyone else about. Ellen noticed how deformed her mother's hands had become from the arthritis as she chatted to the children.

"Ellen, my dear, how are you? And who have we here? Two big boys and a princess?" Henry stood in the doorway; they could hear his laboured breathing. The two boys ran to him while Kathleen shyly buried her face in her mother's skirt.

"Papa, it is lovely to see you. We heard you were taking a nap so we didn't want to disturb you." Ellen embraced her father; he had always been a tall man but he too seemed to have shrunk.

"Your mother makes me sleep every afternoon. Anyone would think I was an invalid the way she fusses about. Joseph, come and sit on my knee. Harry, I want to hear everything that you have been doing in school."

The two boys were soon chatting animatedly to their grandfather. Kathleen continued to cling to her mother but after a while was happy to sit with her grandmother. Ellen could not believe the change in her parents; the change was evident not just in them but in the house which looked a bit neglected. They seemed to spend most of their time in the kitchen which was warm, thanks to the range. When she went into the parlour for extra china, it looked unused and dusty. It was cold and a bit damp;

obviously the fire was seldom lit.

They were just finishing their tea when Annie arrived home from the Big House. "Ellen, children, it is so good to see you! I am sorry that I wasn't here to greet you but Lord Lucan needed me."

Ellen hugged her sister. "Annie, you look well! It seems ages since we saw you. You will have to come to Dublin for a visit soon."

"Yes, I would love to. I do some secretarial work now for Lord Lucan as well as looking after Isobel so I am kept quite busy."

"I don't know what we would do without Annie," her mother interrupted. "She looks after us very well. Maggie is very good too. We are lucky to have our daughters to take care of us."

Annie's face tightened and she started to put away the butter and jam and gather the teacups.

"Let me help, Annie," Ellen offered. "Then I would love to go for a walk around the demesne. I am stiff from being on the train. Would you like to come, children?"

Kathleen was preoccupied with her grandmother and the two boys were more interested in a game of Toss Ha'penny which they were playing with their grandfather, so the two sisters were able to have a private talk as they walked.

"I was shocked to see how changed Mama and Papa are," Ellen confided in her sister. "They look so much older. Are they attending the doctor regularly?"

"Yes, they are, but there is nothing he can do, he says. Papa's heart is very weak and Mama's arthritis has got very much worse. The house is a bit damp and that doesn't help. They are not able to do a lot. I do most of the housework and the cooking."

Ellen was surprised. "Doesn't Maggie help you?"

"She gives me a hand with the cleaning and the garden when she can and she keeps them supplied with her baking. She helps Matt now in the shop since his father died so she hasn't that much free time," Annie explained.

"I thought that you had someone to help Papa." Ellen was beginning to realise the responsibilities that Annie had taken on.

"Well, Lord Lucan sent a young boy who is supposed to help Papa but really, he is useless. If Papa has to be replaced as the lodge keeper, then I worry that we could not stay on in this house. I don't know where we would go or what we would live on. Isobel is almost ready for boarding school and Lord Lucan could easily get someone better to do his administration so I might be out of a job soon."Annie was relieved to be able to talk about all her worries. "I am sorry. I didn't mean to burden you with all of this. I just feel so depressed by it all."

"Do you still think about training as a nurse?"

"I would love to but there is no chance of that now. I am needed here. Mama and Papa couldn't manage without me. I am resigned to that. But that is enough about me. Tell me about Dublin. How is James?" Annie deliberately changed the subject.

"James is very well. He is a bit bored with his job but he is happy to be back in Dublin. I am getting used to it and the children have settled down."

For the rest of the walk they chatted about the children and life in Dublin.

When they returned, Henry was reading titbits from the paper to their mother, as he usually did. "It seems Germany has invaded Belgium and declared war on France."

"Well, let us hope that it stays far away from us. We had enough trouble with the Lockout." Mary Ann was remembering the aborted visit to Dublin.

Henry was more interested in the local news. "I see that the Home Rule Bill was passed again by the House of Commons. This time the House of Lords cannot veto it. We may yet have Home Rule in my lifetime."

That night the children were allowed to stay up late and the adults settled down to a game of cards. When Henry began to look tired, Ellen gathered the children and put them to bed; they were all sharing the bedroom that Ellen had once shared with her sisters.

Next morning, Annie had already left for the Big House when Ellen and the children came down to breakfast. Her mother was putting the kettle on the range and Ellen took over the preparation of breakfast. Henry joined them and was playing a noisy game of "I Spy" with Harry and Joseph when Annie suddenly opened the door looking distraught.

"Britain has declared war on Germany. Lord Lucan just heard. He allowed me to come and tell you."

"But that doesn't affect us, does it?" Mary Ann was dismissive of the news.

Her husband looked grave. "Yes, I am afraid it does. The British Army will be mobilised and there are thousands of Irishmen already in the army. Hopefully, the war will not last long. Is James still a member of the Reserve, Ellen?"

"No, Papa. Anyway, he is over forty now, he would not want to be in the army at his age. Besides, he has a good job. Why would he leave that? Do you think the war is likely to last long?"

Henry reassured her. "Not at all. It will probably be over in a few months."

In spite of her protestations, Ellen was worried. Every night, she lay awake thinking about the war and the news that she heard about Irishmen joining up. James had loved army life and had not really settled into civilian life in Dublin. He found his job boring and missed the camaraderie of the army. She consoled herself by thinking about their house in Dublin and the secure job that James had. He wouldn't want to jeopardise that, would he?

Her concern made her anxious to get back to Dublin. The next few days seemed to drag by until it was time to return. When she had loaded the children into the car and was saying goodbye to her parents, she had the premonition that it was the last time she would see them. They looked lonely and small as they waved goodbye from the door of the lodge. The children hung out of the windows waving for as long as they could see the two figures becoming smaller and smaller, until a bend in the road took them out of view. Annie had decided to accompany them to Galway and sat in the front seat next to Albert. They seemed to know each other quite well and laughed and joked with the children and each other.

"It is very good of you to take us to Galway, Albert. You could have dropped us off at Westport."

"I'm quite glad to get away from the demesne for a while. Anyway, I will have the company of the lovely Annie on the way home." Albert smiled at Annie.

The normally taciturn Albert seemed very different when Annie was around. Albert stayed with the car while Annie helped Ellen and the children and their bags on to the train.

Ellen kissed her sister goodbye. "Look after Mama and Papa and come and visit us soon in Dublin."

"I will. I would like to see where you are living and to have a good chat with you. The week seems to have gone so quickly, especially since I was working up at the Big House for most of it."

They all leaned out of the window watching as Annie walked back to the car where Albert was waiting.

James was on the platform when they arrived at Kingsbridge Station. The children screamed when they saw him and almost knocked him down as they all tried to hug him at once.

"Wait now, boys. Don't knock Kathleen over. Ellen, my love, it is great to have you home again. How are your parents?" There was an air of suppressed excitement about him as he lifted Kathleen up into his arms. "Come on; let's hurry to the tram before all the workers come out."

Ellen couldn't wait. She walked alongside James, holding Joseph by the hand.

"James, have you heard? War has broken out between Britain and Germany."

"Yes, of course, it was all over the papers. My old regiment is being sent to France."

Ellen was watching his face. "You didn't think of enlisting, did you?"

His answer was evasive. "Well, John Redmond is urging Irishmen to join up. Even the church is encouraging people to go."

"But James, you are too old to enlist! You have a good job here. The children need you. I do not want you to go."

"It is hard to see my old comrades marching off without me. Anyway, I enquired about my age. Because I was a sergeant major they would be glad to have me to train new recruits."

Ellen couldn't believe it. "You enquired! Without even waiting for me to come back! You have a good job! We have a nice house! How can you even think of leaving me and the children?"

"My job will be there for me when I come back and the house is secure as long as we can pay the rent." James was trying to calm her down.

"When you come back? If you come back!" Ellen could feel the tears rising.

"This war will not last very long. I will probably be stuck in Aldershot training raw youngsters for the duration of it."

The children were looking anxiously from one of them to the other. Kathleen began to cry. James lifted her up into his arms. "Let us talk about this tonight when the children are in bed."

James deliberately sat with Kathleen on one knee and Joseph beside him when they boarded the tram, leaving no space for Ellen. Harry sat beside his mother and slid his hand into hers. He was looking anxiously at his father; he had heard some of their exchange about the war.

135

James told her that night. He had already had a medical. He was enlisting the following day and would leave for Aldershot within the week. Des Vaughan intended to do the same. Ellen cried quietly, knowing that there was nothing she could say to change his mind. He was bored with his job, with the routine and the lack of variety. He missed the camaraderie of the army, the excitement, the sense of purpose. That night, she couldn't stay angry with him, knowing that he would be leaving within the week.

"You are going to miss Christmas, the children's birthdays, Joseph starting at his big school, so many things." She could see the year stretching ahead of her, empty without him.

"This war will be over in a year, at most," James said confidently. "The pay in the army is better than what I am getting in the Post Office so you will be able to buy things for the children. I will be home before you know it."

Ellen lay in his arms that night and the following nights before he left, waiting until their lovemaking was over and James was asleep before she let the tears come. The week seemed endless, the tension in the house was palpable and at times she wished that he had already left.

The children were distraught when they heard that he was leaving. Kathleen didn't really understand but was affected by the crying of her brothers. James was very busy for the week, gathering his kit and doing small jobs around the house that he should have done months before. Ellen didn't sleep at all the night before his departure. She lay beside him, feeling his warmth and listening to his breathing. She wondered if this was the last night that they would make love, the last night that he would fall asleep in her arms?

As soon as the room began to lighten with the dawn she got up, easing herself out of the bed so as not to wake him. She looked down at him and tried to capture his image in her mind; he looked peaceful and childlike in sleep. A lock of blonde hair fell over his face, his lips were slightly parted, his chin showed signs of stubble and one hand stretched into the place where she had lain. Her love for him overwhelmed her and felt like a pain under her heart. She suppressed a sob and went downstairs to light the range and make breakfast for James and the children.

She was engrossed in thoughts of how she would live without him when suddenly he was beside her in the kitchen, dressed in khaki and already looking unfamiliar. "I'll say goodbye to you now, love. We don't want to upset the children."

He pulled her into his arms, running his hands down the length of her as though he was imprinting her shape on his memory. They kissed slowly and gently until she pulled away. "You are not going without saying goodbye to the children?"

"No. I will wait for them to come down but I don't want to prolong the goodbyes. Anyway, I will be home again before you know it. This war will not last very long."

James had washed and shaved and was sitting eating his breakfast when she brought the children downstairs. The boys looked suspiciously at his uniform.

"Why are you dressed like that, Papa?" Harry wanted to know.

"You know that I was a soldier when we were in India? Well, now I am a soldier again because there is a war on and I must re-join my regiment. I will be gone for a while so I want you two boys to take care of Mama and your sister."

Joseph immediately set up a loud wailing and was soon joined by Kathleen.

"Can we not come with you? How long will you be gone? Where are you going?" Harry looked stricken.

"First I am going to Aldershot in England to train the new recruits. Then I will probably be sent to France with them. I hope I will not be too long away because I will miss my lovely children.

Come and give me a big hug now." James opened his arms to them.

Ellen handed the still-crying Kathleen to James while Joseph clung to his father's waist. Harry hung back and pleaded with his father. "I don't want you to go, Papa. Please don't go."

Ellen took Kathleen back while James tried to embrace Harry who was standing rigidly. Joseph transferred his hold from James's waist to his neck. Still Harry made no attempt to touch his father.

"I have to go now. God bless you all. Take care of each other." He disentangled himself from Joseph's grip.

Ellen stood in the doorway, holding Kathleen and watching as James picked up his kit bag and marched down the street to be joined by Des at the corner. He looked back and waved and Joseph, who was crying quietly, made to run after him. Harry appeared in the doorway and pulled Joseph back. "He is gone, Jo-Jo. I will look after you now."

Chapter 14
1914: Alone in Dublin

Life without James proved to be more difficult than Ellen could have imagined. Harry was very withdrawn for weeks. Then he began to immerse himself in his schoolwork, in his choir practice and in Gaelic football which was a new interest. Joseph had fits of crying and wet the bed a few times. Only Kathleen seemed untouched by the change in their lives although she did cling to Ellen more than she used to.

When he saw Ellen struggling to do everything in the house, Harry volunteered to do some of the jobs that James had done such as bringing in buckets of fuel. He also read to the other children before they went to bed. When they ate their meal in the evenings, he sat in the chair that James had occupied, sitting opposite her and chatting to her about the events of his day.

One evening they were sitting together when they heard loud knocking on the door. Ellen opened the door to find a distraught Mrs Kelly outside.

"Mrs Devereux, will you come inside with me? I don't know what to do."

Ellen followed her into her living room. The door into the small room was open. John, the younger of her two boys, was lying face down on the bed, sobbing convulsively. Mrs Kelly pulled up the sheet that was covering him. The backs of his legs and his buttocks were covered in red welts; some of the welts were bleeding where the skin had broken.

"Oh my God, what happened to you, John? You poor boy, you must be in a lot of pain." Ellen stroked the boy's head and then turned to her neighbour. "Did this happen in school? Who did it?"

"I don't know the full story. Paddy arrived home almost carrying him; he could hardly walk. What can I do to make him feel better?" She wiped her eyes with the edge of her apron.

"Bathe him with cold water; it will bring down the swelling. Where the skin is broken needs to be cleaned. Have you any iodine? No? I will go inside and get some."

Harry was sitting at the table doing his homework when she returned. John had been in his class the previous year but had been held back.

"Do you know anything about what happened to John Kelly?" she asked him.

"John? He hasn't been in school for about a week. I thought he was sick. Why? What happened to him?" Harry was curious and watched Ellen as she found the iodine.

"I'll tell you later. Keep an eye on the others for me."

Mrs Kelly was already bathing John with cold water when Ellen returned. She used the antiseptic to clean the bleeding cuts. When she had finished she called Paddy into the room.

"Paddy, tell us exactly what happened. Who did this to John?"

Paddy looked at his brother and sighed. "John has been mitching for about a week. He didn't want to go to Brother O'Keeffe's religion class on Monday because he hadn't learned his catechism. I tried to persuade him to go to class the next day but he was afraid to. He has been spending his time up in the park for the last few days and coming home at the same time as me."

His mother was distraught. "Why didn't you tell me? I would have brought him back to school!"

Paddy shook his head. "Ma, he made me promise not to tell, but someone told where he was and this morning, Brother O'Keeffe went up and found him. He brought him back to school and leathered him in front of the class. He called me in at the end of the day to take him home. I nearly had to carry him he was so weak."

Ellen remembered the unfriendly brother with the gimlet eyes. "He shouldn't be allowed to get away with this. You should go to the school and complain. I will come with you if you like."

Mrs Kelly was crying. "Who can I complain to? Brother O'Keeffe is the principal. I will have to keep John home for a few days anyway. I'll go with him on his first day back. I would be terrified to go on my own so it would be great if you came with me."

When Ellen went home she told Harry what had happened to John. He was upset but not surprised. "John was held back in school last year. He finds it difficult to learn anything off by heart. His spelling is not very good either. Since the new term began, Brother O'Keeffe has been very hard on him and the more he shouts and threatens John, the less John can remember. Luckily, we only have Brother O'Keeffe for religion, because he always picks on John. The other brothers know that he is not as bright as Paddy and help him when they can."

"Why is Brother O'Keeffe so hard on John?" Ellen asked.

"I don't know." Harry thought for a minute. "I think he is just making an example of him."

"Does he beat other boys as badly as that?" Ellen was concerned for her own sons.

Harry nodded his head. "He has a reputation for using the leather very often. He seems to enjoy it."

"Has he ever beaten you?" Ellen was almost afraid to ask.

"No. I learn what he tells us to learn and I keep my head down. That is the way to survive in his class." Harry was offhand about it.

"Survive? You are going to school to learn, not to survive the likes of him! I will have a thing or two to say to him when I meet him."

Harry looked worried. "Mama, please don't say anything to him. If you do he will only take it out on Joseph or me."

Ellen was thinking about Harry's plea when she accompanied Mrs Kelly and John to school the following Monday. In spite of his mother's reassurances, John looked cowed and pale as he went off to his class. The two women asked to see Brother O'Keeffe and were shown into the hall of the monastery. It was vast and high ceilinged and smelled of floor polish and cooking. The highly polished wood floors were slippery underfoot and the green paint on the walls reflected a gloomy light. At the far end of the hall, statues of Our Lady and the Sacred Heart cast their eyes heavenward. The two women were left standing there, waiting, for half an hour. They spoke to each other in whispers.

The swish of a soutane and heavy footsteps announced the arrival of the brother. "Good morning, ladies. What can I do for you?"

"Good morning, Brother. My name is Mrs Kelly. I am John's mother. My son is John Kelly. I wanted ..."

Nervousness and the gimlet gaze of the brother were making her incoherent. Ellen stepped closer to her friend and gave her an encouraging smile.

The brother looked coldly at Mrs Kelly. "Did you bring John Kelly back to school today?"

"Yes, Brother. You see ..."

"That boy is completely out of hand. He never does his homework, he can't seem to pay attention and now, to cap it all, he mitches from school. He needed to be taught a lesson." The brother looked grim.

Mrs Kelly gathered her courage and said, "That is what I wanted to talk to you about, Brother. When John came home, he was in a terrible state. You beat him so badly that he was bleeding. He also had missing clumps out of his hair where you dragged him across the classroom. I want to make a complaint."

"You want to make a complaint? That boy needs a bit of discipline. He has no father, isn't that right? You are obviously not able to control him. Maybe an industrial school would be the best place for him." He stared coldly at the two women.

Mrs Kelly turned pale and looked as though she was going to faint. Ellen put her arm around her. "Please Brother, he doesn't need an industrial school. I will make sure that he attends and does his homework. I don't want any trouble. Please give him another chance."

The brother smiled sourly at her. "Let us see how he gets on. Now, I have a class to go to. I bid you good day."

Once they were clear of the building and walking down the street, Mrs Kelly began to sob. "If my poor husband was alive, he would know what to do. I will die if John goes to an industrial school. That brother is wicked enough to send him to one just for spite. Who will listen to me? I am only a woman. He has all the power on his side."

Ellen realised that her friend's fears were well founded. If the brother decided to report that John was not attending school and that his mother could not manage him, the courts could decide to send him away. She consoled her neighbour by saying that they would all have to support John for the rest of the year and try to ensure that he attended school and stayed clear of the wrath of the principal. Mrs Kelly cried all the way home.

The first letter from James came about two weeks later. The tears rolled down Ellen's face as she read it. She read parts of it aloud to the children but parts of it she kept for herself and reread the letter a hundred times before the next one came. She imagined she could smell him from the paper and pictured him as he wrote it, writing with his left hand, chewing the end of the pencil as he searched for the right words, smiling as he thought of the children.

My dear Ellen,

I arrived here safely almost two weeks ago. Things were very confused when I first arrived so I didn't get a chance to write. As you can see, I am in Aldershot and expect to be here for about three months.

There is a great need here for people who had experience of training troops so Des and I have both been assigned to that duty. It is a very different experience from when I enlisted myself and was trained in Galway. Here many of the men who volunteered are only boys; some of them have lied about their age I am sure. Since conscription started, others have joined them, many of whom do not want to be soldiers. Training is difficult because some of the men have no uniforms as there are not enough to go around. There are not enough weapons for training. The quarters are very basic, not at all what I was used to in Galway. Sometimes I think about the luxury we had when we were in India and wonder if this is the same army that I joined.

I think of you and the little ones every day. I hope that Harry is now more reconciled to me leaving. It is very hard for him and Joseph to understand. I enclose a story which I wrote for them. Give my little Kathleen a hug from me and tell her that I send her kisses every night. I miss you, my darling wife, more than I can say. Some nights I go to sleep imagining we are dancing together. Other nights I wake up to look for you beside me and you are not there. I pray for you and the children every night.

Your loving husband,
James

Soon letters came from James on a weekly basis and she read parts of them to the children as they sat at the table. His letters were warm and funny but he also wrote about the things that concerned him. He always enclosed drawings for the children and sometimes a new story that he had written for them. Joseph kept all the drawings and stories under his bed inside one of his favourite books.

Then the letters stopped coming so regularly. They scoured the newspapers for information but news about the war seemed to be confined to heroic stories about the exploits of the British army or stories which painted the Germans as fiends. It appeared from the reports that the British army was far superior to the German war machine and would soon overpower the enemy. Ellen and Violet were consoled by the thought that it would soon be over as the newspapers said. They deduced that the absence of letters meant that their husbands had been moved to France or Flanders and were possibly now in the thick of the fighting. Information about what was really happening was scarce.

Then the letters began to arrive again but somewhat sporadically. They contained less information and were not specific about the whereabouts of the regiment.

December 1914

My dear Ellen,
We are in France now after an interesting sea

voyage. It reminded me a little of our journey to India. As our ship left Southampton, all the men who were assembled on deck sang "It's a Long Way to Tipperary" which has become our regimental song. It was both heart- warming and sad as I thought that I was leaving you and the children further and further behind. We are based in a beautiful area which reminds me of Castlebar because it is farming country with lovely meadows and very green. At least it was until we started digging trenches and the rain began and now it is a muddy quagmire. The conditions that we live in are pretty awful but I hope we won't be here for long.

I enclose a story for the children. Give them kisses and hugs from me and tell them how much I love them. I miss you, my darling wife, more than I can say. Look after yourself and the children and pray for me.

Your loving husband,

James

The last paragraph brought tears to Ellen's eyes. Each night, she lay in bed and prayed for the safety of her husband. Subsequent letters made her uneasy because they were full of longing for home and a kind of fatalism about what was happening. The tone was completely unlike the accounts of the progress of the war which she read in the newspapers. He wrote about the countryside where they were digging trenches, the beauty of it when they first arrived and the filth and horror of it as the winter progressed. Coming up to Christmas the family was surprised to receive a box of biscuits from him, presumably posted before he left England.

Because of the children Ellen tried to make preparations for

Christmas as normal as possible. Her mother sent a goose in the post which arrived battered and bruised but still edible. Ellen made a Christmas cake and a pudding and invited Violet and her children to join them for Christmas dinner; it made it easier to have a celebration with all of them together. As they watched the children play with their presents, the two friends wondered aloud about their husbands and whether they would have any celebration at all. In spite of their best efforts, there was a flatness about the day which ended with the younger children becoming fractious and crying for their fathers.

The dark days of January brought another absence of letters. The only letter that arrived was one from her mother telling her that she and Annie were to visit Dublin the following Saturday and would be staying with Jane and Tom. Her mother wanted Ellen to visit them there the following Sunday.

Ellen was surprised at the visit, particularly since the weather was so cold. She wondered about the reason for it. Perhaps, she thought, Annie had decided to train as a nurse after all. Maybe they had been able to make some arrangement for looking after Henry and Mary Ann. Perhaps Lord Lucan had decided to replace Henry as lodge keeper and they had to make other living arrangements. She spent the next few days puzzling about the reason for the visit.

On the Sunday morning, she dressed the children in their best clothes and they all accompanied Harry to the Pro-Cathedral where he was the solo boy soprano. Afterwards, the children lit candles for the safe return of their father. They took the tram from the city centre to Glasnevin, the suburb where Jane lived. Ellen had never been there before; Jane had invited her in a half- hearted manner but it was obvious that she was a bit ashamed of her sister and thought that Ellen belonged to a different class.

As they walked from the tram, she and the children marvelled at the large houses, the well-kept gardens and the general air of prosperity. Children dressed in tailored coats with velvet collars played in the gardens or rode bicycles on the pavement and looked at them in a superior way. It didn't seem possible that this was the same city where people were still starving as a result of the Lockout, the city where poor Nan was struggling to make a living for herself and her son in the filth and poverty of Church Street.

She found the house without too much difficulty and was welcomed and fussed over by Jane who opened the door. The children were surprised when their aunt insisted that they take off their shoes before she ushered them into the drawing room. Mary Ann and Annie were seated in large velvet upholstered chairs. There was no sign of Tom, Jane's husband. Jane vanished into the kitchen as Ellen and her children greeted their grandmother and aunt. Mary Ann looked exhausted and tense as Ellen kissed her. Annie was pale and quiet.

"What's wrong? Is it Papa?" Ellen knew that there must be bad news.

Jane reappeared with a tray with tea and biscuits before anyone could reply. "Come on, children. I have something special for you in the kitchen." The children disappeared with their aunt as Annie poured the tea.

Mary Ann took a sip of her tea and then put the cup down with deliberation. "We have something that we want to discuss with you and Jane." She looked at Ellen and then at Annie. Jane re- entered the room and sat beside her mother. Still Mary Ann could not seem to get the words out.

Jane looked from her mother to Ellen. "Annie is in trouble."

"Trouble? What kind of trouble"? Ellen was confused. She had expected news about her father.

Jane was her usual impatient self. "There is only one kind of trouble that a young girl like Annie gets into. She is going to have a baby."

148

Annie burst into tears and looked at her mother, who continued to look down at her tea cup. Ellen could not bear to see her youngest sister so upset. The image of Annie and Albert smiling at each other came into her mind. She went and sat on the arm of Annie's chair and put her arm around her. "Was it Albert? Surely he will marry you? "

Jane looked grim. "That is the problem. Albert is already married. He has a wife and two children in Dublin. He never told anybody about them when he took the job with Lord Lucan. When the war started and it became difficult to get petrol Lord Lucan dismissed him and he joined the Dublin Fusiliers."

Annie raised her face to Ellen and whispered, "I thought he was going away to war and might never return. I didn't know he already had a wife. We ... we ... I loved him."

"Loved him! And look what it has brought you to! If your father ever found out it would kill him. The shame! How could we face people!" Mary Ann was angrier than Ellen had ever seen her.

Jane looked at her mother. "The question is what are we to do with Annie until the baby is born?"

Ellen could not believe the cruelty in Jane's words. "Do with her? Do with her? How can you speak about your own sister like that? We have to help her as best we can. Couldn't she stay here with you until the baby is born? You could say that she was a girl from home that you are helping out. And maybe when the baby comes, Maggie might take it as her own. You know how much she wants a baby."

Mary Ann now looked defeated. "We already thought of that. We asked her before we came to Dublin. She discussed it with Matt but they felt that there would be gossip if Annie disappeared and a few months later, a baby appeared. Much as she would like to have the baby she couldn't face the gossip. And there is your father's position to think of too. We might be put out of the lodge if Lord

149

Lucan heard about this and then where would we live?"

Jane stood up and began to gather the tea cups onto a tray. "She can't stay here. Tom wouldn't stand for it. He has his position to think of. There is a convent not far from here where they take in unmarried girls until their baby is born. She could go there and we could keep an eye on her. Then when the baby is adopted she could get a job in Dublin."

Annie was crying silently through all of this. Ellen drew her sister into her arms. "Annie, you can come home with me. James is not there to discuss it with but if he was I know he would agree because he is a kind man. No sister of mine is going into a convent to have her baby adopted."

Jane was smiling at her. Ellen had the feeling that she had deliberately engineered this outcome. Mary Ann was crying with relief. "Ellen, thank God for your goodness. You can tell your neighbours the story about helping a poor girl from home. Once the baby is adopted, Annie can come home to live with us again. We can say that she tried the nursing but didn't like it."

Ellen looked at her mother and Jane with distaste. "It will be up to Annie to decide whether the baby is to be adopted or not. I will look after her from now on. She will not be coming home again to look after you and Papa. Annie, help me get the children into their coats and boots and gather your own things."

The business of getting the children ready for the journey helped to alleviate the awkwardness that they all now felt. Mary Ann kissed her youngest daughter a tearful goodbye. Jane promised some financial assistance, should it be needed. Ellen could not wait to get away from the house and its self-righteous snobbery. Annie was shaking and pale but managed to compose herself before they got on the tram. The children were delighted with the company of their favourite aunt on the journey home and vied with each other for her attention, providing her with much-needed distraction.

It wasn't until the children were in bed that the two sisters were able to discuss the events of the day. Annie had recovered and was now concerned for her sister and the likelihood of any gossip. "Will you pretend that I am a girl that you are helping as Mama suggested? I am four months gone so I will start to show soon."

"No, we will say that you are my sister and that your husband enlisted with the Connaught Rangers and is now in France so you came to stay with me until the baby is born. No one around here except Violet knows anyone in the Connaught Rangers and I am sure she will understand. We will buy you a wedding ring tomorrow. Anyway, in the city, among working people, there is less interest in gossip than there is in a small town like Castlebar, with its hierarchies and class distinctions."

Wordlessly, Annie hugged her sister.

Ellen wrote to James about her decision to take in Annie. His reply came weeks later. As she expected, he supported her decision and said that Annie was welcome to stay with them as long as she liked and that he was glad that she had someone to keep her company.

The small parlour became Annie's room and afforded her some privacy when she felt a bit unwell. Her pregnancy was uneventful and after one visit from the midwife, Mrs O'Farrell, she settled into a regular routine. She accompanied the two boys to school every morning, saying that the exercise was good for her. She also took over the ironing and some of the cooking. Neighbours seemed to accept her story about her husband being in France but she was wary of people and spent most of her time in the house.

Letters from Mary Ann and Maggie came regularly, enquiring about her health and offering advice. Now that the problem had been removed from their doorstep, they could allow themselves to be concerned about her wellbeing. There were no post scripts from their father; he obviously knew nothing about Annie's pregnancy.

The letters made Annie cry but she knew she was lucky to have Ellen's support.

They had discussed the options available to Annie and had agreed that she would keep her baby and bring it up with Ellen's family. So many girls in her situation had no choice but to enter a mother and baby home and give up their baby for adoption. Nothing had been heard of Albert since he left for the war and Annie knew that she would probably never see him again. She tried to be cheerful for the sake of the children but when she was alone in her little room at night, she wept for the man she loved.

Chapter 15
1915: Old Friends and New Friends

Annie's presence with the children gave Ellen a certain amount of freedom. A few months after Annie's arrival, Ellen got a letter from her friend Ada who was now living in London. Her husband had also joined his regiment and was in France. She wrote that she would be in Dublin for a few days and would love to see Ellen. She was part of a group of suffragettes who were planning a number of meetings in Dublin, Cork, Belfast and Galway. Ellen was delighted to hear from her old friend. She and Ada had written a few times to each other since they left India and she knew that Ada and her husband Laurence had settled in London and that Ada had been working in a munitions factory.

She was excited when she told her sister. "Annie, do you remember my friend Ada, the one who taught me water colour painting when we were in India? She is coming to Dublin with a group of suffragettes and asks if she can stay here for a night. Her husband has also enlisted with the Connaught Rangers and is in France. I wonder if he has met up with James? They used to be good friends."

"Why is Ada coming to Dublin?" Annie was intrigued.

"She is spending her week's holiday organising meetings with a group of English suffragettes who wish to support their Irish sisters. The suffrage movement in England is much more militant than that in Ireland although since the war started they have been very quiet, according to Ada." Ada's letter had reminded Ellen of their long conversations in India about women's suffrage.

"I haven't heard much about the suffragettes in Ireland. They are very quiet, not like that woman who threw herself in front of the King's horse." Annie was curious.

"That is because the suffragettes in Ireland are closely involved with the Home Rule movement. John Redmond promised women the vote when Ireland gets Home Rule so they didn't feel the need to be so militant," Ellen explained.

"I didn't know you were so interested in the suffragette movement," Annie said.

"Ada was the one who first got me interested. But the things I have seen since I came to Dublin and the things that I saw in India have made me much more aware of the inequalities of women's lives. Recently she wrote to me that she herself had been involved in the militant arm of the movement and had been imprisoned for her actions. She was a victim of the so called 'Cat and Mouse' treatment where suffragists were allowed to go on hunger strike until they became very ill. Then they were allowed to return home to recover. Once they were healthy again, they were once more imprisoned."

"My God, that is unbelievable that the British government would do that to women!" Annie was shocked.

"Well, they did and the prison conditions were awful," Ellen said. "Ada's health has been damaged and she now suffers from a serious kidney condition."

Ellen told Annie about her English friend and what had happened to her since they left India. They also discussed her own experiences and observations of women's lives since she had lived in Dublin. She had seen that domestic abuse was common and that the law allowed men to physically abuse their wives. She described her recent experience with Mrs Kelly and how the principal had threatened to have John sent to an industrial school. Annie was aghast when she heard that and Nan's story and the situation in which she now lived. They talked about Annie's own experience and how men escaped scot-free while the woman was left, literally holding the baby. Married women had no control of their own money or possessions. They were lucky if they had a good husband like James, but otherwise could be left penniless. Women in the United Kingdom had no right to vote, were classed with children and idiots and had no say in how their country was governed. Annie was surprised at her sister's passionate explanation of the suffrage movement but resolved to learn more about it for herself.

Ada's appearance, when she arrived two weeks later, shocked Ellen. She was very thin and emaciated-looking and her skin had a yellowish hue. In India she had favoured the brightest and most glamorous clothes but now she was dressed in black and her hair, which was streaked with grey, was drawn back severely into a bun. The children did not seem to remember her and treated her with suspicion. Ada shared Ellen's bed so that they had ample time to talk. She explained that she and her group had organised suffragette meetings in Dublin, Belfast, Galway and Cork over the following six days. She asked Ellen and Annie to accompany her to the Dublin meeting which was to be held in the offices of the ITGWU. Annie was by now heavily pregnant and did not feel that she would be able for the journey in and out of the city. She was also rather intimidated by Ada so she offered to look after the children instead.

The air was cold and damp as the two women set off for the meeting. Ada had been unsure about the numbers likely to turn up so they were surprised to see crowds of women as they neared the city centre, in groups of twos or threes, all walking in the same direction. The hall was crowded when they arrived and Ellen had difficulty keeping track of her friend in the throngs. When they got to the front Ada identified the women who were already on the platform.

"That's Hanna Sheehy-Skeffington, Margaret Palmer and Jane and Margaret Murphy. They and a few others were all imprisoned for two months for throwing stones at the windows of government buildings when the Home Rule bill was introduced to Parliament without the expected support for women's suffrage."

Ellen remarked that most of the women in the hall looked middle class although there were groups of working class women present as well.

"That is probably because middle class women have more independence and free time compared to women like us," Ada whispered as the meeting began with an introduction to the English visitors. Ada joined the others on the platform and spoke passionately about the activities of the suffragettes in England.

"Suffragettes in England have found their activities more difficult since the war started because some of the women believe that they should channel their energy into the war efforts. Many women in my country are now doing men's work in the factories, on the farms, driving buses and trains, keeping the country going while the men are at war. Yet we women are still denied the vote and many of the other civil liberties that men enjoy as their right."

Then Hanna Sheehy-Skeffington spoke, followed by her husband, Francis. They both made the point that the Irish Parliamentary Party was supportive of women's suffrage even though John Redmond, their leader, was opposed and had not included it in the Home Rule Bill. Then others spoke, encouraging women to continue their campaign until they achieved full citizenship. Ellen was struck by the energy and enthusiasm shown by the women and the few men present. She was exhilarated when she re-joined Ada and was introduced to the others on the platform.

"I hope we will see you at more of our meetings. If you leave us your name and address we will keep you informed," Mrs Sheehy-Skeffington said warmly. "We are always looking for young blood. There is a lot of work to be done."

Ada said goodbye to Ellen then because she was to travel to Belfast the next day for another meeting and would stay with one of the other organisers in Dublin that night. Ellen walked home, talking animatedly with some of the women that she had met. She was anxious to discuss the events of the evening with Annie and hoped that she was still waiting up for her. As soon as she opened the door she knew that something was wrong. Annie was sitting by the range, doubled over in pain. She looked terrified.

Ellen went to Annie and realised that her waters had broken. "Don't worry, love. The baby is coming but it will be a while yet. How long have you had pains?"

"Since just after you left. I didn't want to wake the children and I knew you would be home soon so I just waited." Her relief at her sister's return was obvious.

"You should have called Mrs Kelly or one of the other neighbours. I wouldn't have left you if I thought that it was near your time." Ellen felt guilty at her neglect of her sister. "I will go and get the midwife. It won't take me long. Here, let me help you to your bed."

Ellen ran all the way to the midwife's house which was only three streets away. Mrs O'Farrell was used to being called out suddenly and had her bag ready. "Isn't she a bit early? I thought she wasn't due for another three weeks."

"I don't think she was very clear about her dates. But yes, she is a bit early. She wasn't feeling very well today. I should have realised."

Mrs O'Farrell was very competent and took charge, leaving Ellen to hold her sister's hand and encourage her. She was probably more nervous for her sister than she had been during her own four deliveries. Annie was very brave, stifling her screams in the pillow, mindful of the children asleep upstairs and gripping her sister's hands fiercely when the pains came. Before dawn, Annie was delivered of a beautiful baby girl. Ellen held the small baby in her arms and thought of her own firstborn, Nancy. Mrs O'Farrell was bustling about, washing the baby, helping Annie to change into a fresh nightdress and reassuring her, as she did with all new mothers. Then she said goodbye, adding that she would look in the following day. Ellen gave the baby back to her sister who was crying with relief and happiness and a touch of despair.

"She looks a little bit like Albert, doesn't she? How am I going to bring her up without a father?" The sadness in her voice brought tears to Ellen's eyes.

"Don't worry, love. She will always be part of this family. You will not be bringing her up alone." Ellen stroked her sister's face and settled her down to sleep with her baby beside her.

She stoked up the range and tidied the bedroom, putting the sheets to soak in the hip bath.

When the children came down to breakfast, they were amazed to find a new member of the family.

"What are you going to call her?" Joseph asked Annie.

"I am going to call her Mary after my mother and Ellen after your mother," Annie explained.

Kathleen wanted to play with the baby as though she was a doll and had to be diverted to her own rag doll.

"Where is her Papa?" Harry was looking at Annie thoughtfully. Ellen knew that he would not easily be fobbed off with stories of an absent soldier husband.

"Come on now, children. Time to get ready for school."

Baby Mary was small but fed well and began to thrive. Neighbours called in with gifts and good wishes. Ellen found the clothes belonging to Nancy which she had treasured for so long and gave them to Annie who presumed they were Kathleen's. Every time she saw one of the small items on her niece she suffered the sharp pain of regret but was glad that she could now remember Nancy with as much fondness as pain.

Soon the matter of Mary's christening arose. Usually children were christened within about a week of their birth. Mary was three weeks old when Annie tearfully brought up the subject. "What are we going to do about Mary's christening? Will the church allow her to be baptised when her father and I were not married? Will I have to say who the father is?"

Annie had been quite tearful and depressed since the birth of her baby. Ellen knew that the matter of the christening had been preying on her mind.

"I do not know what the situation is. I will have to go and see the parish priest. I am sure that they would not refuse to baptise an innocent baby. Tomorrow, when the children are at school, I will go to Aughrim Street and see Father Waters."

Father Waters proved to be a kindly man who was realistic about his parishioners. Ellen described the situation to him, without revealing that Albert was a married man.

He was quick to reassure her. "Of course we will baptise the baby. However, we will arrange a private christening rather than include her in a group christening. That way we will avoid giving scandal."

Annie cried with relief when Ellen told her that the christening was arranged for the following Saturday afternoon. "I would like you to be Mary Ellen's godmother. Would you allow Harry to be her godfather?"

"I would love to be Mary Ellen's godmother," Ellen replied. "Harry has made his confirmation so he will be allowed to be godfather. Now I want you to go back to sleep while Mary is sleeping. You need a rest."

Harry was delighted with his new responsibility. Annie, the family and Violet all went to the church the following Saturday and Mary was baptised. Harry insisted on holding the baby during the ceremony. Afterwards, they had a small celebration at home. Annie wrote to her mother telling her about the baby, the christening and the fact the baby was called after her. Their mother wrote back saying that she was glad that Annie and the baby were well but she couldn't tell Henry because it would break his heart and he was unwell. Maggie sent a present of some clothes for the baby and some money for Annie. Jane sent money with a short letter. Ellen realise that her family were leaving her with the full responsibility for Annie and Mary.

At times like this she really missed James and his support and good humour. His letters were very sporadic now and much shorter than they had been. Much to Joseph's disappointment, there were no more stories or drawings. His letters now were disjointed, depressed and full of longing for home. Ellen both longed for and dreaded their appearance. She knew that he and Des were in Flanders and from the few clues he dropped, she imagined that they must be on or near the front line.

In spite of the propaganda in the newspapers, reports were trickling through of awful casualties. She knew women whose husbands were in the Dublin Fusiliers and who seemed to get more information than she did. One of those women, Delia Carey, had received a telegram to say that her husband had been killed in a place called Ypres. There were many other casualties among the Dublin Fusiliers, most of them by shell and bullet but many by gas. Now all of the soldier's wives dreaded the appearance of the telegram boy.

Having Annie and the baby in the house was great company and gave her someone to talk to but she didn't want to burden the young mother with her worries. She found comfort in going to the suffragette meetings and talking to other women who also had loved ones in the trenches and had similar experiences. Some of them had already lost a member of their family in the war. Others were nationalistic and felt that Irishmen should be fighting for the freedom of their own country rather than fighting for the British

Empire. Whatever their differences, their common purpose in fighting for women's rights bound them together.

Then the letters began to come again but they were very short and more worrying than consoling. One day in April, Ellen was making some scones for the tea when she heard a knock. Thinking it was one of the neighbours she wiped her hands on her apron and opened the door.

The telegram boy stood there. "Mrs Devereux? Mrs Ellen Devereux? I have a telegram for you."

The air seemed to dislocate and then freeze around her; she went cold all over and her heart plunged. She tried to put out her hand for the telegram but felt paralysed. The slim envelope with her name on it blurred as the boy put it into her hand. She couldn't open it; her fingers refused to move. The telegram boy was looking at her with concern.

"Please open it for me. I can't ..." She took the opened piece of paper and tried to focus.

"Regret to inform you that Sergeant-Major James Devereux has been reported missing in action."

Relief made her go weak and she leaned back on the wall for support. "Missing in action? Oh thank God, he is not dead. Missing in action! Not dead!"

"Mama, what is wrong?" Harry was beside her. She put her arm around his shoulder and he took her weight.

"It's your father. He was reported missing in action."

"Missing in action? What does that mean?" Harry was trying to lead her inside.

"It means that they don't know where he is. But he is not dead. I would know if he was dead. I would feel it!" Ellen could feel the hysteria rising within her.

Harry looked at her anxiously. "Mama, come inside. Annie, where are you?"

161

Annie emerged from her room where she had been feeding the baby. She took the telegram from Ellen's hand, read it, re-read it and drew her sister into the kitchen. "Sit down, love, and I will make you a cup of tea."

Ellen sank into one of the armchairs; Harry stood beside her, his hand on her shoulder. Annie gave her a cup of sweet tea. "How long has he been missing?"

"I don't know; it doesn't say. It just says that he is missing in action. Oh my God, what will I do if he doesn't come back? How will I live without him? How will the children live without a father?"

Ellen then thought of Joseph and Kathleen who were playing out on the street with their friends. "Harry, we must not tell Joseph and Kathleen. They would not understand. Please God your father will be found safe and well. Time enough to tell them if we have bad news."

At that moment a distraught-looking Violet burst in the door, a telegram in her hand. "Did you get one too? Is James all right? Is he missing? Is he dead?"

Ellen put her arms around her friend. "Yes, he is missing. That doesn't mean he is dead. Is Des missing?"

"Yes, that is all I know. Oh, why don't they give us more information?"

Her friend's distress had the effect of calming Ellen down. "I am sure that as soon as they know anything they will contact us. I am not going to tell the children. Harry knows and I suggest that you should tell Desmond. But there is no point in telling the younger children."

Ellen did her best to comfort her friend and Annie walked back with Violet to her house. Ellen thought about how she could get more information and decided to write to Mrs Major who was now living in Galway while her husband was at war. In the meantime

162

she scoured the newspapers for any information about the war. She learned that the 6th Battalion, which included the Connaught Rangers, had fought a number of battles at a place called Ypres and suffered what the papers called "major casualties".

Every night she lay awake, thinking about James and imagining what he was going through. Sometimes she half woke up in the night and thought that she felt him beside her. Other times, she thought she caught a glimpse of him coming down the stairs as she lit the range in the morning. She felt in her heart that he was not dead and prayed for his safe return. She asked their dead child Nancy, whom she believed to be in heaven, to watch over her father. Keeping things normal for the children's sake kept her going. Some evenings she went round to Violet's house when the children were in bed and the two women said the rosary for their husbands and tried to keep each other's spirits up.

Two weeks later, she got another telegram. This time she ripped it open.

"Sergeant-Major James Devereux found safe. In hospital with minor injuries."

"Oh thank God, thank God. I knew he wasn't dead! He only has minor injuries!" Annie had joined her on the doorstep. The two women hugged and cried with relief.

Kathleen looked at them with amazement. The two boys were still at school.

"I must go to see Violet. I hope she got good news too."

Ellen put on her coat and hat and hurried to Violet's house. When she got there, the door was opened by her elderly neighbour, Mrs Dolan. Violet was sitting, white-faced and crying, being comforted by another neighbour.

"Violet, what is it? What has happened? Did you get a telegram?" Wordlessly Violet handed her a piece of paper.

"Regret to inform you Sergeant-Major Desmond Vaughan

163

killed in action at the Second Battle of Ypres April 1915."

"Oh, my poor dear! Oh my God, I am so sorry."

"Is James still missing? Have you heard anything?" Violet's tone was dead.

"Yes, he was found. He is in hospital. With minor injuries, they said." Ellen could not bear to reveal the extent of her relief to her friend. She felt almost guilty that her husband was alive.

"Why was my husband lost and yours is safe? Why did God do that to me? How am I going to manage? How will I bring up the children without a father? What am I going to do?"

Violet was crying hysterically and clutching her youngest child to her. Ellen wanted to comfort her. She went to put her arm around her friend but was repulsed.

"Go away. Your man is coming back. Mine isn't. Go and celebrate."

Ellen didn't know how to deal with Violet's anger. Mrs Dolan smiled sympathetically at her. "Go on, love. I will look after her. She is not right in the head at the moment. It is very hard to come to terms with news like that. She is angry with God and with everyone around her. She will feel different after a few days."

Ellen cried all the way back home. Her tears were for Violet and Des and their children but they were also tears of relief. James had been spared. He was safe and would come home to her. That was all that mattered.

A week later a letter from James arrived. Ellen was alone in the house, the boys were at school and Annie had taken the two girls to the park. She sat down to read it; tears of relief and sadness rolled down her face as she opened the flimsy envelope which was such a tenuous link to her husband.

My dear Ellen,

By now you will have heard that I am all right. I am sorry that you were informed that I was missing. I can imagine what that news did to you and the children. I got a flesh wound in the thigh but it is healing fast. I am in a field hospital and quite well looked after. There are men all around me here with terrible injuries, lost limbs, eyesight gone, lungs ruined. I was lucky. As soon as my wound heals I will be sent back to the front.

You must know by now that our friend Des Vaughan was killed in action. I will miss him very much. He was a good friend. I have lost many friends in the action. I myself was lost in No Man's Land for almost a week. The Germans have started to use gas and it overcame many of the men. A doctor told me that it just melts the lungs. As we were advancing, a corporal in my battalion, Jimmy Dunne, fell beside me. At first I thought it was the gas because we were all choking from it. Then I realised that he had been hit in the stomach. I tried to help him but he couldn't move and was losing a lot of blood from a wound in his stomach. I tried to stop the bleeding. We called for stretcher bearers but no one came. Then it became night and we realised that we had no hope of rescue until morning.

When morning came it was still like night because the gas obscured our vision and we waited once more. Then Jimmy died. I tried to find my way back behind the lines but was disorientated. I knew I risked being fired on by our own troops. Eventually I found my way back but in the confusion of the battle couldn't find my own battalion. That is why I was posted missing. I do not know what happened to Des. I think of Violet and the children and pray for them.

Sometimes I cannot believe that you and I once had a life that was very different from this one. When I lie in the cold and filth of the trenches I try to think of India, the heat, the beautiful flowers and the scent of the frangipani. I imagine that we are sitting on the veranda at night, listening to the crickets and inhaling the scented balmy air. I imagine that you put your arms around me and hold me close and I manage to go to sleep and forget for a little while the horror that is all around me.

Give my beloved children a kiss from me and tell them that I will try to come home safe to them. My darling Ellen, I send you all my love.

Your loving husband,

James

Ellen read the letter greedily, over and over, until she knew it by heart. Each time she came to the description of how he imagined her holding him in her arms as he tried to sleep she sobbed; that was the image she tried to conjure up for herself when she couldn't sleep. One sentence filled her with dread. "As soon as my wound heals I will be sent back to the front." How could they send him back when he had been lucky enough to survive it once? She had some idea of the fatalities that the British Army had already suffered. Mrs Major had written to her and told her as much as she knew about the progress of the war and Ada had sent her cuttings from the Daily Mail which seemed to have more honest and clear information about the war than the other newspapers.

She settled down to write to James, making her words as comforting and encouraging as possible. She tried to write as imaginatively and romantically as he did, recalling their meeting in her parents' home in Castlebar, their years in India and their life with their children in their cosy house in Dublin. She ended by telling him that their daughter, Nancy, who was an angel in heaven, would look after him. She had just finished when she heard Annie and the children returning.

She wiped the tears from her face and smiled as she opened the door. "Look, children, a letter from Papa! Come and sit down and I will read it to you. After tea, you can write to him and we will post it tomorrow."

They listened attentively to the bits of the letter that she read out. Harry and Joseph both settled down that evening to write to their father. Kathleen took out her crayons and started to draw a picture. "Look, Mama. I am sending a picture of all of us so Papa won't feel so lonely."

Before they went to bed Ellen gathered up the picture and the letters which the children kissed before she placed them in the envelope with her own letter. That night, she went to visit Violet.

Her old friend greeted her with tears. "I didn't think you would come back after what I said to you."

Ellen embraced her. "I understand why you said it. Grief affects us in many different ways."

Violet went to put the kettle on the range. "I am so glad to see you. We have been through so much together."

Soon the two women were sharing a pot of tea and talking. It was almost like old times except it wasn't; Ellen knew that there

167

would always be a shadow between them.

Christmas 1915 came and once again Ellen invited Violet and the children to share it with them as they had before. Violet told her that her brother in Mayo had invited her and her children to come to his farm for Christmas.

"Anyway, I have no money to buy anything and if I stayed here I would be thinking of last Christmas when I knew Des was alive."

Two days before Christmas the two families said goodbye to each other. Harry accompanied them to the train so that he could help Desmond with the bags. Ellen reflected that without Annie and the baby, she would have felt unbearably lonely this Christmas. There was no goose from Castlebar this time and Ellen counted out her money to see what she could afford for Christmas dinner. She had her army payment but with three children and Annie and the baby, her money didn't seem to go very far. She suggested to Annie that they go to the street market in Moore Street on Christmas Eve where there were bargains to be had. The two women set off, Annie carrying Mary and Ellen holding Kathleen's hand. Harry and Joseph skipped along ahead of them, delighted with the excitement of going into the city. There was a festive air in Sackville Street as they got off the tram and set off for Moore Street. Gas street lamps and festive lights shone through the gloom of a foggy December afternoon. The pavements were thronged with hurrying people, many of them with bags and parcels which bounced off those carried by other people as they made their way through the crowds. Pubs disgorged glassy-eyed, smiling men with brown paper bags full of porter bottles onto the streets. Dejected-looking beggars accosted people entering the large department stores. Outside the GPO carol singers filled the air with Silent Night and good-naturedly rattled their collection boxes.

In Moore Street, traders lined both sides of the street, shouting out their wares and proffering items to passers-by. Ellen and Annie decided to walk up and down both sides of the street to see what they could afford. The war meant that many traditional Christmas food items, such as tangerines, were not available. Bruised-looking chickens were on offer but were expensive. Rabbits were a better buy so they selected two. Rosy red apples and hazelnuts attracted the two boys, so they bought bags of each. Fresh Brussels sprouts reminded Ellen of the garden at the lodge so she bought some. The boys chose paper cones of assorted sweets and broken biscuits. Ellen had already bought a small toy for each child so their shopping was done. They walked slowly back to the tram, admiring the Christmas lights and the shop front displays as they went. The big department stores had enticing signs up pointing to Santa's Grotto and they could see lines of parents with their children waiting to make a visit to the bearded gentleman. Harry and Joseph looked wistfully at the queues but knew that their mother could not afford such luxuries.

Next morning, Harry was singing at the Pro-Cathedral and all the family walked through the chilly morning to attend Mass there. It was a sung mass and Ellen glowed with pride when Harry sang the solos. Afterwards, they lit candles for the safe return of James.

"Our second Christmas without James," Ellen prayed. "At least we know he is alive. Please let him come back safely to us."

When they came home, Ellen served Christmas dinner in a room that she had made as festive as possible with the holly and ivy which the boys had brought home from the Phoenix Park. The excitement of the children made the meal a jolly affair and Annie tried to hide the tears that came to her eyes when she thought of Albert and other Christmases in the lodge with her parents. She still had had no news of Albert and had no idea whether he was alive or dead.

Ellen saw her sister's grief but had her own worries. James had been sent back to the front a few weeks before Christmas. His latest letter was short, disjointed, depressed and worst of all, lacking in hope. The carefree romantic man that she had married seemed to have disappeared, changed utterly by the terrible things he had experienced. Even though he spared her graphic descriptions of the trenches she knew enough from gossip and newspaper reports to have some idea of the horror which surrounded him. She wondered how much longer he would have to endure it; how much longer could he survive?

Chapter 16
1916: A New Allegiance

Harry was beginning to grow up into a fine young man. He was now almost twelve and was tall and dark like her father. An excellent student, he had won a scholarship to the Secondary School where he was due to start in September. Recently, he had stopped calling Ellen Mama and addressed her as "Mother". He was mature and intense and they often sat together talking and discussing the week's events. In many ways he had become her confidante.

One Sunday evening in early February he sat with her when Annie was out at a meeting and the others had gone to bed. "Mother, have you noticed that my voice is breaking? This morning Mr O'Brien had a chat with me and said that I might not be able to sing with the choir for much longer."

"Well love, you are certainly growing up. You are taller than me already and almost as tall as Papa. Will you miss the choir if you have to leave it?"

"Of course I will. It has been part of my life since we came to Dublin. But I don't want to wait until I am asked to leave. I have decided to tell Mr O'Brien that I am leaving next week."

Ellen looked at her growing son with new respect. She had been aware of a change in his voice and wondered how he would deal with leaving the choir when the time came.

"The choir used to take up a lot of my time. Now I can do other things. I want to join Na Fianna." Harry looked determined.

"Who? I never heard of them." Ellen was concerned.

"Do you remember the stories you used to tell me about Fionn McCuaill and the brave warriors of the Fianna? That is who they are called after. I went to one meeting with Sean Scallon from school and I was invited to join. Their headquarters are over in

171

Ranelagh but they are going to move to the city centre."

"What do they do? Are they a sports organisation?"

"No, not exactly. It is a bit like the Boy Scouts. They go camping and drilling and it is great fun, Sean says." Harry was trying to allay her fears.

Ellen was dubious about his new interest. She had heard of organisations which had sprung up, most of which seemed to have a political agenda. Annie was a member of Cumann na mBan, a women's group, some of whose leaders had also been involved in the suffragettes but had changed their allegiance to the new group. James Connolly, a trade unionist and socialist leader that Annie greatly admired, was closely involved with the organisation. She resolved to find out as much about Na Fianna as she could. Why did all these organisations have such unpronounceable Irish names, she wondered? Although her mother was an Irish speaker, Ellen herself had no Irish and little interest in the language which had been denigrated when she went to school. Now her children were learning Irish and seemed to love it. Even Kathleen had learned songs in Irish at school which she tried to teach to her mother and to baby Mary.

There was a definite surge of interest in things Irish which was discernible in the city. Ellen and Violet had been to the newly opened Abbey Theatre before their husbands left and had enjoyed the evening even though they had only been able to afford seats in "the gods". The theatre had been founded to encourage Irish writers who wrote on Irish themes such as W.B. Yeats, J.M. Synge and Lady Gregory. It all sounded a bit disloyal and dangerous, she thought, when Irish men were fighting in the trenches far away in France and Flanders.

She continued to attend meetings of the suffragettes but even there she found a change in attitude. At the last meeting she had attended there was a heated debate between a group of women who wanted to continue with the programme of meetings and protests which they had been doing for a number of years and another group who were tired of what seemed like a fruitless battle to achieve the vote. The latter group had put their trust in John Redmond and his party and were bitterly disappointed when they failed to have women's suffrage included in the Home Rule Bill. They now wanted to transfer their allegiance to Cumann na mBan because leaders like James Connolly were promising that, when Ireland was self-governing, women would immediately get the vote. Hanna Sheehy-Skeffington, who led the first group, was a pacifist as was her husband, Francis. They both spoke strongly and passionately about the need to steer the Women's Suffrage movement away from nationalist politics and possible violence to peaceful demonstrations and education of the general public about the issue.

"You want us to stay away from violence but what about the women who were arrested and put in jail for two months for throwing stones at the windows of government buildings when the Home Rule Bill was introduced without any reference to votes for women?"

The woman who spoke, Catherine Waters, had herself been jailed and her six children had been left to fend for themselves while she was in jail. "If I am going to go to jail again, I want it to be for something worthwhile that is likely to get us the vote, not just for throwing stones!"

"James Connolly is committed to votes for women. From now on I am going to give my energy to Cumann na mBan. There is talk of a revolution and I want to be part of it." The second speaker was a young woman who often spoke at the meetings. She was obviously impatient with the older leadership.

"We will be well rid of those two. They would like to see us out on the street battling the police!" Ellen's neighbour said as the two other women and some of their supporters left the meeting.

Ellen had always avoided the more militant wing of the movement. For one thing, if she was arrested and imprisoned, Annie and the children would be left with no one to look after them. For another, she had seen what being militant had done for Ada. It also felt disloyal when James and thousands like him were fighting for the same government that the militants opposed. She was happy to help organise the meetings and to hand out leaflets in public and continued to attend regularly even though their numbers were depleted.

At the next meeting she found herself sitting next to a woman of about her own age who was dressed flamboyantly in flowing garments of jewel colours. She had long copper-coloured hair coiled at her neck and wore a large hat tilted rakishly over her eyes. She looked completely out of place amongst the soberly dressed suffragettes.

She turned to smile at Ellen. "I am Grace Geraghty. I think I have seen you here before."

She had a perfect face with milky skin and large green eyes. Ellen was fascinated by her beautiful clothes and confident demeanour. "Yes, I saw you here a few months ago. My name is Ellen Devereux."

"I can't come to the meetings very often. I work at night and sometimes I am away. I am an actress at the Abbey Theatre," the other woman revealed.

"Of course! I was wondering why I seemed to know your face. My friend and I saw you in 'The Playboy of the Western World'. You played Pegeen Mike. You were wonderful in the part." Ellen was delighted to meet an actress.

"Thank you," Grace said. "It was a great part. Do you like the theatre?"

"Yes, but I can't afford to go very often," Ellen said regretfully.

"Are you in a play at the moment?"

"I am rehearsing for 'John Bull's Other Island' by Mr George Bernard Shaw. We rehearse in the mornings so that is how I could come tonight."

The two women chatted to each other before the meeting and went to have a cup of tea after it. Grace told Ellen that she had been an actress since she was sixteen. She was now part of the Abbey Company and had been on tour with them in the United States and England. Some of the well-known actors and actresses like Sara Allgood and her sister Molly left the company after the tour and that had affected the attendance. However, for Grace, it had meant opportunities to play parts that she otherwise would not have had. By the time they parted, the two women felt as if they had been friends for a long time.

"Come and visit me in my rooms; I am there most afternoons at the moment. I live not very far from you on the North Quays. I will write down my address for you. Bring the children if you like. I would love to meet them."

Ellen had not talked as freely or as openly to anyone since she had left home and her confidante, Maggie. Ada had also been someone she could confide in but their backgrounds were different enough to ensure that she often had to explain herself or the situations about which she was talking. Her new friend had had an upbringing similar to hers and they seemed to understand each other perfectly.

The following week she decided to visit Grace and took Kathleen and Mary with her. They found the house easily; Grace had two rooms on the first floor. Her rooms were like herself, graceful and exotic. Ellen thought that she had not seen so much colour since she left India. The living room had a squashy deep red sofa which had layers of velvet throws on it. The two girls immediately sat on it and slipped cosily between the throws. Grace invited Ellen to sit in a large gentleman's chair in deep green velvet which stood by the window. She herself sat on a chaise longue which was upholstered in mustard. Between them was a beautiful carved table in a dark wood which was scattered with books. The tall bay window had tastefully draped damask curtains with an inner layer of lace. A log fire crackled in the grate of a marble fireplace. On the walls were photographs of Grace in various costumes and also of other people who were obviously actors. The room exuded comfort and warmth.

They chatted comfortably for a while and then Grace excused herself and reappeared a few minutes later with a tray. She placed the china cups and a plate of fruitcake sliced into fingers on the table and then poured tea for everyone. Ellen had brought a bottle for Mary but was nervous of Kathleen and the fragile cups; Kathleen, however, behaved as though she always drank out of china cups and ate her cake like a lady.

Seeing the girls begin to grow restless, Grace asked, "Girls, would you like to play dressing up?"

She showed the two excited girls into her bedroom. While she was sorting out an array of shawls, scarves and jewellery for them to play with, Ellen had time to look around the room. It was gorgeously untidy with beautiful gowns thrown carelessly over chairs and beads and necklaces draped over the dressing table mirror. Under the brass bed with its thick eiderdown, shoes of various colours could be seen.

"It is a mess, isn't it? I am hopelessly untidy and I can't mend or even sew on a button. I am hopeless," Grace laughed.

The two women moved back into the drawing room, leaving Kathleen to her dressing up. Mary was sitting on the floor, entranced by ropes of shiny beads. Grace wanted to hear about Ellen's time in India. No one else in Dublin had ever evinced an interest in that period of her life, maybe because it was too foreign

176

and exotic to even imagine.

"I hope to visit India myself someday," Grace said. "Tell me all about it."

Grace was genuinely interested and Ellen found herself talking more than she had in a long time. She described her painting expeditions with Ada and the different aspects of India that they had seen. She talked about the servants and their kindness, particularly to the children and her own inability to get close to them. She even found herself talking about Nancy and her burial at sea, something she had not done with anyone else. She had tears in her eyes when she finished and Grace came over and put her arms around her.

"I can't imagine how you bore that grief. It must have been heartbreaking. But at least you have the other children. You are very lucky."

Something in the other woman's voice made Ellen say, "Did you ever want to marry and have children, Grace?"

"I almost got married when we were on tour in America. I was very much in love and I thought that he was too. Then he got an offer to stay in America and go to Hollywood. I had to go home and he stayed. When I discovered that I was going to have a baby I wrote to him but he didn't even reply. Maybe he didn't get the letter; he was moving around a lot at the time. I thought about keeping the baby but it just seemed impossible. My family would be unlikely to support me and I wouldn't get parts in the theatre if I had a baby. So a friend introduced me to someone who could help a girl in my situation."

Ellen took a few minutes to register what her friend was telling her. "Oh Grace, I am so sorry. You must have suffered so much!"

There was a pause while Grace relived some of the memories of that time. "Yes, afterwards, I was very depressed and couldn't work. But then a good friend gave me a small part and I began to be

177

offered good roles again. Pegeen Mike, the part that you saw me playing, was the first big chance I got. But I still think about the baby I might have had and I feel very lonely and alone sometimes."

Kathleen burst into the room at that moment, draped in beautiful scarves, with a large hat perched on her head and beads dangling around her neck. "I want to sing for you. Would you like to hear me, Grace?"

"I would love to hear you, darling." The interruption brought Grace back to the present.

Kathleen used the doorway of the other room as her stage. She announced herself. "Miss Kathleen Devereux will now sing 'You made me love you; I didn't want to do it', made famous by Mr Al Jolson."

To Grace's delight she sang the popular song with actions and displayed a lovely singing voice. When she had finished, both women clapped loudly.

"I didn't know that you knew that song, love," Ellen said proudly.

"Miriam Delaney sings it when we have concerts out on the street. They have a phonograph and lots of records." Kathleen was still twirling around in her scarves.

"You have a lovely voice, Kathleen, and you are quite the actress!" Grace was delighted with her.

"I want to be an actress like you, Grace," Kathleen said, and Grace picked up the little girl and danced around with her.

Mary was getting tired and began to cry. Ellen lifted her up. It was getting dark outside and Grace began to light the gas lamps. "Thank you, Grace. We have had a lovely time. Annie and the boys will be wondering what has happened to us so we better go."

Grace was helping Kathleen into her coat. "I hope you will all come again. I get a bit lonely here sometimes. Promise that you will all come again. In the meantime, I will send you tickets when my play opens."

Amid a flurry of hugs and kisses and promises to return, Ellen and the girls left. On the way home, the two girls were animated and full of chat about their new friend. Ellen too felt that she had enjoyed a holiday, so different had her day been. She realised that Grace, in spite of her glamorous career, was a very lonely person. She hoped that they would be able to see each other often.

Annie had been spending more and more time out of the house. She too had been involved with the suffragettes but had made friends with women in Cumann na mBan and attended regular meetings. She told Ellen about their activities and about the Irish Citizen Army to which they were affiliated. Her ambition to be a nurse had been rekindled by a friend in the group, a nurse, Elizabeth O'Farrell, who was a midwife. She was encouraging Annie to apply for training to one of the Dublin hospitals. The two sisters talked it over and Ellen agreed to look after Mary while Annie did her training. When the acceptance letter came from the Meath Hospital in the Liberties, Annie almost changed her mind. She discovered that she would have to live full-time in the nurses' home and would have very little time off. The idea of not seeing Mary for long periods broke her heart. Ellen encouraged her sister.

"Just think, Annie. You will be able to make a better life for Mary if you qualify as a nurse. It is something you always wanted to do. Don't worry about Mary. The children and I will look after her. I know you will miss her but you will be able to see her frequently."

Mary was already a part of Ellen's family and looked on Kathleen and the two boys as her siblings. Annie accepted the offer and was told to report on 2nd January 1916. Annie found it very difficult to leave her daughter and Mary missed her mother. However the two boys took it upon themselves to keep the baby amused and vied for the opportunity to hold her on their knees. Ellen found that she was very much housebound with Mary and, because the weather was very cold, hardly left the house except to go to the local shop. She trusted Harry to look after the baby for a few hours occasionally but he was very busy with his Gaelic football and the activities of Na Fianna. Ellen missed going to the suffragette meetings but consoled herself that it was only while Mary was very young.

Annie made her first visit one month after she began her training. She was tearful when she held her daughter but she could see that Mary was perfectly happy without her. She was animated and full of stories about her patients and the other nurses and especially the matron who seemed to be a dragon. She was a good mimic and had them all laughing at her imitations of the dragon-like matron and the more demanding patients. Ellen was delighted to see her sister so happy and enthusiastic about her new life. Annie had also managed to attend some of the meetings of Cumann na mBan and talked of the Irish Citizen Army and the Irish Volunteers drilling and training for an insurrection against British rule in Ireland.

Ellen thought it all sounded romantic and far-fetched and said so to her sister. "How do you think James would feel if he heard you talking like that? He has been wounded and lost many of his friends in this war. He and his comrades are fighting for king and country and the freedom of small nations like Belgium."

"Not my king and not my country," said Annie. "Do you not think it strange that our men should be fighting for the freedom of Belgium when our own country is not free?"

Ellen knew she was not going to get anywhere with this discussion so she changed the subject.

"I had a letter from Mama this morning. Papa is not well at all. Apparently, Lord Lucan is selling the estate and house to the Sisters of Mercy. They are going to move the secondary school there. The Lucan family are going to live in London permanently from now on."

"Oh poor Mama and Papa! It must have been a terrible shock to them. But where will they live?"Annie still worried about her parents in spite of her mother's abandonment of her.

"Maggie has invited them to live with her and Matt. They weren't able for the lodge anyway. They must have known that they would have to leave one way or another and Maggie will look after them."

"Yes, but you know how proud Papa is. It will break his heart to leave his own home and be dependent on others, even if it is his daughter and son-in-law. I would love to go to see them but I don't know whether they would want to see me." Annie's voice broke as she said this.

"Jane is going to visit them next week and she said that she would call in here on her way home. I'd love to go and see them myself, Annie, but it is not possible at the moment. They would not want me to bring Mary and with your training you won't be able to get more than a day off at a time for a while."

It was time for Annie to go back to the nurses' home. She looked sad as she kissed Mary goodbye and Ellen helped her on with her coat. "Do you think that Mama and Papa will ever forgive me, Ellen?"

Ellen tried to reassure her sister. "I hope in time they will. Mama always asks for you and Mary when she writes. Now hurry or you will miss your tram."

The following week Jane called as she had promised. She arrived in the afternoon, having caught the early train from Galway. She was dressed very fashionably in a long tweed hobble skirt, a black coat with a fur collar and a cloche hat. Ellen was conscious of her own clothes which were clean but a bit shabby and certainly out of date. Jane bustled in, put down her bag and exclaimed over Mary whom she had not seen before. Mary drew back from the effusive embraces and began to cry.

Ellen rescued the baby. "I was just about to put her down for a sleep. Sit down by the range and I will be back as soon as I settle her."

Jane was prowling around the kitchen looking at photographs and ornaments when Ellen returned. "What a cosy little house you have here! It is a pity that Mama and Papa never saw it."

Ellen tried not to notice the condescension in her sister's tone. "How are they? Have they settled in to Maggie's?"

"They are not very well. The move took a lot out of them. Papa's breathing is very bad. He has to be helped to walk and he can't get in or out of bed without help. Mama is upset at having to leave but she will be better off in Maggie's where it is nice and warm and not damp like the lodge."

Ellen could see that her sister was once again offloading a problem on to someone else, this time Maggie. Half-heartedly, she invited Jane to stay for tea.

"Oh, I would love to but Tom is meeting me off the tram so I better hurry. Why don't you come over and visit me some day, and bring the children of course."

"Yes," thought Ellen. "Bring Mary, the baby you wanted to give up for adoption."

Aloud she said, "It is a bit difficult with the children and school and so on. Then at the weekend Harry and Joseph have a lot of activities. Annie only gets to visit us every fourth Sunday so we couldn't miss that."

"Yes of course. Annie is lucky that you are willing to mind her baby while she trains. It must be difficult for you. How is James, by the way?"

Ellen made a non-committal reply. She couldn't confide in Jane who was so judgemental and snobbish and was certainly not going to tell her about James's depressed state. She could have done with someone to talk to, she reflected as Jane left. Violet used to be the one she confided in but things had changed. When Violet came back from Mayo after Christmas she had come to see Ellen. She looked thin and strained as the two friends greeted each other.

After telling about Christmas with her family in Mayo she suddenly blurted out, "I am going to have to take Desmond out of school. I can't manage on Des's army pension. I'll have to look for some kind of work myself as well. My brother offered to let Desmond stay there to work on the farm and said that he would send me Desmond's wages. I couldn't do it. The girls would miss him terrible and so would I. Anyway, like me, he hates farm work. At least if he gets a job here in the city he will be with his family and friends."

Ellen knew that Desmond, Violet's eldest son, was her pride and joy. He had done well at school and, like Harry, won a scholarship to secondary school where he had been for two years. He was now fourteen and should have stayed in school until he was at least sixteen by which time he would have some hope of a reasonable job.

"It was kind of your brother to offer but I think you are right not to leave him in Mayo. His chances must be better here in Dublin," Ellen agreed.

"I don't think my brother was being kind, I think he was thinking of cheap labour!" Violet was realistic about her family.

"Have you contacted the regiment to see if they could help him find a job?" Ellen asked.

"Yes, I did, but the problem is that so many men have been killed that they can't help all of their families. They suggested that I try local shops and businesses. Desmond has an interview next week in May's shop, the one on Infirmary road. Tom May was a friend of Des's. They are looking for a messenger boy. It is not what I would have wanted for him but it is a start."

"What about yourself? How will you manage with the children if you have to go out to work?"

"Mrs Heaney, one of my neighbours, works for the railway as a cleaner on the trains. She said she could get me a start. The work is early morning and late at night. Julia is twelve so she will have to mind the three young ones while I go to work. I should be home by the time she has to go to school."

"If I can help you let me know. Maybe I could take the twins with me to school along with Kathleen." Ellen knew how difficult it was going to be for Violet.

"That would be a great help. Otherwise, I would have to do it myself after I got home in the morning. Now, I better get home. Thanks for the cup of tea."

As soon as Violet had gone, Ellen started to wash the teacups. She knew some of the women who worked as cleaners on the trains. Sometimes when she couldn't sleep she would hear them leaving for work in the early hours of the morning. Other times she would see them walking wearily home in the dark. She didn't think Violet would have much time in the future for chats and cups of tea.

Chapter 17
Easter 1916

Ellen looked forward to Annie's monthly visits. Her sister had matured since she started her training and Ellen felt that she could confide more in her now, woman to woman. Her next visit was going to be on Easter Monday so Ellen made some plans for the weekend. She usually painted eggs for the children's breakfast on Easter Sunday and loved to see the delight on their faces as they examined the individual paintings which she did for them. She planned to get a piece of bacon to have with cabbage for the dinner on Sunday and a rabbit which they would have with the remains of the bacon on Easter Monday. She had also bought some small chocolate eggs as a surprise.

Joseph and Kathleen were excited and rose early on Easter Sunday. They were delighted with their painted eggs; Joseph's had a rabbit's face and Kathleen's looked like a pretty flower. Even Mary had got a pink egg with a bonnet drawn on it. Harry went along with the excitement, admiring his which depicted a tiger's face, even though he obviously felt too old for such frivolity. Ellen kept the small chocolate eggs for a surprise for after dinner.

They all went to early Mass together in Aughrim Street and returned home where she prepared dinner. The best part for the children was when she gave them the small chocolate eggs. After dinner they walked together to the Phoenix Park and around the perimeter of the zoo where it was possible to see many of the animals without paying in. She thought of James and the first time the family had visited the park just after they arrived in Dublin. She remembered trying to capture the perfect moment when the children were laughing and feeding the ducks and James had smiled at her and drawn her close. Maybe she had had a premonition then that it was all going to change. That life seemed a very long time ago.

Next morning, Harry came into the kitchen as Ellen was black-leading the range. "Mother, after breakfast I am going up the park with Paddy and John to kick a ball around."

"That's fine love, as long as you are back here by two o'clock at the latest. Annie will be here for dinner and she will be looking forward to seeing you."

When Harry went off with his friends, Joseph and Kathleen went out to play on the street and Mary sat watching as Ellen prepared dinner. At two o'clock they were all sitting around the table waiting. When three o'clock came Ellen decided to serve the children who were starving. At four o'clock she reheated and ate her own dinner. Perhaps Annie couldn't get the day off after all, she thought. Harry was often late home when he went out with friends because he didn't seem to have any sense of time.

By six o'clock that evening she was really concerned; Harry would never stay out so long because he knew how she would worry. Leaving Joseph to look after the two girls, she went next door to Mrs Kelly. Her two boys were older than Harry but they were friends because they had accompanied him to school when he first started and had looked after him for the first year. They also played Gaelic football together and they all belonged to Na Fianna.

"My boys are not home either." A distraught looking Mrs Kelly brought her inside. "It is not like my boys to stay out at all. John is a bit wild but Paddy is very sensible. Will we tell the police?" Mrs Kelly asked.

Like most people, neither woman trusted the Dublin Metropolitan Police.

Ellen thought for a minute. "No, not for the moment. If the three of them are together, we have to hope that they are all right. If we hear nothing by the morning, then maybe we will."

Ellen put the children to bed and quieted their questions about

Harry's whereabouts by telling them that he was with Paddy and John. Then she sat down to consider what she could do. Things that she had heard from Annie, whispers about a possible rising against the British, about Irish volunteers drilling in the Dublin Mountains, about weapons being smuggled in, came into her mind. She had dismissed it all as more of the romantic, silly nonsense that these organisations like Cumann na mBan went on with. Now she wasn't so sure. Making up her mind, she put on her hat and coat and knocked on Mrs Kelly's door again.

"It is still light so I am going to go up to the park where the boys usually go. They wouldn't stay out like this unless something was preventing them from coming home. Here's my key; will you look in on the children from time to time? They are asleep but just to be safe."

She hurried to the Park Gate on the corner of the North Circular Road. There was no sign of trams coming or going in the area. Excited crowds were walking towards her, coming from the city. They were walking in groups, laughing and shouting and gesticulating to each other. Some of them seemed to have armfuls of clothes, still with their tags on. Others were carrying miscellaneous objects: one man held a saxophone over his head, a woman carried a picture larger than herself, a child ran alongside a scooter, a woman pushed a pram full of shoes. It reminded Ellen of a pantomime in the Queen's theatre to which she had taken the children. She tried to stop the woman with the pram but was nearly knocked over.

The boy with the scooter stopped as she almost fell over him. "You should go into the city, missus. It's great! Clery's and some of the other posh shops are on fire. Their windas is broke and you can help yourself to whatever you can carry!"

"What happened in the city? Why are the shops on fire?"

"Dunno, missus. Somethin' goin' on in the GPO." He scooted

away.

Ellen walked alongside a distressed, elderly man with glasses who gasped out what he knew as he hurried home. "There seems to have been some sort of attack on Dublin by the Irish Citizen Army and the Irish Volunteers. They took over a few places like the GPO and City Hall. I was walking down Sackville Street on me way to me daughter's house when a man in uniform came out and read some sort of notice. I saw all the trams was stopped so I turned round to go home again. Then I heard breaking glass and saw groups of people climbing into Clery's shop window and the jewellers beside it and taking anything they could get their hands on. It was like a riot and I was afraid for me life."

The Park Gates were now closed since it had become dark. The boys couldn't still be in the park. They might have heard about what was happening in the city and gone there out of curiosity. If she walked towards the GPO she might find them. She still didn't know her way around Dublin very well. She knew the route from Kingsbridge Station along the quays to Sackville Street where the General Post Office was so she turned down Infirmary Road again and made her way towards the station. There was a lot of activity around the station but no sign of trains arriving or leaving. People were moving around, trying to engage the few jarvey cars that were available. Along the Liffey, going towards the Four Courts, Ellen found that she was battling to move forwards against the crowds who seemed to be trying to leave the city. When she turned the corner into Sackville Street, she could see the damage caused by looting. Large and small shops had broken windows; in some, looters could still be seen scavenging through what was left. The police were nowhere to be seen. Two flags flew over the GPO, a green flag with a harp on it and the Tricolour. Flimsy pages fluttered around and she picked one up. The heading was "The Proclamation of the Irish Republic." She put it in her pocket. The

188

windows of the GPO were smashed and books and files had been used to fill the gaps. Looking up, she could see people peering out of the upper windows. Suddenly, a group of cavalry appeared in the street and shots rang out. Two horses and riders fell. Other cavalry men dismounted and picked up their fallen comrades. The wounded men were helped to sit up in front of one of the other riders and the group withdrew towards the bridge, leaving the dead horses behind.

A barricade had been erected around the GPO of broken furniture, bins and pieces of masonry. A handcart stuck out at one point and a man was trying to free it from the rest of the debris. In doing so he was pulling down the barricade.

A man came out of the GPO carrying a pistol. "Leave that alone. Get away from the barricade or I will shoot you."

"That's my handcart. I need it to work. I'm taking it." He continued to pull at the handcart.

The man with the pistol walked forward and shot him. Ellen was near enough to see the look of surprise on the man's face as he slithered down to the ground, blood flowing from his chest. Hand over her mouth, Ellen drew back into the shelter of a doorway. The man with the pistol pushed the handcart back securely into the barricade and walked back into the GPO. Ellen waited a few minutes and then walked quickly back the way she had come, feeling glass crunch underfoot, avoiding a body lying in the gutter, looking over her shoulder and breathless by the time she reached the quays. There was no hope that she would find the boys now, especially since it had got dark and some of the gaslights were not working.

When she eventually turned into Aberdeen Street she was sobbing with exhaustion and fear. A figure stepped out of the doorway; it was Harry. She threw her arms around him and hugged him to her. "Oh, thank God you are all right!" Mrs Kelly and her two boys emerged from their house and followed them into her kitchen.

Harry was flushed and excited and anxious to tell her of their adventures. "We didn't mean to worry you or Mrs Kelly. When we went to the park this morning we heard that there was going to be an armed rising in the city. We saw groups of Irish Volunteers marching and we followed them. They stopped in Sackville Street at the GPO. They went in and a little while later a man they called Patrick Pearse came out and read the Proclamation of the Irish Republic. Oh, Mother, it was wonderful! The Volunteers who were still outside clapped and so did we but some people laughed and turned away. Then Patrick Pearse went back inside and some of the volunteers left. We wanted to join the volunteers inside but an officer told us we were too young."

"Thank God he did! What were you thinking of, going in to the city like that? You could have been killed! There were soldiers and looters and bullets flying." Ellen was still shaking.

"Mother, I saw Annie! She was with a group of nurses that went into the GPO. I called her but she didn't hear me. She must be still in there. Will she be all right?"

"I don't know. There are very few soldiers around at the moment and no police but I don't know how this is going to end," Ellen said wearily.

Harry continued to talk excitedly after the Kellys had left. "Do you think Auntie Annie knows Patrick Pearse? Do you think we will have an independent country soon? Brother O'Hara says that we should have our own country, our own government and our own language. What do you think, Mother?"

"I think that if you ever leave me worrying like that again, I will murder you. Now, get ready for bed."

Ellen sat by the range long into the night, thinking about Annie and the scenes she had witnessed in the city. She didn't think the so-called Rising would last very long but she was concerned about Annie losing her training place. What had she been thinking when she got involved in that ridiculous charade? She wished James was there to put his arms around her and calm her fears but he was far away with much worse things to worry about.

Wearily, she went upstairs, checked on the children and went to bed. She slept uneasily and dreamed that James was trapped under a dead horse and that she was struggling to free him while the looters continued to drag their spoils through the shop windows. One of the looters turned to look at her and it was Annie. She woke up, feeling cold perspiration running between her breasts and her nightdress clinging damply to her. For a minute, she couldn't remember where she was. An eerie, ghostly light in the room was dawn breaking. She didn't want to sleep again in case the nightmare returned; she lay there, cold in her own sweat, and thought of James.

Chapter 18
The Aftermath

Next morning Ellen went up to Miss Ormond's shop for bread and eggs. The bread delivery had not yet come so there were quite a few women standing around, waiting and talking animatedly about the previous day's events.

"It is one thing playing at soldiers and wearing uniforms and marching but it is quite another to start burning down the city. Sure, nobody really understands what they are after anyway," one woman said.

"Did youse hear about the looting? They say that all the shops on Sackville Street were emptied. Course, the looters was all from the tenements; nobody around here would do a thing like that."

All the women nodded in agreement, feeling the superiority of those who live in a house with a toilet and running water to tenement dwellers.

"I heard that reinforcements are being brought in from England to deal with this. Haven't the British army enough on their hands with the war an' all without these shenanigans?" The speaker had a son in the British Army.

Ellen was glad to hear that there didn't seem to be any support among her neighbours for the Rising. She asked, "What is happening in the city today, do you know? Are the trams running?" Ellen had been thinking of visiting Annie whom she hoped would by now be back in the hospital.

"The whole city is shut down, missus. My Jem is a train driver and he drove a train from the Curragh this morning that was full of soldiers. He also saw a train from Belfast that brought in more troops. Them lads in the GPO will be lucky if they are not killed." The woman drew her shawl around her with the satisfaction of one who has insider information.

"It's not just the GPO. I heard that they took over buildings all over the place, even Jacobs!" The women continued to speculate, both excited and horrified by the events in the city.

By this time Peter had arrived with the bread and more news. "This might be the last bread you get for a while. I barely got the bread boards out on to the dray when I heard gunfire. I nearly killed the aul' horse trying to get him to hurry. I don't know how I am going to get him back to his stable. I'm not going back into the city until I hear it is all over."

Ellen bought some packets of biscuits, potatoes and the last of the eggs. Those who could afford it were buying in food and the shop was almost empty. If the Rising lasted another few days she realised that she would have no food left for the children. She walked back to the house thinking about Annie. She still hadn't heard from her sister and did not know whether she was in the GPO where Harry had seen her or safely back at the hospital.

Harry had been left looking after the others while she went to the shop. The previous evening, after the initial relief, she had been angry with him and forbidden him to go out for the next few days. Now, he greeted her arrival home with a pleading look.

"Please Mother, let me go up to the park with Paddy and John. I won't go near the city, I promise. There are only a few days left of the holidays and we want to play football."

Ellen was non-committal, "Eat your breakfast now and we will see." When the Kelly boys called, Ellen relented, warning Harry to be home in good time for his dinner. Harry was back by two o'clock, wide-eyed and excited by the stories he had heard from people he had met in the park.

"There are soldiers all over the city and they are arresting everyone who gets in their way," he told his mother.

"Then I think it would be safer for you to stay around here rather than go to the park. You can play football at the end of the street, can't you?"

By the next day, they could hear gunfire coming from the city. People said it was coming from the Mendicity Institute, near the Four Courts.

When the paper boy came around shouting out the headlines, Ellen bought a copy of the Irish Times which was the only newspaper that he had. "The others weren't printed, missus. There was no power in the city. The Irish Times has its own power supply."

Ellen scoured the paper for news of what was happening. The main item was about the opening of the Spring Show at the Royal Dublin Society grounds. Other articles were an update on the war. There were two articles about the insurrection in Dublin led by what the reporters variously called "rebels", Sinn Féiners or "revolutionists". One was a report on how insurgents had occupied strategic buildings around the city, the resistance they had met, the number of casualties and the looting of shops by the "Dublin underworld". There were a couple of light-hearted articles about what Dubliners could do when they were confined to their homes because Martial Law had been declared with a curfew from 7pm to 5am. The editorial hoped for "the speedy triumph of the forces of law and order".

Christy Murphy hadn't come around with the milk. Mary was crying because she was hungry. Ellen buttered a piece of bread for her and gave her a drink of water. She didn't know what to think. There were all sorts of rumours flying around. Heavy artillery fire could be heard coming from Kingsbridge Station and the city. She stood in the hall at the front door, knowing that someone was sure to come along to discuss the situation and relay the latest rumours. Neighbours hurrying by stopped long enough to share the latest gossip. The rising was said to be all over the country. Liberty Hall was destroyed. Someone said that Cork was held by the insurgents.

Another had heard that German warships had defeated the English and had landed in Ireland. Someone's cousin had seen more troops landing at Kingstown to quell the Rising.

Ellen realised that there must be some truth in some of these rumours. The general mood in the city seemed to be a mixture of exhilaration and terror. That night, it was difficult to sleep because of the noise of the heavy guns which the British Army had brought in. Ellen took the two girls into her own bed and lulled them to sleep by singing to them.

In the middle of the night she heard Joseph screaming. When she went in to their room, Harry was sitting up in bed with his arm around his brother. "It is all right, Mother. Joseph was having a bad dream."

Ellen looked out of the window. She could see that the sky was lit up by fires in the city. It was an eerie sight and strangely beautiful. She settled the two boys down to sleep again, returned to her own bed and slipped in between the two sleeping girls. She eventually drifted off to sleep thinking about James and the terrible sights that he must witness every day.

On Thursday morning Ellen realised that she had very little food left in the house. Miss Ormond's shop had closed the previous day because she had no stock left. May's shop on Arbour Hill was only selling to regular customers because they had run out of most things. There was still some oatmeal so the children could have that for breakfast but there was no milk to go with it. Harry and Joseph manfully ate the watery gruel that she served up but the two girls cried and wouldn't eat it. She gave them a couple of biscuits each and hoped that would keep them going. She ate nothing herself, just had a cup of black tea, because she didn't know how long the meagre rations would have to last.

Dinner consisted of mashed potatoes with a small bit of butter and a few carrots. At tea time they all had biscuits. The children stayed indoors, frightened by the swirls of smoke and the acrid smell of burning which was coming from the city. That night in the darkness they could see sparks flying through the air, rising flames licking into the sky and reflections of the fire making strange shapes on the skyline. The roar of the guns seemed even louder, the sound of the great guns vibrating around.

"It must be like this for James," she thought, "only much worse. At least we are in our own house and we are warm and safe. He has lived with horror like this for over two years. How can he bear it?"

The children were too terrified to go to bed so they all sat beside the range, the room lit only by the fiery sky, huddling together when a loud bombardment made the sash windows shake. At about ten o'clock there was a knock on the door. Thinking it was one of the neighbours, Ellen went to answer it. Annie stood on the doorstep, shaking and crying. She was wearing her nurse's uniform which, even in the darkness, Ellen could see was torn and stained.

"For God's sake, Annie, come in. Don't you know that there is a curfew?"

She drew her sister in and sat her down in an armchair by the range. Annie was shaking and freezing cold. Mary immediately ran to her mother and sat in her lap. "Harry, get a blanket from my bed. Annie, I will make you a cup of tea. There is no milk, I am afraid, but it will warm you up."

Annie huddled gratefully into the blanket and stroked her daughter's hair. She told her story in quick bursts, mopping her tears with the edge of the blanket. "Mr Connolly told some of the nurses to leave the GPO tonight and to try to get home. Most of us left but Elizabeth and two others stayed. Mr Connolly was wounded in the shin by a bullet that ricocheted off the wall and he was in terrible pain. Mr Pearse spoke to us and encouraged us by saying that reinforcements were coming from Dundalk. Oh, Ellen, the fighting was terrible! The soldiers were using Guinness lorries as armoured cars to attack the GPO. There was a big barricade in the street and it was hit by a shell and caught fire. The fire spread to surrounding buildings. Clery's and the Imperial Hotel were hit by so many shells that they crashed to the ground; there is nothing left of them. All the time there was looting going on and many of the looters were shot. Some of them were only children. Then everything on Sackville Street went quiet; it was deserted and still although we could hear the sounds of fighting coming from further away. That is when Mr Connolly told us to go and find our way separately home. I don't know Dublin very well so I was terrified. I wanted to stay but Elizabeth made me go."

"What possessed you to be in the GPO in the first place? I didn't know that you were so involved with the Sinn Féiners. How long were you in the GPO?" Ellen couldn't disguise her anger.

"Since Easter Monday when Mr Pearse read the Proclamation," Annie said proudly.

"I saw you there, Annie. Wasn't it wonderful?" Harry's eyes were shining as he interrupted the conversation.

"There is nothing wonderful about it: people have been killed, buildings destroyed, the whole city is on fire. What is it all for?" Ellen didn't mean to sound so stern and softened her face as she handed her sister a cup of black tea. "Are you hungry? We haven't got much but ..."

"No thanks. We had plenty of food in the GPO."

"How did you manage to get home?"

"One of the other girls, who lives on Arbour Hill, helped me. When it got quiet, we made our way down Henry Street and cut back out onto the quays. There were soldiers coming from the direction of Trinity College and we could hear gunfire from further up, maybe Grafton Street or the Green. We made our way back along the quays, dodging in and out of doorways until we got to Kingsbridge station. That seemed to be occupied by British soldiers. All along the way, we saw bodies lying on the ground. We looked at one or two of them to see if we could help but they were all dead. There were young boys running around in the midst of all the firing, looting and scavenging; they seemed to think it was a game. The Four Courts and another big building near it were full of British troops as well. We didn't realise that there was a curfew but suddenly the streets were completely deserted. We had to hide down an alleyway in a derelict house until it got dark. Then we made our way to Parkgate Street and Arbour Hill. Alice's family wanted me to stay there but I knew you must be worried about me so I decided to come home."

"I am glad you did although it must have been dangerous. What will happen about your place in the hospital now? Do they know where you were?" Ellen voiced her main concern.

"No, I was supposed to be visiting you on Easter Monday. They probably thought that I couldn't get back to the hospital. I am sure a lot of people couldn't get to work this week because it was impossible to cross the city."

Ellen looked at her sister's face; it was drawn and pale with dark smudges of tiredness under her eyes. "I am sure you haven't slept for nights. The children are worn out as well; they couldn't sleep with the noise. Let's all go to bed now. Maybe things will be better tomorrow."

Sun beaming in through the windows woke them up the next morning. It was Friday so Ellen hoped that the woman who sold fish would call because she had little food left in the house. The sunshine seemed to highlight the columns of grey smoke rising from buildings in the city. The acrid smell of burning pervaded the air and even seemed to get into the house. Ellen looked at her meagre food stocks. The little oatmeal that was left she made into gruel for the boys. The girls would not eat it, she knew. There was still a packet of biscuits and a few eggs. She gave the two girls a boiled egg and a biscuit each with a drink of water. She and Annie had black tea and a biscuit. There were a few potatoes and carrots and an onion which she would cook later. There was also a packet of rice which she could use to make puddings but she had no milk. Maybe if she cooked it with water and spooned the last of the jam into it, the children would eat it. Annie wanted to try to get back to the hospital while it was still daylight but Ellen talked her out of it. They still didn't know what was happening in the city. Again rumours were flying around. There was still fighting in the city because they could hear it. Annie wore some of Ellen's clothes while they washed and mended her uniform.

The children were very subdued and didn't ask to go outside. They ate their dinner early because they were all hungry. Ellen watched the makeshift dinner disappearing and wondered how they would manage if the fighting went on for much longer. By evening the children were hungry again: Kathleen and Mary were crying, Harry and Joseph quiet and listless. They went to bed early, Annie with the two girls either side of her, Ellen with the two boys.

Saturday morning they were woken by the clip clop of Christy Murphy's horse and cart outside. Ellen couldn't believe it. She ran to get her two big jugs. "Christy, I am so glad to see you. How did you manage to get here?"

Christy smiled at her as he filled her two jugs with foamy milk. "I didn't have to go into the city at all. My farm is out in north county Dublin so I came in the back roads. I didn't want to let my customers down. Here missus, would you like a bit of bacon?"

Christy kept a few pigs as well as cows and collected slops to feed the pigs from the people who bought milk from him. She often bought a bit of bacon when he had killed a pig.

"I would love it but I will have to pay you next week, if that is all right. I have no food left in the house and the children are hungry."

"That's grand, missus. Next week will be fine," Christy assured her.

That morning the children had sweet rice and a drink of milk for breakfast and they were quite happy. She enjoyed the luxury of a cup of tea with milk as she ate a biscuit. By the afternoon, an eerie silence seemed to have gripped the city. The guns had stopped but what did it mean?

Annie was determined to get back to the hospital and put on her uniform as soon as the guns stopped. Knowing that food supplies were very low she ate nothing but had a cup of tea with a drop of milk in it. "Don't worry about me, Ellen. I will be fine. My uniform will protect me. I have to get back to the hospital or I may lose my training place. Anyway, I want to see that Elizabeth is all right and also Mr. Connolly. I will try to get back to see you in a few days even if only for a few hours."

Mary was very upset when her mother left so to distract her Ellen took her in next door to pay a visit to Mrs Kelly. The older girls in the house were very fond of Mary and made a great fuss of her. Ellen and her neighbour exchanged what information they had about what was happening in the city. Ellen described Annie's experience and Mrs Kelly relayed the rumours she had heard. People said that a ceasefire had been called and then the rebels had surrendered. Paddy and John had seen the prisoners being marched to Richmond Barracks and crowds of Dubliners had booed them. People were being arrested all over the place, accused of being part of the Rising. They had seen dead bodies on the streets, some of them with white flags in their hands. The two women surmised that the Rising must be over and that things would return to normal.

During the next few days people became aware of what had happened in the city. Some outrages, like the murder by a British officer of the pacifist Francis Sheehy-Skeffington, came to light. Ellen remembered the gentle, kindly man she had met at a suffragette meeting and said a prayer for him. Thousands of people were arrested, among them a number of women. Some local men, whose wives Ellen knew, had been arrested, many of them with no connections to the Rising. Public opinion seemed to be turning in favour of the rebels. Listening to stories that were circulating about the leaders, Ellen found herself admiring their bravery. This was in spite of the fact that she heard herself and other British army wives being called "Separation Women", a derogatory term referring to the fact that they were paid an allowance for being separated from their husbands.

Then the court-martials began on the second of May. By this time the newspapers were covering the events very thoroughly. On the third of May, an incredulous Harry read out from the paper that three of the leaders, Patrick Pearse, Thomas MacDonagh and Thomas Clarke had been executed early that morning. Harry and Joseph were grief-stricken. During the following week, the rest of the leaders were executed. The last to die was James Connolly on Friday 12th May; he was so ill that he had to be tied to a chair to be shot. News of this inflamed public opinion, which was already becoming hostile to the British since they had recently tried to impose conscription on the Irish.

When Annie came to visit the following Sunday, she was inconsolable. "Mr Connolly was so brave and such a gentleman. How could they do such a terrible thing? Elizabeth told me that the doctors said he had only days to live anyway. He had gangrene in his leg."

"Is Elizabeth all right? Did she get back to the hospital?" Ellen asked.

"No, she is in prison in Kilmainham. So is her friend, Kathleen Lynn. Only for Mr Connolly, I would be there too. I was able to see her for a few minutes yesterday and I brought her some food. She is being held with a few other women and they are in good spirits.

They haven't been tried yet. She says that they could be sent to prison in England."

"I hope she will be released soon. After all, she was not really involved; she was just doing her duty as a nurse."

"I don't think the British will see it like that!" Annie said. "Did you know that she was the one that Mr Pearse chose to carry the white flag to the British General when they decided to call a ceasefire? She was with Pearse when he surrendered."

"No, I didn't know that. She must be very brave." Ellen found herself admiring the insurgents more and more.

"She is. I better go now. One of the other nurses swopped shifts with me so that I could come to see you and Mary. I will see you again in a few weeks."

When Annie had gone, Harry and Joseph went out to boast to their friends about their aunt's part in the Rising. Ellen made herself a cup of tea and sat down to think about the news that she had got from Annie and various neighbours over the previous few days. Could this British Army that they said had committed so many atrocities, be the same British Army that she had known in India, the same British Army whose uniform James wore, the same British Army for whom thousands of Irishmen were fighting? She wondered if the Irishmen fighting in the trenches had heard of the events at home and how it was affecting them. Some Dublin Fusiliers had been deployed to attack the GPO; some of them, it was said, had brothers or relatives among the rebels. She had heard that a number of Connaught Rangers, James's own regiment, had also been involved in putting down the insurrection. How would James have felt if he had been ordered to fight his own countrymen? James never mentioned the Rising in his letters but wrote about a terrible battle, fought at about the same time, in which thousands of men were killed, including many Irishmen. In the newspapers they referred to this as "The Battle of the Somme".

Chapter 19
1917-18: The Tide Turns

The newspapers were now saying that the British government, in a bid to restore stability, had offered to introduce Home Rule to Ireland, but excluding six of the counties in Ulster. By the beginning of 1917, they had released all the remaining rebels. Public opinion continued to turn against the British government and in favour of the rebels. Ellen saw this happening in her own home: Harry had always admired the leaders of the Rising, especially Pearse; Joseph now joined his brother in singing patriotic songs about the executed leaders and joined Na Fianna; Kathleen followed the lead of her brothers and even baby Mary could join in the revolutionary songs. Annie was a very active member of Sinn Féin, the party which had won the public support which used to belong to John Redmond's Irish Parliamentary Party. Sinn Féin wanted nothing less than an Irish republic and won two by-elections that year with overwhelming public support.

All the upheaval and turmoil at home in Dublin was a distraction from concern about the war and suddenly, on the eleventh of November 1918, the war was over. Celebrations of the Armistice were muted in Dublin, particularly in nationalist areas.

Ellen waited patiently for news of James's homecoming. Irish soldiers began to return home from the war to a country that did not want them. At best, they were an embarrassment to their families; at worst, they were treated with hostility. Many of them were shell-shocked or suffering from the effects of gas. Many more were missing limbs. Some brought with them a terrible legacy of the war, Spanish flu.

Ellen's neighbour on the other side was a Mrs Hackett. She and her family were not popular in the area because she was the widow of a member of the Dublin Metropolitan Police and it was suspected that she was a police informer. One night when the children had gone to bed and Ellen was steeping the oatmeal to make porridge the next morning, she heard a banging on the back of the range. This was a well-known method in the neighbourhood of summoning help from a neighbour. Usually it was a woman who had unexpectedly gone into labour and needed help or a sudden illness of one of the family.

Ellen barely knew Mrs Hackett. She had chatted to her on a few occasions when they had met in Miss Ormond's shop. Now she came out onto the street and found her neighbour distraught and waiting for her.

"It's my Maisie! I don't know what is wrong with her. She was out until late with her fella last night. He is just back from the war and I suppose that they were up in the park courting till all hours. She was cold and shivering last night but I thought it was just a cold. Would you take a look at her for me, missus?"

Ellen found herself being drawn into the house and up the stairs to the front bedroom. There were two double beds in the room. Three girls peered at her over the blankets from one. In the other a young girl lay with the bedclothes thrown off and her nightdress clinging to her wetly. There was a smell of vomit and the air was glutinous with the heat and perspiration coming off her body.

"Maisie, let Mrs Devereux have a look at you". The mother tried to speak to her but the girl was muttering incoherently and thrashing about in the bed. "She started to vomit this morning. I don't know what to do for her. She won't even drink any water. Do you think she has pneumonia or T.B.?"

Ellen knew that people in Dublin had a dreadful fear of T.B. which had wiped out whole families, especially in the tenements. "I don't think you would be vomiting with either of those ailments. I think you should call the doctor. Maisie is very sick."

"I can't afford the doctor. My pension is small and I have four girls to feed." Mrs Hackett was wringing her hands and weeping.

"Doctor O'Meara only lives down on the North Circular Road. He would probably let you pay later." Ellen said sympathetically. "Would you like me to go for him?"

"If you wouldn't mind; I don't know what else to do."

Doctor O'Meara was not very pleased to be called out from his bed, especially when Ellen told him that Mrs Hackett would pay him later. However, he was a kindly man and soon took Ellen in his car back to the house.

He examined Maisie carefully. He turned to her mother. "You say her young man is a soldier, just returned home? How is he?"

"I don't know how he is, they live in Kilmainham. Why are you asking me that?" The mother looked worried.

"Because, I think that Maisie has caught Spanish flu from her young man. I have seen a number of cases like this already. They are calling it Spanish flu or trench fever and it seems that the soldiers are bringing it back with them," the doctor explained.

"I've never heard of Spanish flu," said Ellen. "There is nothing in the newspapers about it."

"I have a friend that I went to medical school with who lives in Belfast. He wrote to me a few months ago about this mysterious illness. They had quite a severe outbreak in Belfast and they were calling it the Plague. Some of the English newspapers have had articles about it but they are saying that it is rampant in Germany and Austria."

"Will she be all right, Doctor?" Mrs Hackett interrupted.

"The next twenty-four hours are crucial. Try to bring down her temperature and make her drink liquids. I will come back in the morning to see how she is doing. It is very contagious so move the other girls out of that room," he advised.

Once the doctor had gone, Ellen helped her neighbour to move the other girls. Then they sponged Maisie and changed the soiled bedclothes. She was coughing uncontrollably and did not seem to recognise her mother.

It was almost time to get the children ready for school so Ellen went home, scrubbed herself with carbolic soap and changed her clothes before she made breakfast. She asked Mrs Kelly to look after Mary while she went back next door.

The doctor was there before her and looking very serious. Maisie was coughing up blood and making choking sounds. "I am afraid that there is nothing more that I can do for her. I am very sorry, Mrs Hackett."

The older woman was sobbing. "What about the other girls, Doctor? Nora, the youngest, is not very strong. Will she get it? She was sharing Maisie's bed."

"It is impossible to know who will get it," he said as he closed his bag. "If it is any consolation to you, it seems to be the strongest and healthiest who are stricken down by this disease. But we know very little about it or how to treat it."

Ellen's heart went out to her neighbour and she was reminded of the awful days around Nancy's death. She sat with her neighbour for the few hours it took Maisie to choke to death on her own blood. Then she helped the distraught mother to wash and lay out her daughter in preparation for the undertaker.

The doctor had told them that the funeral should be as soon as possible. The family had no money for a funeral so Ellen and Mrs Kelly went around the neighbours who contributed what small amount of money they could. Even though Mrs Hackett was not popular, a pauper's funeral was something that they all dreaded.

Harry had been left in charge of the children while Ellen went to the funeral. When she returned, he was standing in the kitchen, white-faced and clutching an unopened telegram. She tore the flimsy paper open and read the first words.

"Papa is coming home!" She could hardly believe it even though it was the news she had been waiting for.

The children hugged her and each other. Their celebrations were soon tempered when she read the rest of it which said that James had been wounded again, during the last days of the war. He was in a hospital in France with a bullet wound in his shoulder and would not be released for a few weeks. He was also suffering from pneumonia. It added that he had been awarded the Military Cross for bravery.

She proudly told the children about his medal and that he would not be home for Christmas after all. "Papa has been wounded and he also has pneumonia so he will have to stay in hospital for a little while until he is well enough to travel. He was awarded the Military Cross for bravery. Isn't that wonderful?"

Harry looked at her coldly. "What did he get the medal for?"

"It seems that they were being fired on by their own side and Papa risked his own life to signal to them," Ellen explained. "I don't know the details but Papa will tell us all about it when he comes home."

Harry ignored the explanation. "Will Father be wearing his uniform when he comes home? I do not think that it would be a good idea. People around here hate the British army now."

Joseph looked at his brother and then turned to Ellen. "Will Papa, er, Father be carrying a gun when he comes back?"

Ellen looked at her two sons and realised that they had grown up while their father had been at war. Harry was now fourteen but looked older with his height and broad build. Joseph was almost twelve but was small for his age. However, a quick intelligence and a quiet intensity about him made him seem older than his years.

"I forget what Papa looks like. I remember that he used to carry me when we went to the park." Kathleen was oblivious to the tension in the room.

Ellen looked gratefully at her. "You were only six when he went to war. Now you are ten and very grown up. Papa will not believe that you are the little girl he left behind."

"Will Papa still be a soldier when he comes home?"

"No, he will have left the army. Do you remember before he went away, he used to work in the Post Office? Maybe he will be able to get that job again. Won't it be lovely when we are all together again as a family?"

Kathleen smiled and nodded but the two boys simply looked at her blankly.

Ellen was glad that Christmas was coming and would provide a diversion until James could come home. It would also give her time to talk to the children about James and hopefully to help each of them to remember the attentive and loving father that he had been.

When Grace Geraghty came to visit, she confided her fears to her. "Perhaps I should have talked to them more about him: perhaps I should have revealed the terrible time that he has endured and the horrible sights that he has seen. Then perhaps they would have been more sympathetic to him and looking forward to seeing him again instead of seeing him as just a member of the British army."

"He has been away a long time," Grace consoled her. "Four years is a very long time in the life of a child. They probably don't really remember him very well. Telling them about the horrors he has endured would not have done them any good."

"That is true. I didn't want to worry them and I found it difficult to sleep myself when I read some of James's letters and thought about the sights that he was careful to only vaguely describe."

Grace put her arm around her friend. "Give them time to get to know him when he returns. At the moment, the Rising, its leaders and the aftermath of the executions seem more real and admirable to the two boys because it is all around them. Now, I have to go and get ready for my performance tonight."

"We will see you on Christmas Day, then, Grace?" Ellen asked.

"Yes, thanks for inviting me. I am looking forward to it."

Christmas 1918 was their fifth Christmas without James. On Christmas Eve, Ellen went in to visit Mrs Hackett. None of the other girls had caught the Spanish flu but they had heard that Maisie's young man had also died. Mrs Hackett had returned to her taciturn self and seemed almost resentful of Ellen's interference in her life, especially the fact that the neighbours had contributed money for the funeral. Her pride was hurt.

Annie was able to join them for a couple of days. She was not surprised to hear about Maisie's death. Before Christmas, the Meath hospital had been overwhelmed with cases of Spanish flu, many of them returned soldiers. "There was very little we could do for them," she said to Ellen. "Some young, strong people died of it within twenty-four hours. Others, who were more fragile, recovered. The doctors do not know what to make of it. They are calling it an epidemic in America, so I heard. It is strange that there is not more about it in the papers."

"There was not a lot about what was really going on in the war, either," Ellen said. "I think the government only allows the newspapers to tell us what they want us to think."

Violet and her children also came for Christmas dinner. Desmond was now a tall sixteen year old who resembled his dead father. He was still working as a messenger boy and, like Annie, was closely involved with Sinn Féin. Julia was the same age as Harry and working in a laundry. She was a pretty girl with the same untamed head of red curls as her mother. She followed Harry with her eyes all the time but was too shy to speak to him. The twins, Esther and Ellie, were the same age as Joseph and spent their time teasing him and making him blush. William, the youngest, was eight and a good friend of Kathleen's. Mary, at four, was the baby of the group and was passed around the older children like a good-natured doll, until Annie claimed her daughter and sat holding her on her knee.

When Grace arrived, she joined Annie, Desmond and Harry chatting animatedly about the recent General Election, held a few weeks previously, in which Sinn Féin had won seventy-three parliamentary seats.

"Countess Markievicz is the first woman in the United Kingdom to win a seat in parliament! Isn't that wonderful, Ellen?" Ellen smiled at Annie's enthusiasm.

Grace was quick to respond. "Yes, but we still have not got votes for women, unless of course you are over thirty and a landowner!"

"Don't worry, Grace. Once we get independence, all women in Ireland will get the vote." Harry was almost as enthusiastic about women's suffrage as he was about independence.

He, Desmond and Annie had all been involved in the election campaign and discussed the fact that the successful candidates would not take their seats at Westminster and what the consequences were likely to be.

Ellen looked around at all the animated faces as she and Violet served up the dinner of roast rabbit and tried to steer the conversation away from politics. The younger children were now pulling the paper crackers which Annie had brought and laughing at the jokes contained in them. Grace poured out a glass of port wine for each of the women from a bottle which she had brought. The room was festive and warm and Ellen found herself wondering, as she sipped her drink, what James was doing and whether he had a Christmas dinner. His last letter had been a bit more cheerful and he wrote that he was recovering very well and hoped to get back home by the end of February. She had not seen him for four and a half years and she realised that they both must have changed.

A few women she had met through the suffragette meetings had husbands who returned early from the war, wounded or gassed. The wives had told her that the homecoming had been strained and that the men had found it very difficult to fit back in to civilian life. They did not go into details but had hinted at fractious relationships with children who had got used to living without them and marital problems with wives who had become accustomed to being independent. She felt sure that her love for James and his for her would help them overcome any difficulties that he might experience. The attitude of her sons to their father was more worrying but, looking at their happy, bright faces, she hoped that they would be able to return to the close loving relationship that they had enjoyed with him before the war.

Grace was proposing a toast. "Here is to peace at home and abroad!"

Harry lifted his glass of lemonade, drank and raised his glass again. "Here is to a free and independent Ireland."

Annie was not to be outdone with toasts. "Here is to equal rights for women!"

"We will all drink to that," Ellen and Grace said in unison.

Chapter 20
1919: The Legacy of War

Once Christmas was over, Ellen set about spring-cleaning the house in preparation for James's homecoming. She knew that she would have to reorganise the bedrooms. The two girls had developed the habit of sleeping in her bed for the frightening nights during the Rising. The two boys shared the front bedroom and Annie occupied the small parlour whenever she could stay for a night. The girls would have to move down to the parlour and Annie could squeeze in with them for the odd night. Ellen was looking forward to sharing the bed with her husband again and allowed herself to remember what their lovemaking had been like. That was something that they had both enjoyed and she hoped that they would again.

She wondered whether he would find her very changed. Four, almost five, years was a long time. Leaning in to the mirror on the door of the big wardrobe, she examined her face. She had grown thinner over the last few years. There were some grey hairs threaded through the brown hair at her temples but Grace had shown her how to roll it at the sides to hide the grey. She experimented until she got it to her satisfaction. Grace had also offered to dye her hair for her but she had demurred, thinking that it was all right for an actress to dye her hair but not a woman like her. Her hands in the mirror were rough and reddish where once they had been white and soft. She could make a paste of oatmeal and milk and apply it to her hands and her face and it would soften and whiten her skin. But her eyes, that James had told her were like cornflowers, were as blue as ever and though she had a few lines around them, the skin on her face was clear and smooth.

At the back of the wardrobe were some of the dresses that she

212

had brought from India. She took them out and [...]
up against her. She could smell the sandalwood [...]
always remind her of India. The dresses were flims[...]
not at all suitable for the Irish climate but she w[...]
could make a blouse out of one of them. She sele[...]
had long sleeves and was a soft shade of blue. M[...]
door was good with a needle; she would ask for he[...]
clothes were out of the question but the blue blouse [...]
good with her black Sunday skirt.

Next she began to think about the food she would [...]
his first meal. James had always been fond of bacon and [...]
so she would ask Christy Murphy to bring her a bit of bac[...]
wasn't sure of the exact date of James's arrival but the [...]
would keep for a few days. A few bottles of stout would ma[...]
celebration and she would ask May's to deliver it becaus[...]
wouldn't like to be seen buying it. Moving about the h[...]
polishing and dusting, she found herself singing "After the B[...]
the song she sang on her wedding day. The feelings that she h[...]
about James coming home was a lot like her feelings on h[...]
wedding day, a mixture of happiness and fear, joy and dread.

James actually arrived a few days earlier than Ellen had
anticipated. The children had gone to school, Mary was in bed in
the small parlour having a nap and she had been scrubbing out
the kitchen. She had scrubbed her way out to the small hall and
was scouring the granite front step when she looked up and saw a
pair of boots on the pavement outside.

She scrambled to her feet, almost knocking over the bucket of
water when she realised who it was. "Oh my God! James, is it
really you?"

"It is me all right, Ellen, my love." He pulled her to him,
hugging her so fiercely that she couldn't breathe. The familiar
feel of him made her eyes fill up with the remembered loneliness

he previous years without him. He was crying too. A
hbour passed by and looked at them curiously but she didn't
.

She kissed him and pulled him into the hall. "How did you get
e? Why didn't you write to say you were coming earlier? I
nted to have everything ready for you. I have nothing ..."

"I just wanted to get home to you and the children. I asked the
octor if I could be discharged a few days early. Some friends of
ine were travelling to Dublin so he agreed if I went with them."
His eyes were still fixed on her as though he was afraid she would
vanish if he took his eyes off her.

She took him by the hand. "Come inside, James and sit by the
range. You must be tired and hungry after all that travel." She
knew she should go out to the yard and fill the kettle to make him
a cup of tea but she couldn't take her eyes off him, couldn't move
away from him. Suddenly conscious that she was wearing her old
pinafore over her clothes, she pulled it off and tried to brush back
the damp tendrils of her hair which were sticking to her face.

He leaned forward from the chair and pulled her down to sit
on the arm. His hand caressed her face. "I used to try to visualise
your face every night when I could not sleep. When the guns
made so much noise I used to block them out by imagining you
singing to the children. I missed you all so much." The tears were
rolling down his face again.

"We missed you too," she said as she kissed away his tears.
"We prayed for you every night and asked God to bring you back
safely to us. Now, I must make you a cup of tea with a bit of soda
bread. I am sure that you haven't had that in a long time."

While the kettle boiled, she cut the bread and put butter and
jam on it. She took the chair opposite him while he ate and drank
and studied him hungrily. He looked different, older. He had
always had a straight military bearing but now his shoulders were

drawn forward, almost as though to protect himself. With his overcoat off she could see that he was much thinner. His elegant moustache was gone and his hair was now more grey than blond. His skin had a yellow pallor and there were shadows that looked like bruises under his eyes. When he looked up and directly into her eyes she saw the most profound change in him. His light blue eyes had been one of the most attractive things about him. They always seemed to have a smile in them; they lit up with amusement or enthusiasm when he was talking. Now, his eyes were dead, as though they had seen too much.

They both jumped as the door was thrown open. "Mother, do you know what happened in school today?" As usual, Harry couldn't wait to get inside to tell her his news. He and Joseph rushed into the kitchen to throw their schoolbags down.

James stood up. "Harry, Joseph, I am so glad to see you!"

Joseph threw himself into his father's arms. "Papa! We thought you weren't coming for another few days."

Harry stood back, his arms rigidly by his sides. He was taller than his father.

"Welcome home, Father. I trust you had a good journey?"

James looked uncertainly at his eldest son and then proffered his hand. Harry took it without moving towards him so that they had to stretch towards each other.

"You look well, son. You are taller than me now." There was an awkward silence.

Ellen broke it. "Sit down boys and I will get you a cup of milk. What was the news about school that you were going to tell me when you came in?"

"There was a competition in school. We had to write a poem in Irish about one of the leaders of the Rising. I wrote about Patrick Pearse and I won the prize," Harry said proudly. "Look, it is a book called the Anthology of Irish Fairy and Folk Tales

215

edited by William Butler Yeats."

James reached for the book and traced the Gaelic lettering on the leather cover with his finger. "Well done, son. That looks like a lovely book. Who did you say you wrote your poem about?"

"Patrick Pearse. He was one of the leaders of the Rising. He was executed by the British. Have you heard of him?" Harry's tone was cold.

"No, we didn't get much news when I was at the front. I heard a little bit about it when I was in hospital but I don't remember the names."

Joseph interrupted. "Are you all right now, Papa? Is your shoulder better? Will you be staying at home now?"

"Yes, Jo-Jo, I am much better, just a bit tired and I will be staying at home from now on," James smiled at his youngest son.

Just then Mary woke up and Kathleen arrived home having walked with Violet's girls. At first she looked shyly at James but was soon hugging him and sitting on his knee, demanding a story, just as she used to do four years previously. Ellen brought Mary into the kitchen where she ran to Harry, sat on his knee and looked suspiciously at James.

"There will be plenty of time for stories, Kathleen. Papa is very tired after his long journey. He needs to go for a rest now and maybe he will tell a short story after tea," Ellen said, realising that James was white-faced and exhausted and making a great effort to respond to his family.

She climbed the stairs after him, found him a nightshirt and made sure that he had a drink of water beside him. "I will leave you out some clean clothes and if you feel like it you could get up after a few hours and have some tea. If you are too tired, you can see the children in the morning."

"Thanks, Ellen. I will be better able for them when I have a sleep." He sounded weary. She kissed him on the forehead and

216

closed the door quietly.

Harry and Joseph had a Fianna meeting to attend so she gave them their tea early. The two girls played in what was now their bedroom and Ellen took the opportunity to tidy herself up. Her newly-altered blouse and her good skirt were in the big wardrobe in the boy's room. Soundlessly she climbed the stairs and changed her clothes. She brushed out her hair and rearranged it in the style which hid the grey hairs.

James was snoring gently in the other room. The door was shut tight but she pushed it and looked in at her husband. He had taken one of the blankets off the bed and wrapped it around himself, even covering his head. The clean clothes and nightshirt were where she had left them and there was no sign of his day clothes; he was probably still wearing them. How could he breathe like that with his head completely covered? She moved closer and gently tugged at the blanket where it covered the top of his head. There was a sudden movement and James was crouching on the bed with his back to the wall, a look of terror in his eyes.

"It is all right, James. It is me, Ellen. I was just trying to make you more comfortable."

A look of recognition spread slowly over his face; he began to cry, great racking sobs. "I thought I dreamed it, you and the children. I thought I was back in the trenches. I covered my head because of the gas. I couldn't breathe ..."

Ellen reached for him and cradled his head on her breast. "It's all right, my love. You are home now. I will take care of you. Let me take your boots off. Now, you can go back to sleep. Would you like a hot drink or something to eat?"

Slowly, he lay down again and she managed to pull his boots off.

"No, I am not hungry. I will just drink a sup of this water. I

217

am so tired that I think I could sleep for a week."

"You sleep for as long as you want. You will feel much better in the morning." She kissed him, feeling the salt tears still on his face and tucked him in, just as she would one of the children.

Kathleen and Mary were in bed when the boys returned home from their meeting. They immediately wanted to know where their father was.

"He is sleeping. He is still recovering from his wound, you know, and it is a very long journey from France, through England to Dublin. After a few days rest he will back to himself but until then, we must look after him." She was hoping that Harry would be more sympathetic towards his father but he ignored her explanation. He was visibly excited.

"Mother, tonight at our meeting we heard that the Sinn Féin members who were elected met as the first Irish parliament called Dáil Éireann. That means that we will soon have an Irish Republic and be independent from Britain. I am going to join the Irish army as soon I am old enough."

"So am I." Joseph did not want to be outdone by his brother.

Ellen put an arm around each of her sons. "I don't think there will be an independent Ireland for a while. For the moment, while Papa is recovering, please try not to discuss politics in front of him. He has been fighting the Germans in France and Flanders like many other Irishmen. He does not know what has been going on in Ireland and it will take him some time to adjust."

Joseph smiled up at her. "I am glad Papa is back. I know a few boys in school whose fathers did not come back from the war. They are very sad and I would not like to be like them. I am sure that when he understands what is going on in Ireland he will feel the same way as we do."

Harry looked at his brother, moved away and sat in one of the armchairs. "Father will have to get used to the fact that the British

218

are not wanted here."

"Harry, your father is as Irish as you and proud of it," Ellen remonstrated. "He was fighting to free Belgium, a small country like ours, from the Germans. You know that he was awarded the Military Cross for bravery. He is just as brave as the men who fought in the Rising. He has been wounded twice and saw terrible things. Please remember that when you speak to him."

Harry never liked to earn her displeasure. Now he moved over to stand beside her and put his arm around her shoulder. "I'm sorry if you thought I wasn't nice to Father. It was just such a shock to come home and see him sitting there."

"I know. I got quite a shock myself. Come on now, it is time for bed for the two of you. Go upstairs quietly so you don't wake Papa." Ellen followed the boys upstairs and kissed them goodnight.

She opened her own bedroom door and put the candle on the bedside table. It was softer and less likely to wake James than the gaslight. He had wrapped himself like a mummy again in the blanket and nothing could be seen of him except a tuft of hair. She undressed and managed to squeeze in beside him, pulling the sheet and remaining blanket over her as best she could. Tentatively, she put her arm around his huddled form and cuddled in to him. Memories came flooding in to her mind of other nights when they had slept in each other's arms in Galway, India and their early days in Dublin. They had always gone to sleep with their arms around each other. It was one of the things that she had missed the most during the lonely years without him.

She was just drifting off to sleep when James began shouting and thrashing about in the bed. She tried to restrain him and one of his flailing arms caught her across the mouth. She could taste blood; her lips were stinging from the blow. His eyes were closed and he was still shouting. She shushed him and tried to hold him still, all the while quieting him as she would a child. His eyes opened but he didn't seem to see her; he was still shouting. She thought that he was saying, "Get down, get down!" She got out of bed and switched on the gaslight. The shouting stopped and he looked bewildered.

The door opened and Harry and Joseph were standing there, looking terrified. "Mama, what happened? Why is Papa shouting? What happened to your mouth?"Joseph was trembling; his big eyes were fixed on her face.

"It is all right, Jo-Jo. Papa was just having a bad dream, just like you sometimes do. Mama will make him better. Let's go back to bed."

Ellen looked gratefully at Harry. "Papa was having a bad dream. He shouted out in his dream and moved his arm and I got in the way so I banged my mouth. It will be better in the morning."

James was looking from the terrified face of Joseph to her bleeding mouth. "What happened? Did I do that? I thought we were being attacked and I ..."

Harry put an arm protectively around Joseph. "You were shouting very loudly and Jo-Jo got a fright. He is all right now. Goodnight, Father, goodnight Mother."

Once the boys had left the room, Ellen set about straightening the bed. She persuaded James to take off his sweaty clothes and put on a nightshirt. While he was changing she could see the livid scars of his two wounds on his thin body. He lay down under the blankets and turned away, avoiding looking at her as she changed. Gently she lay down beside him, her arm around his chest, her knees behind his. She kissed the back of his neck and felt the tension in his body.

He half turned to her. "I am sorry, Ellen, I can't ..."

220

"I just want to hold you, my love. There will be plenty of time for other things." She held him like that for the rest of the night. From time to time he cried out or moved violently but each time she held him and soothed him like a sick child.

In the morning she woke to find him propped up on one elbow, gazing at her. He kissed her and stroked her face. "I still cannot believe that I am home with you and the children. "

"I can hardly believe it either."

He put one arm under her shoulder and moved her so that she lay on his chest. "It is going to take me a while to adjust to life at home. You will all have to be patient with me."

"I know that, my love." Ellen kissed him and got out of bed. "Now, let me get you a good breakfast. I got in some Hafner's rashers and sausages especially for you. I have to get the children off to school first so you have a sleep while I do that. You can see them later when they come home."

It took her a few minutes to wake Harry and Joseph. They were grumpy and tired after their broken sleep of the night before but still anxious to see their father. Kathleen and Mary had obviously heard nothing of the drama and chattered away, full of questions about Papa.

When Kathleen and the boys had left, Ellen settled Mary down to playing with her dolls and prepared breakfast for James. She went upstairs to wake him and to ask if he would like breakfast in bed.

He laughed at the suggestion. "That would make me feel like I was an invalid again," he said. "Anyway, I will enjoy sitting at a table and having a meal properly. In the trenches, eating was a very rough and ready affair."

He ate his rashers, sausages and eggs with great enjoyment, dipping his sausages and soda bread into the egg yolk. Mary sat watching him and he gave her some choice pieces, much to her delight. "You are the image of your mama," he told her.

"Which Mama? Mama Ellen or Mama Annie?" she wanted to know.

"Annie," he said as he popped a piece of sausage into her mouth.

Ellen sat opposite him, drinking a cup of tea and attentive to his needs.

He smiled at her. "Mary reminds me of Nancy. You know, I think Nancy was watching over me in France. I don't know how else I was spared. Most of my battalion was wiped out but I was one of the few survivors. I was wounded twice and missing in action for almost a week but I came home. That is more than poor Des and most of my friends did." His voice choked on the last sentence.

She could see the tears in his eyes. "I am sure Nancy was looking after you. We were praying for you too. We are blessed that you came home to us. I know so many families who lost loved ones, fathers, husbands, sons, brothers."

Mary then created a diversion by insisting on showing James her doll. He wiped his eyes and took her onto his knee while Ellen boiled a kettle on the range so that he could shave. She watched him perform the familiar ritual as he spread the foam over his face and grimaced to one side and then another as he glided the open razor over the contours of his face. She was glad to see that he was beginning to grow his moustache again, avoiding his upper lip with the razor and fingering the growing stubble there when he finished. She had found the pomade which he used to use on his hair and left it out for him. He combed his still-thick hair into the style he used to favour and turned to look for her approval. Then he returned upstairs and put on his waistcoat and jacket. When he came down, she handed him his gold pocket-watch and chain which she had looked after for him

222

and he arranged them carefully on his waistcoat.

She watched him as she was brushing his hat. "You are still the handsome man I fell in love with."

He smiled at her with a perceptible straightening of his shoulders as he took the hat and placed it at a jaunty angle on his head. "I think I will pop down to Ryan's to see if any of my old butties are about. Then I think I will take a walk in the park. The fresh air will do me good."

He kissed her and she watched him walking down the street, hardly able to believe that the receding figure was James, her husband, who had come home safe to her.

The children had eaten their tea, done their homework and were all in bed when he eventually arrived home. He was unsteady on his feet and almost dragged the tablecloth off when he sat down clumsily at the table. She took his hat and helped him off with his coat and then set about getting him his tea.

"Have you had anything to eat at all? You must be starving. I have some bacon and cabbage, would you like that?"

"I'd like a small bit of bacon and cabbage. I haven't got much appetite at the moment. I'd love a bottle of stout to wash it down, if you have one. You are very good to me, Ellen."

He grasped her hand and pulled her down to sit on his knee. The sweet grainy smell of porter wafted from him.

"I'll get you a bottle, love. You can have it while I heat up the bacon and cabbage. I am so happy to have you home, James."

She put the dinner in the oven of the range to heat while he poured the porter. She watched him pour the black liquid sideways so that a foamy head rose up at the top of the glass. He downed it in two gulps. He drank the second one more slowly, savouring the bittersweet taste.

"I met a few of me aul' comrades that survived, below in Ryan's. A lot of other friends that joined up at the same time as me never came back, like poor Des. We were talking about old times and remembering them that are gone. Willy Ryan gave us a few drinks on the house. We were drinking a toast to fallen comrades when this fella came over and asked, 'What about the men that died for Ireland in Easter Week?' I said to him that we were only back from the Front and didn't know the details of Easter Week as he called it. Before we knew it he had called a few of his friends over and they started throwing insults at us, calling us British bastards. One of them hit Mick and it looked like it was going to be a free for all but Willy Ryan saw what was going on and came over and threw them out."

Ellen sat down opposite him. "Things have changed in Dublin, James. Feelings against the British are running very high. It is because of the executions of the leaders of the Rising, you see, and also because they tried to impose conscription here. I am sure it will all calm down in a little while."

"That is what Willy said. I hope he is right." He began to eat the dinner that she had placed in front of him. "This is lovely, Ellen. I'd forgotten what bacon and cabbage tasted like."

The food had the effect of sobering him up and he began to tell her a little about what it had been like at the Front. "You cannot imagine how lonely it was for all of us, not just because we were missing our families but because so many of our comrades died. It got so bad that I was afraid to get too close to anyone in case they too died. Comrades became your family when you were in a filthy trench and trying to stay alive. We lost any idea of time and hours stretched into days, weeks and even months. Sometimes I thought that I had died and gone to Hell and my punishment was to keep fighting for eternity."

"Well, you are home safely now. Do you remember what I used to say to the children when they hurt themselves, that I would kiss it and make it better? I will kiss you and make you

224

better, I promise, my love."

They kissed, gently at first and then deeply, and went upstairs. She undressed him slowly and kissed his scars. Then she undressed herself while he watched and they lay down together. It seemed almost like the first time they made love except that this time, she took the lead. He lay passively, his body still tense, while she caressed him all over and then coaxed him into an erection. She guided him into her and gasped his name as he came very quickly. She felt herself shuddering in response to him. Afterwards, they lay in each others' arms and kissed gently; his face was wet with tears. She kissed them away and murmured to him, telling him how much she loved him. After a while, she realised that he was asleep. She settled herself, her back to his belly, his arm around her. She matched her breathing to his and soon she too was asleep.

She didn't know how long she had been asleep when the shouting started. James was still asleep but twitching convulsively and shouting out what sounded like a warning. Mindful not to wake him too suddenly from his nightmare, she stroked his face and made soothing sounds in his ear.

The shouting stopped and he sat up, looking around in bewilderment. "Ellen, where am I? What happened? Who was shouting?"

"It is all right. You are safe now. You were shouting because you had a bad dream. Go back to sleep now." She realised that Harry and Joseph were in the doorway again. "Go back to bed, boys. Papa will be all right. It was just a bad dream."

"Goodnight, Father. I hope you sleep well now." Harry drew his brother back into their own bedroom and Ellen could hear him soothing Joseph and reassuring him.

James's nightshirt was soaked in sweat. She found a clean one and he put it on. "I'm sorry, Ellen. I didn't mean to upset you and

225

the children like that. Maybe I came home too soon."

"That is nonsense, love. Home is the best place for you to recover. Now, try to get back to sleep."

Neither of them was able to sleep. They both pretended, lying quietly and breathing evenly, but each knew that the other was awake.

Next morning, when she called the children for school, the two boys were sleepy and irritable. They hadn't slept very well either. She hoped that James's nightmares would not go on for much longer. Surely being back in his own bed in his own house would make him feel safer?

That day was the first time since James returned that the family sat down together for dinner. The boys arrived home from school just as Ellen was serving up the meal at the table. Harry and Joseph sat in their accustomed places with Harry opposite Ellen. Kathleen sat opposite Joseph with Mary on a small stool beside her. James came downstairs and paused and looked at the table. He could see that there was no place for him.

Ellen, busy with plates, looked at his face and saw what was happening. "Harry, let your father sit there and you sit in Kathleen's place. Kathleen, get a stool from the little room and sit beside Joseph."

Harry looked at his father and slowly relinquished his place. There was an uncomfortable silence for a few minutes until Mary, oblivious to the awkwardness, began to chatter.

The next day was easier when they all took their places without any direction from her and Harry began to tell his father about his Gaelic football team and their progress in the league. Ellen relaxed and thought that all they needed was time to get to know each other again.

A week later they were all exhausted and irritable from lack of sleep. James had suffered nightmares almost every night and the boys were reluctant to go to bed, knowing what the night would bring. Joseph was so tired and anxious that she had to keep him home from school one day. Ellen herself was feeling the strain of sleepless nights or, at best, nights of broken sleep. She had to do something about it.

She explained to James after the children had left for school and he was getting up. They were standing in their bedroom. "I am going to move the girls upstairs to our room and you downstairs to the little room. If you have a nightmare and you are downstairs, the children probably will not hear you. It is only until the nightmares are over."

"Where are you going to sleep?" he said quietly.

"Upstairs with the girls until I catch up on my sleep again."

He looked stricken. He began to gather up his own belongings and took them downstairs without a word. She wanted to follow him and tell him that she had no choice but he ignored her when she went into the little room to collect the bedclothes and passed her by to go upstairs again. He came back down with his suit and good shoes.

"I am going out to look for a job. The regiment will not be able to do anything for me so I will have to find one for myself. I will be home for tea."

He shaved in the kitchen and then went into the little room and closed the door. A few minutes later he emerged, fully dressed, and left. She went out and watched him walking down the street from the hall door. There was a vulnerability about his figure that made her heart ache. She sat down by the range and cried. Lack of sleep, concern about James and worry about the children had made her emotional and tearful. She had been brusquer with James than she intended. She had wanted to sound matter of fact: to make the change of bedrooms seem unimportant, to reassure him that it was only temporary. Instead,

227

she had made him feel unwanted in his own home.

That evening, she waited for him to come home so that she could make it up to him for the events of the morning. She had got a few fresh herrings, which he loved, from the fish man and was looking forward to frying them for him. She and the children had their tea at their usual time. When eight o'clock came, it was clear that he was going to be late. Harry wanted to wait up with her when the other children had gone to bed but she persuaded him to go upstairs with Joseph. She made herself a cup of cocoa when the range began to die down and had just finished it when she heard a knock on the door. James had forgotten his key. She opened the door and he almost fell in on her and would have but for the restraining arm of Mick.

"He's all right, don't worry. He has had a skinful so I thought I better see him home. How are you, missus? I haven't seen you in a long time."

Between them they half-dragged James into the little room and laid him down on the bed. He didn't seem to know where he was. Ellen removed his shoes and jacket and covered him with a blanket.

Mick patted the inert figure. "I think he had a few disappointments today. He didn't arrive in Ryan's till the evening but the drink seems to affect him more now than it used to."

"Thanks, Mick, for helping him home. He hasn't really been sleeping since he came back. That is probably why the drink affects him more."

"A lot of the lads that came back have the same problem. I suppose when you have spent four years in the trenches, it is hard to be normal. I'll say goodnight to you now, missus."

That night he slept through the night and there were no nightmares. Next morning the boys were cheerful and happy as they set off for school. Once they had gone and Kathleen had gone to call for Violet's girls, she settled Mary with her dolls and went in to the small room where James was just waking up.

He sat up quickly when he saw her, rubbing his forehead and squinting at the daylight as she opened the curtains. "I had a few jars too many last night. I don't remember getting home."

"Mick left you home and helped me get you into bed." She tried to keep her tone reasonable.

His tone was contrite. "Oh, that's right. I remember now. I ended up in Ryan's and he was there."

"Where were you all day? You said that you were going out to look for a job."

"I spent the day at that but I didn't have any luck. I started off at the Post Office where I worked before but the Army has no influence there anymore. Then I tried Cahill's, you know, the printers where I have an aul' mate, but there was nothing going there. I tried the Park Rangers because a lot of them are ex-British army but they had no vacancies. I even tried a few pubs where I am known to see if they need a temporary barman or had a few hours' work but there was nothing doing there either. I had a few drinks in the last of the pubs and then I ended up in Ryan's. The general word is that no one wants to employ anyone who is ex-British army because of the anti-British feeling in the country at the moment."

He looked so despondent that Ellen sat down on the side of the bed and took his hand. "You will surely find something in a few weeks or so and we have your army pension to live on in the meantime."

He shook his head. "While I was in the trenches I was getting seven shillings a day. My pension will be seven pence a day, not enough to live on. I will have to find something else."

She leaned down and kissed him. "I have a little put by so we can use that for the moment. Now, come and have some

229

breakfast. Do you know that you slept through the night last night? There were no nightmares."

"Maybe I should get drunk every night so." He smiled at her as he pulled on his trousers.

While he ate his breakfast he told her in more detail about his fruitless search for a job. There were very few jobs available anyway, but the chances of an ex-British army sergeant finding work were slim. "I heard that there is labouring work going down at the new buildings at Arbour Hill. They won't care who I am if I can do a good day's work. I will have to buy a shovel before I go down there."

"Labouring work? But James, you have never done work like that in your life! And you are nearly fifty! You won't be able for it. You are not long out of hospital. I do not think that is a good idea."

He shrugged off her concern. "If it is the only work I can get, then I have to be able for it. I will go into Phibsboro and buy a shovel today and then I can go to the site tomorrow to ask for work. The sooner I do it, the better. There are going to be a lot of ex-soldiers like myself looking for work."

His despondency seemed to have disappeared now that he had a plan of action. He lifted Mary and one of her dolls up onto his knee and began to sing "The Galloping Major" which had been a favourite of the boys when they were in India.

The boys were curious when he returned that evening with a shovel on his shoulder. He explained to them that he was now going to be working on a building site. They accepted his explanation and didn't seem to realise what a difficult thing it would be for him.

Next morning he set off for Arbour Hill wearing his old clothes and his military boots, the shovel held jauntily on his shoulder. Ellen kissed him and gave him some sandwiches and a bottle of milk to have at lunch-time. She watched him walk down the street from the shelter of the doorway, feeling the February chill on her face. Later in the day it began to rain, cold sleety rain blown into slanting sheets by the north wind. The children arrived in from school wet and cold and huddled around the range while she made them hot milk and hung their sodden clothes to dry on the clothesline over the range. They had been soaked on the short walk home from school. What would James be like if he had been out all day working in the rain?

He arrived home about six and took off his wet, muddy boots in the hall. His hat, an old one, had lost any shape it once had and the brim drooped like cabbage leaves. When he took off his coat, his jacket, shirt and vest were all wetly moulded to his body. Ellen got a basin of hot water so that he could wash himself clean of the mud. Then he towelled himself vigorously and put his feet in the basin to soothe them.

Harry went to his room and came back with an old thick gansey which he offered to James. "You should wear that when you are working, Father. It will keep the rain out better than a jacket."

James pulled it on. "Thanks son. That is a good idea. If this rain keeps up I will be more like a duck than a man."

"James, it cannot be good for you getting so wet. It is not long since you had pneumonia. Were you out in the rain all day?" Ellen asked anxiously.

"Yes, the only work available was as a ground worker. Don't worry, I was often wetter in the trenches and there I had no wife to bring me hot water, nor no son to give me his gansey."

Harry smiled at his father. He took James's dripping clothes and helped Ellen to drape them over chairs as she said, "We'll just try to dry what is needed for tomorrow. Now, I made a stew. That will warm you all up."

The following weeks of February and into March were as wet as the first. James stoically went off to work every day and returned as wet and cold as the first day. Most nights he was exhausted and went to bed at the same time as the boys. The nightmares came less frequently now. Ellen went to the Francis Street clothes market and got him some second-hand clothes which were suitable for working out of doors. At the end of the first week he was happy to show her what he had earned. They celebrated his first week's earnings by buying a chicken for the Sunday dinner.

Relations between James and Harry were friendlier now and Ellen was glad to hear them discussing football or Harry's latest school project. As long as they avoided politics they got along very well.

Soon they fell into a routine and James got used to the demanding physical work. Ellen was glad to see that he had put on weight and got much of his old good humour back. His moustache was now flourishing and his walk had become jauntier. At weekends, when they walked into the city or around the perimeter of the zoo and James was dressed in his Sunday best, she could almost believe that the years of the war had never happened. Only the occasional nightmare and the sudden sadness in his eyes when he thought of something reminded her.

By summer, she had changed the bedrooms back again so that she and James once more shared the back room upstairs. Their lovemaking became more frequent and satisfying. Her last thought most nights before she fell asleep was how lucky and blessed they were that James had returned home safely. The children had also re-established their relationship with their father and Ellen watched happily as they asked him for stories or told him about the events of their day. She was aware that the world outside was becoming increasingly violent.

Chapter 21
1919-1920: The Black and Tans

In September 1919, the Dáil, the independent parliament of elected Sinn Féin MPs, was outlawed by the British administration. The newspapers were full of the war being waged against the Royal Irish Constabulary by the IRA, formerly the Irish Volunteers, who wanted the British out of Ireland. Harry and Joseph were excited by the descriptions in the newspaper of the guerrilla warfare which the IRA employed against the RIC. By the beginning of the New Year, the British government realised that the RIC could not control the violence and recruited a new force to help them. These were the Black and Tans, so called because of their uniform which, because of shortages, was part khaki from the army and part black like the RIC. Over the winter, the work on the new buildings had become more intermittent for James. Some days when there was no work for him, he went up to the Hollow in the park with a few of his friends where they played cards.

One day he came home early before the children returned. Ellen was peeling potatoes for the dinner. He looked anxious and paced up and down the kitchen a few times before he turned and faced her. "Ellen, I heard today that the British government is recruiting in Ireland for the new force which is to help the RIC. They are looking for ex-servicemen like myself."

"The ones they are calling the 'Black and Tans'?" Ellen was aghast. "Why would you want to join them?"

"Well, the work down at the buildings is very scarce. I only got two days last week. The pay in the new force is very good, ten shillings a day, more than we were getting at the front. Tommy Byrne has signed up already. He is being sent to Cork because they don't want Irishmen serving in their own areas."

"But you would be away from home again if that is the case! We

233

are just getting used to being a family again and now you are talking about going away! Anyway, I don't think you should join up; the RIC are very unpopular so the new force will be too. The IRA are targeting the RIC and blowing up the barracks. I don't want you to come home safely from the war and then to be killed in your own country!"

James looked uncertain. "I only thought of it because it would be regular work and pay. We have used up any few shillings we had in reserve over the last few weeks and I know it is hard for you to make ends meet."

"I would sooner starve than have you join a group like that and be away from home again," Ellen said forcefully.

"Well, to be honest, I don't really want to do it myself. I had enough of violence in Flanders and I don't want to leave you and the family." He looked relieved.

"Good, that's settled then. Don't mention it to the boys. It would only worry them. The building work may pick up again but anyway, don't worry. We will manage."

In her own mind, Ellen had been thinking of the likely reaction of Harry if James mentioned that he had even considered joining the Black and Tans. Relieved, she kissed James and hugged him to her, noting how he had regained weight, especially since he was doing less physical work. She didn't tell him that she had been so short of money for food that she had already spent the money which Harry had earned as a choir boy in the Palestrina Choir and which she had earmarked for his further education.

She had also been forced to make a few visits to the pawn shop. Many women around the neighbourhood went to the pawn shop regularly and seemed unashamed, walking into the city with their husband's good suit or a good blanket over their arm. Before her first visit, Ellen had to ask Violet where the pawn shop was and Violet offered to accompany her. When they got to the shop on the quays, there was a queue of women chatting amicably while they waited for the shop to open. Most of them treated the transaction as though it was an everyday affair and nothing to be ashamed of. Ellen wished that she could be as unembarrassed as they seemed to be. She had brought a cameo brooch that her mother had given her and an opal ring which had been a present from James. She was disappointed at the small sum which the pawnbroker offered her for them but it was better than nothing.

She was very thrifty but there were few ways for her to save money. Sometimes she walked to the bakery to buy bread rather than wait for Peter to deliver it to the shop because it was cheaper. Often she sent Kathleen out to the Rag and Bone man when he called, with empty jam jars for which she got a few pennies. It wasn't much but it helped. While James was away and she was in receipt of the separation allowance as well as his army pay she had never got any groceries on tick; now she sometimes had to record her purchases in Miss Ormond's shop in "The Book" in order to put food on the table. She tried to keep these actions secret from James because she knew that it hurt his pride not to be able to provide for his family.

The two boys, in spite of warnings from their parents, went a few times to peer in through the railings of the Depot in the Phoenix Park where many of the "Tans" were being given a brief training. Rumours abounded about these men, most of them British but a few Irish: that they had been released from prison, that they were soldiers returned from the front, that they were being paid much more than regular police or soldiers, that they had been given permission to shoot to kill. James knew that many men had been brutalised by their experiences in the war and would have no difficulty in shooting innocent people if they were allowed to do so. He also knew that high rates of unemployment meant that there were plenty of willing recruits in Britain but also in Ireland. He had almost been tempted himself by the thought of regular employment.

Harry, Joseph and Annie followed the rapidly changing political scene avidly. When Annie came to visit, she always had the latest news about her new hero, Michael Collins, whom she had known in the GPO during Easter Week. The Irish Volunteers were now known as the Irish Republican Army. Their activities were backed by the Sinn Féin government and coordinated, so the newspapers said, by Michael Collins who was the Finance Minister in the Provisional Government and also the IRA Chief of Intelligence. Much of the IRA activity against the RIC tended to be around the rural areas; it was easier to employ guerrilla tactics in the mountains and countryside than it would be in the city. The RIC, who had the prime responsibility for law and order, were very unpopular but also their barracks were the most likely source of weapons.

The first wave of Black and Tans started work in March 1920. The newspapers had reports from small towns all over the country of reprisals by the Tans and the RIC for the attacks by the IRA on policemen or barracks. The reprisals were indiscriminate and often innocent people were tortured and shot or had their houses burnt down. Mayo seemed to be one of the worst areas for Black and Tan atrocities and Ellen received regular copies of "The Mayoman" newspaper from her family which reported these outrages in detail. Annie kept them informed about what was happening in Dublin.

"Collins's men," she said, her eyes shining, "concentrate on the provision of intelligence; he has a network of informers which has infiltrated even the police and Dublin Castle." She turned to Harry who was listening avidly to her stories about her hero. "You know that book that I loaned you called 'The Scarlet Pimpernel'? Collins is like that. The British are always looking for him but they don't even know what he looks like! He had a squad of hitmen who

236

eliminated Dublin's detective constables, the dreaded "G" men, and after that they really wanted to catch him but they never did."

Ellen listened in fear and dreaded that her two boys would become involved in IRA activity. Harry was now sixteen and Joseph fourteen. They were members of Na Fianna and it was well known as a breeding ground for IRA activists. She tried to keep them close and was glad to see that their relationship with James was getting better all the time.

In early July Maggie sent a letter to Ellen and the latest copy of "The Mayoman" newspaper. There was an article in it which she thought they should read. "You and James will be upset, I know, by the news about the Connaught Rangers mutiny in India. Jack is in that part of India, the Punjab, I think it is called, and I was afraid that he might have been involved. You know he never had much sense! Thankfully, he was not involved."

Ellen read the article but did not fully comprehend the seriousness of it. When James came home from work he read it out loud in disbelief.

"Some of the 1st Battalion of the Connaught Rangers heard about the depredations of the Black and Tans in Ireland and decided to protest by refusing to do their duties as soldiers. They said that they would not return to duty until the British forces left Ireland. They stormed the armoury but were taken prisoner. Eighty-eight men were court-martialled for mutiny. Nineteen men were sentenced to death, fifty-nine were sentenced to fifteen years' imprisonment and ten were acquitted."

He scrutinised the newspaper again. "I can't believe it. I just can't believe it!"

"I don't understand, James. Why were they sentenced to death?"

"Mutiny is one of the most serious offences you can commit as a soldier. But I can't believe that they would sentence so many men to death. What did those men hope to achieve by mutinying anyway? Is Maggie sure that Jack wasn't involved? They don't give any names here."

"Yes, she is sure because she knew that he was away at a hill station when it happened. Anyway they say in the article that it was all enlisted men who were involved, not N.C.O'.s or officers."

James was very quiet that evening and the following few days. Ellen knew how much the Connaught Rangers meant to him. It had been a major part of his life. Now it must seem to him that his regiment, like so many things in his life, had changed beyond recognition. Two weeks later, James received a letter from Jack.

Wellington Barracks
Punjab

Dear James,

I know you must be shocked to hear about the mutiny by men of the Connaught Rangers here in the Punjab. I was away with my men dealing with some trouble near a hill station when it happened and could not believe it myself.

I know some of the men involved though not very well. The ringleader was a Private James Daly and I had a chat with him a few times. He struck me as a serious, thinking kind of man. I heard rumours that his family back in Mayo had been the victims of a brutal attack by the Black and Tans in their home. Eighteen of those sentenced to death have had their sentences commuted to life imprisonment, though I think that you and I might prefer to die rather than spend a lifetime in prison. Private Daly was shot by firing squad on 2nd November in Dagshai prison. May God have mercy on his soul.

The whole thing has had a very bad effect on morale here. Sometimes I wonder why I am still here in India and why I didn't go home at the same time as you and Ellen when I had the chance, instead of signing up for another tour of duty. On the other hand, at least I was spared the horror of the trenches.

There is something else that is troubling me. There is no one here that I can confide in and I hope that you will not be shocked. For the last year I have been visiting a young lady called Geeta. Her father, a Scotsman, was working for the East India Company and had lived here for thirty years before he died. Geeta's mother is a Christian Indian. Her parents were married in the Episcopalian church here. I am very much in love with Geeta but I don't know what to do. She is not accepted by the army and I cannot bring her to any social occasion. Unfortunately, she is not accepted by the Indian community either. My tour of duty will be up in 1920. I thought of coming back to Ireland with Geeta as my wife. I do not think that we would be accepted in Castlebar or Galway but I wondered whether we should come to Dublin. If I could get work, we could get a small house near to you and Ellen. What do you think of that idea? I will also have to bring Geeta's mother with us because, other than Geeta, she has no relatives.

Give Ellen and the children my love. I miss you all, especially Harry who made me feel like a hero.

Your friend,

Jack

Jack's letter gave Ellen and James plenty to talk about. Ellen said that she was not really surprised to hear about Geeta. She had often wondered why Jack had not found a wife. James was still focusing on the mutiny and trying to digest what Jack had told them.

"It would be lovely if Jack came to Dublin and lived near us with, what was her name, Geeta. I was always very fond of him," Ellen said.

"I don't think it is such a good idea. I don't think she would be accepted. And what if they have children? It is bad enough for our children being the children of a British soldier. What do you think it would be like for children who are half-castes?" James was more realistic. "Anyway, he wouldn't find it easy to get work here."

"What will you say to him when you write back?"

"I will tell him about the work situation here and advise him to stay in England when he travels back from India. Geeta might be more accepted there."

"Poor Jack, he is caught in an impossible situation. I wish that he and his wife could come here to Dublin." Ellen was disappointed but realised that James was right. She could not really imagine an Indian woman living on their street.

On Sundays James often went along with the two boys to watch them playing Gaelic football. Harry was selected to play for the Dublin minor team and James was very proud of his son. Ellen was glad about his selection because she felt it would keep him busy and out of harm's way. All three of them were keen supporters of the Dublin senior team. When James broached the subject of them going to see Dublin playing against Tipperary the following Sunday, Ellen encouraged him to go, thinking that it would help him to forget the events in India.

"It is a bit expensive for the three of us to go; one shilling each. I could let the two lads go on their own," James said.

"No, it will do you good to have a day out with the boys," Ellen replied. "You have never been in Croke Park before. The boys love going there so I am sure you will enjoy it."

She made sandwiches for them to have at half-time and waved them off. It did her heart good to see the three of them together with no animosity. They were in high spirits and could be heard laughing and joking until they went around the corner out of sight.

The girls were clamouring for an outing too so Ellen took them to feed the ducks in the park after they had their midday meal. As they were walking home she met a friend she knew from the suffragette meetings who stopped her with an anxious wave.

"Have you heard the news? About twenty British Intelligence Officers were shot by Collins's Hit Squad this morning! It was mostly over the south side of the city although I heard that someone was shot in the Imperial Hotel."

"Oh my God, James and my boys went to Croke Park this afternoon! I hope they didn't come across any trouble." Ellen remembered her journey into Sackville Street during the Rising and had a feeling of dread.

"I am sure they will be all right. It was all on the south side so they probably don't know anything about it."

Ellen hurried home with the girls, noting the ominous quiet that seemed to have settled over the city. James and the boys would have to be home by curfew time and that was only an hour away. She sat down in the small room to wait, watching out the window for any sign of them. Kathleen and Mary sensed her anxiety and sat beside her. Then she saw them, Harry and James on either side of Joseph, whom they appeared to be holding up.

"Oh no! Oh my God! What has happened to him?"

She rushed to open the door. They sat Joseph down in the armchair. James was trying to staunch the blood which was pouring from a long gash on the side of his head. He was pale and frightened.

241

"Get me a clean rag and some hot water. He will be all right; it looks worse than it is. He is a brave soldier, aren't you son?"

Ellen put on the kettle to boil and found a clean rag. "What happened? Will I do that?"

James was expertly cleaning the blood from around the gash in Joseph's head. "No. I am well used to looking after wounds. When the crowd panicked, Joseph was pushed over and hit his head on the step. He was a bit concussed for a while but he was able to walk home with us helping him."

"They shot at us, Mama. Joseph could have been killed." Harry was in tears.

"What do you mean? Who shot at you? Why did the crowd panic?" Ellen was fighting to control the hysteria in her voice.

James was trying to calm his sons and tell the story clearly. "We arrived early at Croke Park and went in by the Canal end. The match started about half an hour late and by then there was a huge crowd. Shortly after the throw-in there was a commotion at the turnstiles that we had come through and then RIC men and Black and Tans burst in and started firing into the crowd."

"Firing into the crowd? My God! Why?"

"I don't know. Some people ran onto the pitch to escape and others tried to leave by the canal gates. There was terrible confusion. We tried to turn back the way we had come but the crowd was surging forward and people were getting trampled on. Joseph was pushed up the steps and hit his head. We managed to drag him outside and then we sat him down to see if he was badly injured."

Ellen was looking anxiously at Joseph as James cleaned the gash on his head.

"We saw two young boys being carried out; they looked as though they were dead," James continued. "Another young woman looked badly injured. On the pitch we could see that two players had been shot, maybe killed. There was screaming and crying all around us. A woman came out of a house on Clonliffe Road and told us we could rest there until Joseph could be moved. She made us a cup of tea and had a look at Joseph. She was very kind."

James had finished cleaning Joseph's wound and was tying a makeshift bandage around his head.

Ellen moved to sit beside her son and put her arms around him. "My poor Jo-Jo. Are you all right? Would you like to go to bed?"

"I just have a bit of a headache, Mama. Papa said I shouldn't go to sleep for a while because of the concussion." Joseph was trying to be brave although his face was white and he was visibly shaking.

"Those British bastards! They were shooting at innocent people! I would love to shoot them!" Harry was white with anger.

"Harry, do not use that kind of language. I know you are worried about your brother but even so. Are you all right?" Up to this, Ellen had given all her attention to Joseph.

"Yes, Mother. I am just very angry. They were just shooting indiscriminately. They didn't care who they hit, children, women, players," Harry raged.

The next day Ellen kept the children home from school. They heard that thirteen people had been killed in Croke Park and six wounded. One of the dead was a member of the Tipperary team. Another was a young girl who was to be married a few weeks later. The two boys that James had seen were among the dead.

After that event, the violence seemed to escalate around the country. Every day there was news of more atrocities. The Mayor of Cork, Tomás MacCurtain, was assassinated by the RIC later in the month. Then the IRA killed fifty-five policemen and destroyed sixteen barracks around the county. Many barracks were abandoned by a demoralised police force. By the end of the year, a substantial part of Cork city was burned and destroyed by the Tans, in reprisal for the IRA actions. Newspapers reported that at least three hundred buildings had been razed to the ground. Many small towns and villages all over the country were devastated by Black and Tan attacks. The new force seemed to be out of control.

From August, the British army had been given powers to intern people on suspicion without trial. James was regularly stopped and searched by Tans when he was on his way home from work. He carried his demob papers because he thought they would protect him but found that they simply exposed him to ridicule by the Tans. One evening he came home bruised and bleeding.

Ellen rushed to his side and examined his head and face. "What happened to you?"

"I am all right; it looks worse than it is. Just get me some water and disinfectant."

James explained what had happened as he wiped the blood off his face.

"I was walking home as usual when I came across a group of Black and Tans who were very drunk. They started calling me a Shinner and a coward. I kept walking but they followed me and kept taunting me. I told them that I was no coward and had spent four years at the front. They set on me then, all six of them. Only for the fact that they were so drunk I would never have got away."

A week later, Harry was also stopped and searched by the Tans. Ellen was always afraid that if he was stopped, he would say or do something that would lead to his internment. Luckily, he had the sense to say nothing and was let go.

Then Martial Law was declared by the British authorities in December 1920. Thousands of people were arrested and interned. Many more "went on the run" and formed "Flying Columns", mobile groups of about one hundred men who lived in remote places in safe houses and conducted guerrilla warfare. Mrs Kelly's two sons, Paddy and John, were two of those who had to go on the run or be interned. They were somewhere out in the Wicklow mountains. They were a great loss to their mother because they were the men of the house and brought home a wage which supplemented her pension.

Christmas 1920 brought sad news. Maggie sent a telegram to say that their father, Henry, had died after a long illness. Ellen was distracted from her grief by wondering how they were going to get to Castlebar for the funeral. Drivers of trains were refusing to take soldiers, Tans or ammunition or guns and consequently, trains were delayed or didn't travel at all. Then Tom, Jane's husband, called in to say that he was driving to Castlebar and could take three people with himself and Jane. They now had two children of their own but were going to leave them with their maid.

"Funerals are no place for children," Jane said, as they all arranged themselves in the Ford car. James had offered to stay and look after the children so that Ellen, Annie and Harry could go to the funeral. There was an awkward silence as Annie got into the back seat behind Jane. They had not spoken to each other since the day that Annie had left Jane's house to live with Ellen and have her baby. Harry sat between his mother and aunt and relieved the strained atmosphere by talking to Tom about the car and Gaelic football.

Tom wanted to hear all about Harry's experience of Croke Park and what was now being referred to as "Bloody Sunday". Ellen was amused to hear the conservative Tom call the British "bastards". It was typical of the way that public opinion in Ireland had turned against the British.

They stopped in Galway to have a cup of tea and arrived in Maggie's house an hour before the removal. Henry was being waked in the front room. Ellen linked Harry's arm as she and Annie went in to say goodbye to their father. Henry looked very thin and aged in his coffin, not at all the commanding presence that she remembered.

"He looks so old, doesn't he? I wish we had been able to see more of him over the last few years." She was thinking of the night before her wedding when he had been so kind and comforting to her and remembered his enjoyment of the children when they had visited.

All three of them kissed his forehead and recited a decade of the rosary for him before going in to the kitchen where Mary Ann was waiting. She too had shrunk and was almost bent over with arthritis. She cried when she saw Annie and opened her arms to her daughter. Annie hesitated but embraced her mother. Then it was time to go to the church for the removal.

A horse-drawn carriage arrived to carry the coffin and Jane, Maggie and their mother followed in Tom's car. Everyone else walked behind the hearse the short distance to the church. The prayers were said by Father O'Dwyer who had performed the wedding ceremony for Ellen and James and who had baptised Nancy. Then the mourners queued up to convey their condolences to the family. There were curious glances at Annie who had not been seen in Castlebar for five years. Harry was complimented on his remarkable resemblance to his grandfather.

Everyone was invited back to Maggie's house for a drink and sandwiches where Mary Ann presided, flanked by Maggie and Jane. Ellen circulated among her old neighbours, answering questions about James and her other children and asking about her old school friends, many of whom, like herself, had moved away. Whiskey and porter with port for the ladies were being served with fruit cake when suddenly, the door crashed open and about ten Black and Tans erupted into the room.

"We are looking for Eamonn Kenny. We know he is hiding in this house. Tell us where he is or we will smash the place up."

Eamonn was Maggie's brother-in-law, Matt's younger brother. Ellen had heard Matt explaining to Mary Ann that Eamonn was

246

working in Scotland and could not come to the funeral. Some of the Tans began to run up the stairs, crash open doors, ransack wardrobes and throw china and glass to the ground. The rest of the Tans stood with guns at the ready watching the mourners. Mary Ann rose and tried to straighten herself to her full height.

"This is my husband's wake. How dare you burst in here when we are mourning him?" she said imperiously.

"We don't care what you are doing, missus. We ain't leaving here until we find Eamonn Kenny." Some of the Tans were now outside, searching the outhouses. Within minutes there was a smell of smoke and one of the outhouses burst into flames.

"Wait a minute. Eamonn is not here. There is no need to set fire to the outhouse."

Matt began to remonstrate with the Tan who seemed to be in charge.

Crack! A rifle butt hit Matt on the head and he fell down unconscious. Maggie screamed.

"If you don't tell us where the bugger is, we will set fire to the house."

"I don't know where he is. Let me look after my husband!" Maggie tried to help Matt.

The leader caught Maggie by the arm. "We are taking him with us unless you tell us where Eamonn Kenny is."

Maggie sobbed hysterically and again tried to reach her husband. Two Tans dragged the still unconscious Matt outside the door and closed it. Then they heard a rifle shot.

"My God, they have shot Matt!" Maggie was screaming.

The leader moved towards Mary Ann and said, "Do you want us to shoot the old woman as well?"

Ellen stood between her mother and the Tan. "We don't know anything. Leave us alone."

The leader signalled to the others and with a last swipe which

247

brought everything on the table to the floor, they were gone. When the sound of their lorries could no longer be heard, Maggie and Ellen ran outside. Matt was lying where they had left him, bleeding and half- conscious but not shot. Others ran to help them as they carried him in and laid him on a couch.

Annie examined his head. "He got a bad blow to the head. I'll bandage the wound if you get me some bandages. Keep talking to him and don't let him go to sleep. He will be all right in a few hours."

Mary Ann was on the verge of collapse. Ellen helped her to a chair and asked Maggie, "Have you a whiskey or a brandy to give to Mama?"

"It is a good thing that your father is not here to see this," Mary Ann said as she sipped the whiskey which Maggie gave her. "He would have said the wrong thing and got himself killed."

Ellen and Maggie couldn't help smiling at the irony in what her mother said. People began to pick up the broken glass and crockery which littered the floor.

"We got off lightly," Father O'Dwyer said. "Last week they set fire to a whole row of shops in Castlebar."

Most of the mourners then drifted away in a very subdued mood.

Harry helped Maggie to make Matt comfortable on the couch. "Do you really not know where Matt's brother is?" he asked.

"He is with one of the Flying Columns up in the mountains. He has been on the run for months now," Maggie told him.

"At least he is doing something about these awful men who are occupying our country. I want to join a Flying Column." Ellen came in in time to hear what Harry said.

Next day, there were fewer people at the funeral than they would have expected. A good neighbour stayed behind to look after Matt. The Tans had scared some people off. Again the only people who travelled by car to the church and later to the graveyard were Mary Ann, Jane and Maggie. Everybody else walked in slow procession behind the hearse.

They took a route from the church to the graveyard which allowed them to pass the lodge at the edge of the demesne where they paused. The flower garden in the front was overgrown and the house looked neglected, as if no one lived there anymore. Mary Ann and her daughters looked sadly at the house that had been their home for many years. Grey rain fell in the graveyard in sheets and made their prayers and farewells a hurried affair. This time few people came back to the house. The party from Dublin had to stay until morning because the curfew in Dublin and Martial Law made it impossible to travel by night.

They left early the next day. Mary Ann did not want to part from her daughters and was very tearful. They all promised to come to see her as soon as possible. Looking at the bent figure of her mother, Ellen realised that she would soon lose her as well. Why did losing a parent make you feel so much older, she wondered? Maybe it was because the line of defence between you and death was gone. You were now in the front line. There was little talk to distract her from her gloomy thoughts. They had all been traumatised by the visit of the Tans and Matt's treatment at their hands and were not in talkative mood.

Along the road they came across a number of units of the Tans putting up roadblocks but were only stopped once. Tom did all the talking and they were not delayed very long. They waited until they reached Athlone before they took a break and arrived in Dublin in the early afternoon. Tom and Jane were anxious to be off so they did not come in but stopped on the roadway to talk to James for a few minutes as he took in their bags. Harry could not wait to tell his father and Joseph about their experience with the Tans. He described them with a look at his mother as "British bastards". This time she didn't reprimand him. James said mildly that not all the British were bastards.

"Why did they send such people here then?" Harry wanted to know.

"Many British people are ashamed of what the Tans are doing in their name. Even the King and Churchill say they should not be allowed to behave in such an undisciplined way," James tried to explain.

"That does not make sense," Harry said. "Surely the King or Churchill could stop this if they really wanted to? No, they want to subdue us and break our spirit but they never will. Aren't you ashamed, Father, that some of these men are the same men that you fought alongside in Flanders?"

"I will never be ashamed of the men I fought alongside. You have no idea what we endured," James told his son. "Some of the bravest men I ever knew were my comrades in the British army. Don't ever try to put them in the same category as the Tans."

Harry looked at his father and went off to his room with Joseph where they could hear him describing the attack of the Tans on Matt's house in great detail. "Uncle Matt was really brave and his brother is with a flying column up in the mountains. That is what I am going to do as soon as I am old enough."

Ellen could see the sadness in James's eyes as he listened to his son.

Chapter 22
1921: A Truce

During the following months Ellen became aware that Harry was attending Sinn Féin meetings regularly. He had stopped going to Fianna meetings but she suspected that he now had some involvement with the IRA. She tried talking to him about it but he was evasive. When the school holidays came in July, she feared that he was planning to join the Kelly boys and their flying column wherever they were in County Wicklow. Just as she had decided that she would tell James about her fears, a truce was called between the British and the Irish. Annie came to visit that Sunday and they celebrated with a few bottles of porter for the adults and sweets for the children. Annie proposed a toast to the Irish Republic. Harry said a few words in Irish which neither Ellen nor James understood but they got the general gist of it.

Annie looked shy and told them that she had some good news. "I am walking out with someone. His name is Padraig Breathnach and he is a teacher."

"That is wonderful news, Annie! Where did you meet him?" Ellen was delighted for her sister who suddenly looked like a young girl again.

"He is also a member of Sinn Féin. We got talking at a few meetings and then he asked me out." She added shyly, "We hope to get married as soon as the negotiations for the Republic are over."

"Can I be bridesmaid?" Kathleen never missed an opportunity to be in the public eye.

"Of course," Annie laughed. "You and Mary will be bridesmaids although we want a quiet wedding."

"I have some news too. I have got a job for the summer holidays in the bookies in Parkgate Street," Harry said and looked apprehensively at his mother.

Ellen pretended to be shocked. "The bookies? I don't think that is very suitable for someone of your age."

"It will be good for my mathematics, Mother. I had to show that I could work out odds to get the job."

"I wonder where you got that talent from?" James asked with a twinkle in his eye.

"I got that from you, Father," Harry laughed.

Annie left the next day, promising to bring her young man to meet them next time she visited. As soon as she had heard about the young man and their plans for a wedding, Ellen began to wonder whether Annie would want to take her daughter back once she had a husband and a home. Ellen loved Mary as much as she loved her own children. She dreaded having to part with her but could not bring herself to mention the subject to Annie. She thought of it every time she looked at Mary as she chalked out squares and played "Beds" out in the street or rolled down the hill in the park with the other children. Mary was to start in St. Gabriel's National School in September.

The summer seemed to go by very quickly and soon the children were preparing to go back to school. Harry was very proud that he could afford to pay for his own schoolbooks from his earnings. Mary was excited at the idea of going to school and accompanying Kathleen every morning. Only Joseph was sad at the beginning of school term. He would have preferred to stay at home and read his books.

Annie brought Padraig to visit a couple of times and they all agreed that he was a lovely young man and suited Annie. His first visit coincided with the beginning of the negotiations between the British government and the Sinn Féin leaders. Ellen and James found it all very confusing. Ellen thought that the negotiations were to achieve an independent republic which is what most people seemed to want. Padraig said that it was not that simple. Lloyd

George, the British Prime Minister was insisting that Ireland must remain within the British Empire and accept the King as head of state. James looked surprised.

"What is wrong with that? The King spoke out against the Tans, didn't he?"

"That is not what the men of Easter Week fought for," Annie said defiantly.

"They are also saying that the six counties in Ulster will remain partitioned and separate," Padraig went on. "We will never accept losing part of our country, that is certain. And we don't want British naval bases here, either."

"Who is doing the negotiating anyway? Lloyd George is said to be a wily aul' fox, so it better be someone as cute as himself." James knew a lot about Lloyd George but little about Sinn Féin.

"Arthur Griffith and Michael Collins are the chief negotiators but De Valera should have gone. He is the wiliest of them all," Padraig said.

Annie interrupted Padraig's explanations. "I am sure that Michael Collins will get us the deal we want. He won't settle for anything less."

The negotiations in London dragged on for three months. The ceasefire meant that the city was more peaceful and it was possible to go into the city without fear of the Tans. Ellen was in Moore Street doing some early Christmas shopping when she saw the headlines in the newspapers. The Irish delegation had signed the Treaty in London.

"Thank God," she thought. "Maybe now we can return to normal life."

The following Sunday Annie and Padraig visited again. This time there was a lot of tension between them.

"Griffiths and Collins should not have signed the Treaty without bringing it home for discussion first," Padraig said.

"Don't be ridiculous, Padraig. They did the job they were asked to do, a very difficult job, but they did it to the best of their ability," Annie retorted.

"They signed away the six counties and made it impossible for us to be a Republic!" Padraig was getting angry.

"I believe Michael Collins when he said that it was either sign or face another war. Nobody wants that, do they?" Annie asked.

"Nobody wants to give away part of their country and to be made to swear allegiance to a British king!"

Annie and Padraig were now standing opposite each other, leaning forward aggressively when they spoke, eyes flashing.

Ellen looked from one to the other. "Let's all have a cup of tea and take a walk up to the park. Mary wants to feed the ducks, don't you love?"

"No thanks, Ellen," Padraig said. "I have to get back. We have a meeting of our local Sinn Féin branch tomorrow evening to discuss the Treaty and I want to be prepared. Are you coming, Annie?"

Annie didn't look at him. "No, I want to spend some time with Mary. I will see you at the meeting."

Christmas Day was the next time they saw Annie and Padraig. They arrived in apparently good form, laden with presents. Padraig's family lived in Kerry and he had ten days' holidays from school but he wanted to spend some time with Annie and would spend the New Year with his family. James had got fairly regular work in the days preceding Christmas so Ellen had bought a goose and a ham for the dinner. She had also made a pudding to her mother's recipe.

Fitting them all around the table was not easy but they managed with much good humour. The young couple had brought presents for everyone as well as chocolates, six bottles of porter in a brown paper bag and a small bottle of port. Annie had bought a beautiful blue velvet dress for Mary which she immediately changed into.

Kathleen got a pair of fur mittens which she was delighted with and the boys received books. When James was proposing a toast before the meal, Annie shyly took a ring from a chain around her neck and Padraig placed it on her finger. Once the exclamations of surprise and delight had died down she told them that Padraig had proposed on Christmas Eve. They were planning to get married the following summer. Ellen was delighted for her sister but tried to push away the thought of Annie taking Mary to live with her.

The party mood went on well into the evening. Ellen had invited Grace to join them for the day but she had a new beau, an actor who was appearing in the Christmas production with her and was spending Christmas Day, their only rest day, with him. Once dinner was over, James sent Harry to ask Violet and her children to join them and Joseph went next door to invite the Kellys. Paddy and John were at home again much to their mother's delight.

The small room was crammed with people. Harry, Desmond and the two Kelly's, all big men, stood with their backs to the wall. Julia, Violet's daughter, stood beside Harry, stealing glances at him from time to time. The seats were left for the older women, who each held a child on her knee. James began a singsong with a rollicking version of "Daisy, Daisy, give me your answer, do", which had been a great favourite with the troops at the front. Everybody sang and clapped along. Paddy Kelly sang "Kevin Barry", a popular ballad about a young student who had been hanged during the War of Independence. Harry and John and Padraig joined in the emotional chorus.

James tried to divert the young men from the patriotic songs by insisting that Ellen would sing so she and Annie sang "After the Ball". When the song finished, he came over and kissed her, his face full of emotion. "I remember you singing that at our wedding and you haven't changed a bit!"

"Ah now, isn't that lovely and romantic," Mrs Kelly said while

Harry and Joseph looked faintly embarrassed.

Padraig volunteered to sing his favourite song, "Ar Éireann Ní Neosainn Cé Hí". It had a beautiful, plaintive air and Padraig had a rich, tenor voice. There was an appreciative silence when he finished singing and then enthusiastic applause.

"That is a beautiful song, Padraig. I never heard it before. What is it about?"

Ellen had been reminded of her mother and the song she sang in Irish at their wedding.

"Well, I suppose it is a love song," he said, smiling at Annie, "but a love song to Ireland, Éireann in the song."

James was quite merry and sentimental at this stage and he proposed that they all sing a few Christmas Carols. They ended with Harry singing "O Holy Night" which he used to sing when he was in the choir and was his mother's favourite. Ellen went over and reached up to kiss him.

"Thanks, love. I always love to hear you sing that. It reminds me of your time singing in the Pro-Cathedral."

There was some comfortable chatting about other Christmases and the people they had shared them with. There were tears mixed with laughter when James spoke about his friend, Des, and some of the antics they used to get up to when they were together in India. He was in the mood for reminiscing and began to tell them about the experience of his first Christmas at the front, Christmas 1914. James was a great storyteller and they were all enthralled as he told his tale.

"On Christmas Eve in Flanders, a ceasefire was called so that both sides could go into No Man's Land to collect the bodies of their fallen comrades for burial. We were knee deep in mud and I was helping to place bodies on stretchers when I realised that a German soldier was standing very close to me. He was very young, no more than seventeen or eighteen. He held out an opened packet

256

of cigarettes for me to take one. I did and then he took one himself and lit both. We smoked in silence, just looking at each other and smiling. Then I picked up my end of the stretcher and walked back to our own side. As darkness fell and soldiers from both sides returned to their trenches, we heard a sound in the air which rose and swelled until we realised that the German were singing 'Silent Night' in their own language. We began to sing it in English and soon the voices blended in the night into one choir. Myself and all the men I could see had tears running down through the mud on their faces. We were all thinking of home, ourselves and the Germans. The next day, we returned to killing each other. I often think of that young German and wonder whether he survived. He reminded me of Harry."

There was silence for a few minutes after he finished his story. Then Harry said, "I don't know 'Silent Night' in German but I know it in Irish and in English. Let us sing it in memory of that night."

The other children all knew the Irish version, "Oíche Chiún", which they had learned in school and joined in with Harry. They all sang "Silent Night" and thought about that one night of shared humanity at the beginning of a ferocious war.

Then the spell was broken as both Mrs Kelly and Violet stood up and began to gather their children ready to go home.

"I'll see Julia home, Violet," Harry said.

Both mothers suddenly realised that he and Julia had been holding hands all the time they had been standing side by side. They looked at each other with raised eyebrows as though to say, "When did this happen?" but then looked approvingly at the young couple as Harry helped Julia into her coat and put a protective arm around her as they left.

When everyone had gone and Joseph and the girls had gone to bed, James sat opposite Ellen on the other side of the range with a

257

last drink in his hands and said, "That was a wonderful day and evening, Ellen. You really make our home a special place. Thank you, my love."

Ellen reached over to hold his hand. "Having you here with us makes it special, James. I missed you so much when you were away. I love you very much."

New Year's Eve 1921 was very quiet. Annie was working, Padraig had gone to Kerry to his parents and Harry was with Julia. James and Ellen went out on to the street to welcome in the New Year with some neighbours while Joseph kept an eye on the sleeping girls. It was a cold, starlit night and they could see their breath on the air as they wished each other a happy new year.

James proposed a toast. "Here's to better times for all of us."

Someone brought out a melodeon and all the neighbours danced a few waltzes up and down the street before the cold drove them, breathless and laughing, indoors again.

Chapter 23
1922: The Irish Free State

A week later they heard that Dáil Éireann had narrowly passed the Anglo-Irish Treaty by sixty-four votes to fifty-seven. People were now talking about a peaceful handover of power from the British to the Irish Free State. Annie came to visit with news about the Treaty.

"Padraig and I went to a few meetings and the atmosphere was very tense. The people who oppose the Treaty are led by a man called De Valera, whom Padraig greatly admires. Many of the IRA officers are also opposed to the Treaty. The IRA seem to have split into two factions, Pro-Treaty and Anti-Treaty. I don't know how the situation is going to be resolved."

At the same time, some of the military barracks were being handed over by the British and there were a number of confrontations between Pro- and Anti-Treaty supporters. One situation that they read about in the papers was in Limerick where the opposing factions agreed to occupy two barracks each of the four barracks in the city. James thought that this was hilarious and earned Harry's wrath by laughing at what he called "playing soldiers."

People soon realised that it was no laughing matter when there was a serious clash of the opposing groups in Kilkenny and eighteen men were killed. Increasing lawlessness was one of the results of the opposing groups since there was now virtually no police presence in Ireland. Then it became dangerous for Annie to cross the city to visit them. She arrived one Sunday, breathless and worried.

"The Four Courts and some other buildings in the centre of the city have been occupied by a few hundred IRA men opposed to the Treaty. They seem to want to start a new war with the British."

Ellen made a cup of tea for her sister. "What are they doing that for? I thought we were going to have a bit of peace for a change."

"They think that if the British attack them it will unite the two opposing IRA groups in a common war," Annie explained.

"Isn't Collins supposed to be in charge now? Why doesn't he do something about it?" Ellen asked.

"Oh for heaven's sake, Ellen, can't you see that that would only start a civil war?"

Ellen was surprised at her sister's tone. She was usually even tempered but obviously all the uncertainty was wearing her out. Over the next few months she was only able to visit twice because of the danger involved in crossing the city.

Then the General Election in June gave the Pro-Treaty group a large majority. Both Annie and Harry were heavily involved in campaigning for the general election. Harry had finished school that June and gave himself full-time to the election campaign. He was frustrated by the fact that both Pro- and Anti-Treaty sides called themselves Sinn Féin, thus confusing many people. Both Annie and Harry had taken the Pro-Treaty side.

"Not to accept the Treaty will invite further and more serious hostilities from Britain," Harry told Ellen and James who both found it difficult to keep up with the events which seemed to be moving closer and closer to a Civil War.

Harry explained that the occupation of the Four Courts put Collins and Griffiths under pressure from the British to take control in their own country, or else, they were told, the British would intervene. They were forced to act when some of the Anti-Treaty garrison in the Four Courts kidnapped JJ O'Connell, a general in the new National Army, of which Collins was Chief of Staff. This insult could not be countenanced and Collins ordered the National Army to bombard the Four Courts, using heavy artillery which they had inherited from the British. Two days later, the ill-equipped Four Courts garrison surrendered. Shortly before the surrender, the whole family were at home when a massive explosion destroyed the western wing of the building, which housed the Irish Public Records Office, and tremors like an earthquake shook the surrounding streets. The newspapers called this battle the act which ignited the Civil War.

Annie took advantage of a lull in the hostilities and came to see Mary. She was looking even more tired and pale than usual. She had been promoted to Ward Sister and took her responsibilities very seriously. Her workload had increased dramatically during the War of Independence and was increasing again. However, she loved her work and that was not the reason for her altered appearance.

She cried as she told them, "Padraig has taken the Anti-Treaty side and has returned to Kerry to take part in the campaign there. That means that he lost his job so the prospect of us marrying is gone. Anyway, we can't seem to say a civil word to each other anymore. All we did was argue before he went home."

She was heartbroken but refused to change her stance on the Treaty. Battles in Dublin continued between the opposing sides with huge numbers of casualties. Sometimes Annie recognised old friends on both sides who had been injured or killed in the fighting and were brought in to her ward. Sackville Street was occupied for a week by Anti-Treaty troops or Republicans as they called themselves. Soon the Free State government was in control of Dublin and the Anti-Treaty forces fled to other parts of the country. She had heard nothing of Padraig since he went back to Kerry.

During the election campaign, Harry met many of the leading figures in the Free State government. He was intelligent and quick and soon became an indispensable member of the organising committee in the north city. Like Annie, he was very impressed by

Michael Collins, the Chief of Staff of the Irish National Army. One evening in the middle of the campaign he found himself alone with Collins who was having a quiet cup of tea before he made a campaign speech. He was a very tall, well-built man, resplendent in his uniform. He turned and saw Harry admiring him.

"What is your name, young man? You seem to be putting a lot of energy into this campaign."

"Harry Devereux is my name, Sir. I just finished school so I have plenty of time on my hands." Harry was delighted to be noticed by his hero.

"Just finished school? Have you thought about joining the National Army as a cadet? We are recruiting at the moment and the country needs young lads like you."

"My mother says I am too young yet, sir. She wants me to wait for a while."

"Now is the time to join, Harry. You will be an officer in no time. Let me know if you decide to enlist. I will make sure that you are looked after."

General Collins was called then to take his place on the platform and Harry moved into a position from where he had an excellent view. Collins was a passionate speaker and knew exactly how to captivate his audience. Harry watched him from the wings. "I want to be like him some day," he thought.

The Pro-Treaty faction won the election and Harry whole-heartedly joined in the celebrations. The following day, he handed in his application to join the National Army, giving General Collins and his aunt, Annie Ainsworth, as referees. He didn't tell his parents until he got his letter of acceptance. His mother, he knew, wanted him to go to university, although how she hoped to pay his fees he had no idea. She was finding it difficult enough to feed the family, he knew. He confided his reasons for joining the army to Joseph.

"I love my country and joining the army is something that my heart tells me to do. I want to serve my country and to be at the centre of it as the new state emerges, Jo-Jo. Joining the army is an opportunity to do that and will also give me training and a career."

Joseph wanted to support his brother but knew that their parents would not be very pleased about his choice of career. "I thought that you wanted to be a solicitor or a barrister. You used to talk about that."

"I would like to be a solicitor or barrister but I wouldn't be paid for years and I don't want Mother and Father to have to support me," Harry said firmly.

He waited until the evening of the day he got his letter of acceptance to tell his parents about his decision. The two girls were playing skipping with some of their friends outside on the street and Joseph was playing a football match in the park. His parents were sitting at the table, chatting and having a second cup of tea. He sat down at the table, took the letter out of his pocket and swallowed hard.

"Mother, Father, I have something to tell you. I have accepted a place to be an officer cadet in the Irish National Army."

There was silence for a few minutes. Ellen was the first to speak.

"Harry, I always wanted you to be a doctor or a solicitor or something like that. You are so clever you could be whatever you wanted to be. You haven't even got your exam results yet. Wait until you do and then try to get into university."

"Mother, there is no point in me even thinking about university. How would we pay the fees? You would have to support me for years and we barely get by as it is. I know you have to visit the pawn shop from time to time and find it difficult to make ends meet. I know how hard it is for Father to find work. I don't want to be a burden on you. As a cadet, I will get my board and lodgings and training for a career as well."

Ellen flinched and looked down when he mentioned the pawn shop. She had never told James about that. "Mary is at school now. I was going to get a job cleaning the trains and that would help pay your fees. Please don't throw your life away by joining the army, Harry. There is still a lot of violence going on. You could be killed." Ellen's voice broke on the last sentence and she sobbed.

James came around the table to comfort her. "I agree with your mother. A young man with brains like you can do better than the army. The two factions of the IRA are still fighting each other and who can say how it will end? At least in the trenches I knew who the enemy was. Here it seems to be brother against brother, friend against friend. Don't get involved in the violence, son."

"I am sorry, Father. I have already accepted my place. I will be going to Beggar's Bush barracks for my training next Monday."

"Beggar's Bush? That is a British barracks!"

"Not any more. It was the first barracks to be handed over to the National Army."

Ellen was still crying. "Harry, is there nothing we can say that will change your mind?"

"I am sorry, Mother. There is a lot of work to be done in establishing the Irish Free State. I want to be part of that."

Kathleen and Mary were very upset when they heard that Harry was leaving home to begin his training. Joseph knew that he too would miss him but he tried to be supportive and understood his reasons for joining the army.

On the Monday morning, Harry refused all offers to accompany him to the barracks and left very early, kissing them all but never looking back as he strode down the street. The house seemed empty without him that evening as they sat around the table. He was the one who always had stories to recount, questions to ask, jokes to tell.

The first Sunday he was free to visit them he arrived in his new uniform. He had called in for Julia on his way and arrived home with her on his arm, looking every inch a young hero, the brim of his hat pulled down severely to his eyebrows. The grey-green of the Free State uniform suited him.

Looking at her son, Ellen realised that he reminded her of James when she first met him. Although Harry was taller, he had the same broad back and straight shoulders, the same confident walk. Strange, she thought, how a uniform changes a man. James had somehow shrunk when he got out of uniform. Even the khaki which he had worn home from France had suited him although never as well as the scarlet uniform of their years in India.

Harry talked non-stop about his training, his accommodation and the friends he had already made. Joseph, Kathleen and Mary sat still, admiring their grown-up brother and drinking in his every word. Julia had lost some of her shyness and helped Ellen to serve up the meal. It made Ellen feel better to see her son so happy. From the expression on James's face, she could tell that he still had misgivings about their son's new life.

When the two young people were about to leave, Harry said, "I won't see you for a few weeks. A few of us cadets are being sent down the country on a mission with a reconnaissance party. We are delighted to be getting out of the barracks and it should be very interesting."

Ellen was immediately worried. "It's not dangerous, is it?"

"No, of course not, Mother. It is just an inspection and getting some information, that's all," Harry reassured her.

"Well, be careful, son. Come to see us again as soon as you can, and bring Julia."

James shook hands with his son and stood with Ellen in the doorway watching until the young couple were out of sight.

On his next visit a few weeks later, he didn't bring Julia and he looked pale and strained. Ellen thought that he and Julia had fallen out and whispered so to James.

She waited until the two girls had gone outside to play before asking him. "What's wrong, son? Did you fall out with Julia?"

"What? Oh no, I didn't bring her because I wanted to talk to you and Father. Something terrible happened when we were down in Kerry. That is where we were sent on the mission I told you about, Kenmare in Kerry. I can't stop thinking about what happened there."

Suddenly the tears were running down his face. He tried to mop them away with his sleeve. Ellen and James had never seen him like that before. They both sat down opposite him at the table and Ellen took his hand in hers. "Go on, son. Tell us what happened."

"There were four of us cadets and we thought that we were just there to help the officers and soldiers by being messengers, doing odd jobs and so on. We were sent to take over a barracks in Kenmare which was being held by the Anti-Treaty IRA. It was all a great lark at first. We travelled by sea so as to take them by surprise. There were more of us than the Republicans and we were better armed so, after a bit of a skirmish, we captured them quite easily and put them in cells in the barracks. Even then, it seemed a bit of a game." He paused and took a deep breath. "They were to be interrogated about the whereabouts of their leaders. That evening, a few of us cadets were told to bring them water and some food. When we saw them in the cells, I couldn't believe what our soldiers had done to them. They were all bruised and beaten and some of them had broken bones. Some of their faces were so swollen and black that their own mothers wouldn't recognise them. I was helping one of them to drink some water when I heard someone whispering my name. It was Padraig."

"Annie's Padraig?" Ellen asked.

"Yes. I wouldn't have known him at all because his face was so badly swollen and bruised. I managed to talk to him for a few

266

minutes. He told me that he was part of a flying column which had been living rough in the mountains around Kerry since the Treaty was ratified by the Dáil. They were all Anti-Treaty and carried on guerrilla warfare against the Free State Army. They had recently taken over this barracks when it was vacated by the British. Now the Free State government wanted to control the whole country and get rid of Anti-Treaty groups like his."

"Did he say anything about Annie? She has been so worried about him."

"He told me to tell Annie that he loved her and that he was sorry they had parted. One of our officers came in then and I couldn't talk to Padraig anymore. I asked the officer what was going to happen to the prisoners. He said that they would be interned." There was a long pause while Harry tried to regain his composure. "The next time I saw Padraig he was in a pile of bodies in the cellar of the barracks. I was told that they had been killed trying to escape but I knew that wasn't true. Oh God, how am I going to tell Annie?" He started sobbing convulsively.

James had tears in his eyes when he put his arm around Harry. "I am sorry you had to experience that, son. War is a horrible business and you see things that you can never forget. Don't tell Annie what you saw. She will hear soon enough about Padraig's death. Telling her that you saw him in that condition will only make it worse for her."

"Your father is right, Harry. Poor Padraig. He was such a lovely man. And my poor Annie. This will kill her if she hears about it. Terrible things like that have been happening in this country. That is why I didn't want you to join the army. I didn't want you to have any part in it." The sight of her strong son crying and sobbing broke her heart.

"We can't avoid it. We are part of it just by living here. General Collins says that we must be strong and put an end to this war before it takes any more lives."

Joseph had been listening to all this in silence. Now he tried to distract Harry by talking about the match he had played that morning. Harry drank a cup of tea but said that he could not stomach any food.

The girls came in and provided another distraction. Mary sat up on Harry's knee, playing with the shiny buttons on his jacket. Joseph offered to walk part of the way back to the barracks with his brother. They left together, Joseph's arm around his brother's shoulder.

When they had gone, James told Ellen about some upsetting news that he had had himself. "My regiment is to be disbanded. The Connaught Rangers will be no more. Our regimental colours are to be sent to the chapel at Windsor Castle." His voice broke.

"Why are they doing that? Surely the Connaughts were one of the most famous and loyal regiments?"

"They are disbanding all the Irish regiments now that we have independence." James swallowed hard. "Anyway, there were hardly any of us left after the war. One week in France we lost nearly seven hundred men. It makes me sad, though, to hear that the regiment is to be disbanded. The Connaught Rangers was a major part of my life. I feel almost as though someone belonging to me has died."

Ellen went to him and hugged him. "I know how you feel. It was part of my life too."

A few days later, they heard that Arthur Griffith, one of the negotiators of the Treaty and President of the Dáil, had died suddenly of a brain haemorrhage. Harry was to be part of the guard of honour at the funeral so Ellen and Grace made their way to Glasnevin Cemetery to see the funeral cortege arriving. It was an impressive sight with soldiers of the Free State forming a guard of honour and all the members of the Dáil in attendance. A huge crowd gathered to pay their respects and Ellen could barely make out the figure of Harry among the other cadets.

Grace pointed excitedly. "Look Ellen, that is General Michael Collins! You couldn't mistake him. He is at least a head taller than anyone else."

Ellen thought that she had never seen such a handsome man and could understand why Harry and Annie were so fascinated by him. Grace told her that she had met him a few times and he was very charming.

Ten days later came the shocking news that General Michael Collins had been assassinated at Beal na mBlath in his native Co. Cork. The whole country seemed to come to a standstill. The funeral of Collins was huge, even bigger than that of Arthur Griffith. Harry did not get home to see them but they heard that once again he was involved in the guard of honour.

Ellen accompanied Annie to the funeral Mass and on to Glasnevin Cemetery. The crowds were massive and the two women had to hold on to each other so as not to be separated. There were scenes of sorrow and anguish such as might be seen at the burial of a chieftain or head of a clan. People were weeping openly. Ellen found herself crying for the man that she had seen only briefly but who had had such a profound influence on her family and her country.

All Annie's grief about the death of Padraig, the deaths after the Rising, the Black and Tan War and the Civil War seemed to be pouring out of her as they followed the cortege to Glasnevin Cemetery. She could hardly see because of the tears flowing from her eyes and would have fallen and been trampled on by the crowds but for the firm grip that Ellen had on her. They were too far away to hear the orations but caught a glimpse of Harry in the distance. Crowds milled about and it was difficult to make their way home. When they got as far as Phibsboro, Ellen suggested that they stopped for a cup of tea in a hotel.

Annie stopped crying and turned her swollen face to Ellen and said, "I can't believe that Padraig is gone and General Collins too. I never thought that the differences over the Treaty would go this far."

The Civil War dragged on in rural areas of Ireland. Autumn and winter made it difficult for the Republican forces to survive and one by one they were wiped out or taken captive. The last of the military barracks were handed over by the British to the National Army.

Harry came to visit and said that he had an announcement to make. "I am to be transferred to what was the Royal Barracks in Arbour Hill and which is to be known after the handover as Collins Barracks in honour of General Michael Collins. I hope that you will all come to the ceremony. I have been given the honour of raising the Tricolour. The new chief of Staff, General Richard Mulcahy, will be attending."

Ellen and James were delighted that he had been given such an honour and also that he would be so much nearer to home. Ellen reflected as she looked at her son that he looked older than his eighteen years now. He had become much more serious and reflective and had lost the playfulness which had been part of his charm.

When she said as much to James he looked sad and said, "That is what war does to a young man. Whether it is a world war or a civil war you see and do things that you would never think of in peacetime. Please God this war will soon be over but it will leave its mark on people."

The morning of the handover, Harry arranged to collect his family and walk with them the short distance to Arbour Hill where they would meet up with Julia and her family. Ellen hurried to black-lead the range and tidy the kitchen before it was time to leave. She could hear James upstairs, getting his trousers from

270

under the mattress and checking their crease, polishing his shoes and brushing his hat. She smiled to herself; anyone would think that he was going to be on parade. The girls were dressed in their Sunday clothes and giddy and anxious to be off. Joseph was waiting impatiently at the door. She had her good coat on and was just putting the hatpin into her hat when Harry arrived. His eyes were shining and he was very excited. She offered him a cup of tea and a scone before he left but he refused.

"I couldn't eat anything, Mother. I am too excited." He was pacing up and down the kitchen, putting on and taking off his hat and tightening his Sam Brown belt. "This is a great day for Ireland. The last of the British army are leaving today. We must get there in good time, Mother."

"Don't worry, Harry. I know how much this means to you. We are all ready. Your father will be down in a minute." Ellen called up the stairs to her husband.

James came down the stairs and into the kitchen. He was dressed in his best navy suit; his trousers had a sharp military crease in them. His bowler hat was sitting straight on his head and his shoes were polished to a high shine. Across his chest he wore his military medals.

Harry looked disbelievingly at his father. "What in the name of God are you wearing those for? Do you want to disgrace me?"

James faced his son. "It is nothing to do with you. I fought in France and Flanders for more than four years and my comrades were all Irishmen. Most of them died there. I am wearing my medals in memory of them. The flag that we fought under is being lowered today. I can't pretend that I am glad to see the end of the British in Ireland. Britain has been good to your mother and me, Harry. I hope the Free State will be as good to you."

Harry stared at his father, turned on his heel and went out the door, not bothering to close it.

Joseph looked anxiously at his parents. "I will go after him and tell him to wait for us. He didn't mean it. He is just excited."

James was standing, fingering his medals. His head drooped and his shoulders were hunched. There was a silence while she fought the tears and the memories. Then she went to him and put her arms around him. "You earned those medals, James, and I am proud of you. Wear them with pride. Sometime in the future, when feelings are not so raw, people will acknowledge what you and your comrades sacrificed. Now, come on, or we will be late."

James straightened up, put on his hat and opened the door. Ellen put her arm in his and they hurried after the others. They could see that Harry had paused at the corner of Infirmary Road, with Joseph's restraining hand on his shoulder. He started to move off as soon as they got near so that they were forced to almost march behind him until they got to the barracks. Hundreds of people were making their way to the Royal Barracks, some of them carrying Tricolours, the flag of the new Free State. A few, like James, were wearing medals from the Great War. There was a carnival atmosphere, with hawkers selling small tricolours or cones of sweets. People were chatting animatedly as they walked and greeting friends. Outside the barracks, a street musician was playing a violin and people were throwing the odd farthing or ha'penny into the open violin case on the ground. Julia and her mother, Violet, were waiting at the gates.

Harry greeted them and turned to his parents. "I have to go and join the colour party now. I will show you to a place where you will have a good view. We are having a céilí after the handover so I won't see you until next week. Enjoy the ceremony."

He led them into the square, kissed his mother and the girls, shook hands with Joseph and, after a slight hesitation, with his father. Then he was marching away, straightening his cap and smoothing down the front of his uniform. There was a huge crowd but the family was at the front and had a clear view. The Union flag was still flying overhead. British soldiers were standing to attention, their officer in front of them. There was a barked order and a soldier stepped forward and began to lower the flag as the company stood to attention and saluted. Another soldier caught the falling flag and folded it with his comrade in a theatrical fashion. There was a loud cheer from the crowd. There was another order and the soldiers wheeled and turned, ready to march out of the barracks.

From the other side of the barracks, the National Army colour party appeared with their officer. They stopped and saluted the departing troops. The British officer took the salute before stepping in at the head of his men and leading them over the square and out of the gates. The crowd made way for them in silence. Then there was a loud and prolonged cheer. James made a small sound beside her. She turned and looked at him. There were tears streaming down his face as he watched the departing British soldiers. She knew that the tears were not about the British leaving Ireland: they were for their years in India and their dead daughter, his fallen comrades, his beloved regiment and the lost years in the trenches. She found his hand and squeezed it.

Overhead, the Tricolour was being raised to the sound of the National Anthem, Amhrán na bhFiann, played by a military band. They could see that Harry was raising the flag. It unfurled and blew bravely in the wind. Harry was looking up at it, his eyes bright with tears, his right arm in a rigid salute. As the notes of the anthem died away, there was silence and then prolonged cheering and waving of flags. The sound echoed around the square. Then a holiday feeling broke out with people laughing and joking and waving their tricolours. It was a new era, a new beginning.

Ellen slipped her arm through her husband's. "Let's go home, my love."

Indigo Dreams Publishing
24 Forest Houses
Halwill
Beaworthy
EX21 5UU
Devon
UK